A Bed of Flowers

Also by Auberon Waugh
and published by Robin Clark Ltd

The Foxglove Saga
Path of Dalliance
Who are the Violets Now?
Consider the Lilies

Auberon Waugh

A Bed of Flowers

Robin Clark Ltd
London

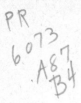

Published by Robin Clark Ltd 1985
A member of the Namara Group
27/29 Goodge Street, London W1P 1FD

First published in Great Britain by
Michael Joseph, London, 1972

British Library Cataloguing in Publication Data

Waugh, Auberon
A bed of flowers, or, as you like it.
I. Title
823'.914[F]   PR6073.A9

ISBN 086072 089 6

Printed and bound in Great Britain
by Nene Litho and Woolnough Bookbinding
both of Wellingborough, Northants

Methusalem, with all his hundreds of years, was but a mushroom of a night's growth to this Day, and all the four monarchies, with all their thousands of years, and all the powerful Kings and Queens of the world, were but as a bed of flowers, some gathered at six, some at seven, some at eight, all in one morning . . .

JOHN DONNE *Sermons* (On Eternity)

PART ONE

CHAPTER ONE

Few Englishmen would care to be reminded that as recently as the night of March 31st 1966, there was no colour television in the British Isles. Perhaps there are other, even more disreputable truths to be revealed about England's recent history, but these are known only to a few people.

The first time colour television was shown publicly in Britain was at Sophie Nizam's party on election night. Bill Nizam was then Controller of Information Services at the B.B.C., which meant that he was responsible for all news and current affairs. Any disc-jockey's impromptu wisecrack about the state of the world had to be submitted to him some days in advance, so that he could ensure that it was sufficiently impartial as between the political parties. On other matters, people were occasionally allowed the luxury of an opinion, provided that the contrary opinion was immediately given equal prominence.

There was nothing really wrong with Bill. He wore floppy jerseys and sandals, collected jazz records, could do quite a good imitation of the B.B.C.'s director-general, took a serious interest in modern painting and let it be known that he had voted Labour. For all that, nobody liked him much, and certainly his party would not have attracted anything like so many guests if it had not been for the lure of coloured television. No fewer than three gossip columns had thought the matter worth mentioning in advance, and one even referred to Sophie as 'the attractive Hungarian-born Mrs Nizam'. Where or how Sophie had been born was anyone's guess, but to describe her as attractive was absurd. Clearly, Bill was a man of influence, but there were other people with even greater influence giving parties on election night. It was the colour television set which drew them to the Nizams' elegant drawing room in Notting Hill. Only a cynic would suggest that they were also influenced by the knowledge that their host would not be there – he was needed at the Television Centre, attending to the General Election; but, sad to say, London contained many cynics at that time.

'It is only a pilot scheme, of course,' said Sophie. 'This is a closed circuit operation, carried on wires.' The row of backs did not move. Eight guests had already arrived, only a quarter of an hour after the party was advertised as starting. All sat like rabbits mesmerised in a car's headlight, staring glassily at the screen. It would be at least half an hour before the first election result came through. Viewers were being treated to a talk on general subjects by the commentator, a round young man with spectacles and a bow tie. He was well known in black and white. It now emerged – something which one would never have guessed before – that he also had a purple face.

'As soon as we have enough results to make a meaningful average, this dial will show you the percentage swing to date – a swing to Labour on this side, a swing to the Conservatives on that side – and this little panel here will show you the overall parliamentary majority which a swing of this size would give to Labour if it were repeated throughout the country.'

Suddenly, a bright orange blister appeared on his cheek. It swelled rapidly until it enveloped the whole of his head, when it burst, leaving him purple again, but now slightly transparent.

'Almost psychedelic,' said one of the rabbits in a chirpy

voice. Everybody laughed, because 'psychedelic' was a new word then.

'I am afraid that there are still a number of problems to be ironed out,' said Sophie, determined not to see her wonderful contrivance mocked. Nobody paid the slightest attention. From the television set there came the noise of a telephone ringing. The commentator lifted the receiver and listened with a frown of concentration on his handsome, purple face. Sophie loyally hoped that nothing had gone wrong. She had spent the last two days grinding paprika into an orange cheese mixture, spreading hard, inedible pellets of imitation caviar over sour cream, cutting fresh pineapple into chunks and sticking them with bacon on a cocktail biscuit. She had denied herself use of either bathroom so that the champagne should be sufficiently chilled; she had deep-fried over eight hundred scampi that very afternoon; she had arranged for an Italian waiter to arrive with the cold chicken from Searcy's. All this had been done for the greater glory of the B.B.C. She knew that it was normal in England to make fun of the things you hold most dear, and always laughed dutifully when Bill did his clever imitation of the director-general, but her heart was not in it. She felt for the B.B.C. rather what Horatius must have felt for Rome, and she was fiercely jealous for her husband's position inside it. Bill, of course, found her a great embarrassment.

The plump commentator put down his telephone with a sigh and a look of profound disgust on his tender young face of Tyrrhenian hue. 'It appears that I slipped up earlier. When I said that the indicator board would give Labour's overall majority resulting from whatever average swing emerges, I should, of course, have said that the indicator board will give the majority accruing to either Labour or Conservative as the result of the given swing. I'm sorry about that. And now we move to Scotland for a progress report from our Glasgow studio.'

In Glasgow, for some reason, people reverted to black and white. The rabbits blinked and shook their heads. Sophie's eyes were shining with pride. 'That was Bill who made him say it again,' she said. One of the rabbits sneezed.

After half an hour it was plain that Labour were going to win as most people had always supposed they would. Everyone present, they told each other, had voted Labour. All had been concerned to see a restructuring of British society, and also a government where moral consideration counted for something.

'Now we've got a decent majority, I hope we can do something about privilege,' said Tim Pardue. 'Thank you, thank you.' He gave the waiter a compassionate smile in exchange for his glass of champagne, to show that he understood all the distress and indignity involved in being a waiter. 'We must tackle it at the roots, and, oddly enough, I think Wilson may be the man to do it. The whole system is rotten.' The wave of his hand took in the Nizams' drawing room and many more drawing rooms for streets around. It took in the John Sturgeons on the wall, the white nylon carpet, the Scandinavian coffee table, the guests, his little wife – everything, in a word, which was not Tim Pardue. Pardue was some sort of senior executive in the Thomson organisation. When asked, he always said that he was in communications.

'If the Conservatives had won, I honestly think I should have emigrated,' said Charlie de Rothschild. He was a merchant banker.

'I just feel that the good people are here again,' said little Mrs Pardue, crinkling up her eyes. She was either a Peek or a Frean – anyway, the biscuit family.

Soon they grew bored of cheering every time a Labour gain was announced. Occasionally a victorious Labour face would flash at them from the screen, and then the room would grow quieter. Somehow those truculent Welsh faces with shifty eyes did not harmonize with the mood in Bill Nizam's drawing room. Conservative faces were invariably greeted with a heartfelt groan, but the cheer which greeted Labour ones was slightly less convincing. It was only on election night that one could be certain of finding no politicians at a party in London – they were all at the vote-counts in their respective constituencies – and this was not a frequent enough occurrence for Londoners to appreciate how very little they knew about politics, or how very little they were really interested in the subject.

Rothschild was soon cornered by Daniel Chamberlain, whom everyone liked. Chamberlain was City editor of a popular newspaper, very keen and serious. He, too, collected jazz records, could do quite a good imitation of the late President Kennedy, took a serious interest in modern painting, and always voted Labour. He was also the kinsman of some dim and disastrous twentieth-century statesman people forgot exactly which – probably Sir Henry Campbell-Bannerman – and even radical iconoclastic Englishmen like that sort of thing. They spoke about some City news which had broken in the evening papers. A boardroom coup was rumoured to have replaced the chairman of Robinson Securities, John Robinson, by his brother Frederick Robinson. Initial comment was unfavourable, since John was said to be the more humane of the two – the likelier, perhaps, to have voted Labour in accordance with the general mood – but all feeling was soon swamped in a frenzy of indignation that such people as the Robinson brothers should still exist.

'Nobody knows the whole value of Robinson Securities except perhaps the Robinsons themselves and their very closest advisers. John Robinson's new adviser is a former Roman Catholic priest. I *ask* you. It must have been his training with the secrets of the confessional which recommended him. They have their own merchant bank, of course, and their own accountants. You could say the whole structure is worth two hundred million pounds, or you could say it is worth four hundred million, but it would not mean anything much.'

'When workers in the Lancashire mills can only earn fourteen pounds a week,' said Tim Pardue bitterly. His own salary was thought to be nearer three hundred pounds a week, but this did not prevent him thinking long and bitterly about the Robinsons.

'It can't be right. I'm sorry, it can't be right,' said Father Rasputian. He was a familiar sight in fashionable London at the time. Jesuits were not generally acceptable in polite society, but Father Rasputian believed in contraception, in abortion, in liturgical reform and in the redistribution of wealth in South America. Much later, after fashionable London grew bored with him, his superiors sent him to a leper colony in Chad.

'Four hundred million pounds? It makes me go all sour inside,' said little Mrs Pardue, of the biscuit fortune.

'I think John Robinson said he might be coming to the party later this evening,' said Sophie Nizam, but nobody ever paid the slightest attention to her.

'At least a Labour government should be able to sort out the Robinsons of this world,' growled someone, when all of a sudden one of the rabbits said: 'Hush, the result from Hungerford East . . . Good news, Oliver Twickerley has been re-elected.'

A handful of rabbits cheered. One, braver than the rest said: 'Who on earth is Oliver Twickerley?'

A chorus of voices answered: 'I was at school with him.'

'We were up at Cambridge together, but I never knew him well.'

'Very good man, Oliver, but a bit of an ass.'

'He's my brother actually.'

'Well, it's good to know we've got a few intelligent people in the Commons for once,' said the original rabbit. 'Hush, here comes the result from Llanwtyth. A. J. H. Williams. I wonder who he is.'

The atmosphere in Robsec House, English headquarters of Robinson Securities, was somewhat less convivial. Frederick Robinson's voice droned on about trustee-holdings, circulating trusts, Canada, group interests, nominees, trade recessions, growth, Switzerland, United Kingdom holdings, Robinson (Argentina) Inc., Robinson (West Africa) Limited, Robinson Nickel and Allied Mining (Southern Australia). From time to time a stony-faced executive would put a new paper in front of him which seemed to provide further material for his endless monologue.

Frederick Robinson was flanked by three expensive looking sycophants – cruel indifferent men who had swimming pools in their gardens and gave fifty pounds a year to the local vicar – and a stenographer who allowed herself to give no indication whatever that she was a human being. John Robinson had only one adviser, a skinny, wild-eyed creature who could not bring himself to look across the polished mahogany at Frederick. Occasionally, though, he nodded his head as if in agreement, or as if in confirmation of something previously understood, and scratched himself. This man was called Jaques.

'What on earth is Frederick saying now?' whispered John Robinson to his financial adviser.

'He is saying nothing. It is not a statement, it is a symposium. He has searched around in three continents to find everything which is most boring and ugly in each, and now he is presenting them to us in the form of an exhibition, I think. You must see him, John, as an outcast on a desert island, and this is all the flotsam and jetsam he has collected to give himself a sense of purpose in his life. Don't listen to a word he is saying, in case your mind, too, becomes polluted. The best thing on these occasions is to hold your breath and think of dying, or of being born. I always think of dying.'

'So the choice left to you, John.' Frederick went on, 'is between resigning the chair voluntarily, which would certainly be the best for all concerned, or awaiting the result of the vote from an extraordinary general meeting which you can't possibly win and which will mean no end of trouble to no end of people.'

'I don't wish to cause people trouble,' said John Robinson, disturbed at the thought.

'There would be no trouble if brother Frederick did not wish to change things,' said his financial adviser with the certainty of a trained theologian. 'The trouble is being caused by Frederick, not by yourself.'

'So my answer is no?' asked John Robinson, relieved.

Frederick tried to keep irritation out of his voice. Robinson Securities carried responsibility for the employment of a hundred and fifty thousand people. Its chairman was in a position to influence the commercial structure of the entire non-communist world.

'Unfortunately you have no choice in the matter, John. Perhaps I should say fortunately. The only occasion where you have seriously interfered in the running of any of our companies was with Robinson Tube, in Halifax.'

'We thought the men would like a greater say in the running of the factory, Jaques and I,' said John Robinson.

'And now ten thousand men are out of work,' said Frederick. 'I suppose you still think it a worthwhile experiment.'

Had it been a worthwhile experiment? John Robinson looked at Jaques.

'We thought that human dignity was more important

18

than material prosperity, said Jaques.

'And now their families must live on the dole. There is not much dignity in that,' said Frederick. Soon, he would become indignant. When he thought about these things, the prosperity of his workers was very close to his heart. Unemployment, or so he had been told, sapped a man's vitality and destroyed his self-respect. For some reason, nothing made Frederick more unpleasant than the thought that he was on the side of the angels. John Robinson knew the symptoms from their nursery days.

'There is no reason why a man should be less dignified on the dole than when he is helping to mass produce steel tubes for some unknown and unhallowed purpose,' said Jaques. 'Our mistake was to suppose that the workers of Robinson Tube were capable of being concerned about their own dignity. They have been taught to equate dignity with servitude. Their minds have become so polluted that they are useless for the purpose of thinking, capable only of conditioned response. Now, being unemployed, they are unhappy because they have been taught to be unhappy when unemployed. That is the tragedy, Mr Robinson.'

In a tiny corner of his mind, cunning Jaques began to suspect that Frederick Robinson's position was not quite so strong as he made it appear. If it had been possible to oust his brother from the chairmanship of Robinson Securities without convincing him that this was the best thing to do, Frederick would scarcely have wasted time trying to convince him. Jaques resolved to find out exactly how many voting shares Frederick personally controlled.

'And so what is your solution, Mr Jaques,' said Frederick. He would have liked to sound dispassionately sarcastic, but something in the pitch of his voice made it querulous. It was absurd that such important and un-answerable truths as his head contained should require the vehicle of a throat, a larynx, a tongue lubricated by spittle to utter them. 'Your qualification, let me see, is that you used to be a Roman Catholic priest, before running away. You served as a missionary in Africa. Ah, yes. Have you any other experience of industrial problems?'

'I did not run away from the Church,' said Jaques with quiet dignity. Clearly he was as happy to talk about himself as about the trivial matter at hand, the future of Robinson Securities. 'It might be truer to say that the Church ran away from me.'

'No doubt,' said Frederick. 'And you were going to tell me your ideas for the solution of our industrial problems.'

'Marijuana,' said Jaques. 'Whether or not it is true that there is an all-loving God seems to me fairly unimportant, but you must admit that it is a most beautiful idea. The trouble is that your workers are no longer interested in the idea. I had hoped, once, that it was possible to introduce the dullest minds to something of the beauty which God created or which, even if He didn't, can be discovered in the very idea of existence. If only your workers could be animated with a tenth part of the wonder of the fact that a bird grows feathers, they would realise quite how empty and fatuous is a life spent in the pursuit of a larger washing machine, a faster car, or even (excuse me if I laugh) greater opportunities for their children to pursue these same ends. But as they can't, we must look elsewhere.'

'And this man was preparing to control Robinson Securities,' murmured Frederick.

'Experience has taught me,' said Jaques, 'that this is no longer possible. So far as your workers are able to comprehend the notion of goodness, they identify it with helping other people towards longer and more comfortable lives. They equate material possessions with happiness although there is not the slightest glimmering of a connection between the two; they are wrong in everything they believe, and their minds have become too much polluted to clear themselves again. Cannabis is the only answer.'

One of the minor sycophants – no swimming pool in the garden, but a birdbath, and a fine show of peonies in early summer – put some papers in front of Frederick.

'I forgot to mention that with the prospect of another five years of Labour government under Mr Wilson, we must expect endless trouble in relation to trust companies, especially with regard to any assets maintained in the United Kingdom which have not yet been transferred to our Canadian holding company – all this may be susceptible to a capital levy – and the prospects for our South African, West African and South American concerns are bound to be overshadowed by difficulties in transferring funds. This is simply not a time when the group can afford to make any mistake.'

'Our greatest mistake was in supposing that we could ever penetrate the defences of your poor, mutilated mind,' said John Robinson.

'Your greatest mistake, if you like to call it that, was in making me the trustee and legal guardian of your daughter until her majority. With the votes of all the ordinary stock held in her name as well as that in my own and in my daughter's, I have a considerably larger holding than anybody else. And I scarcely think that many of our uncles or cousins will wish to retain you as chairman when they hear your schemes for moving all our men in the Doncaster plant to West Africa and all our West African workers to Doncaster.'

'It would have settled the question whether aptitude is determined by heredity or by environment for once and all,' said John Robinson. 'But we have given up the scheme. Mr Truefitt said that people from Doncaster would be unhappy in West Africa. I don't know why. Most people can adjust themselves.'

'The sun would be extremely hard on Yorkshire people,' said Mr Truefitt gently, as if talking to an invalid. He was one of the richer, crueller-looking sycophants, seated beside Frederick. 'Many of them are somewhat pale skinned, and would burn most terribly.'

'They could wear sunhats, if they wanted,' said John Robinson moodily.

Truefitt and Frederick exchanged glances. Jaques stood to his feet, accidentally knocking his chair over. Frederick and the sycophants were obviously delighted by this mishap, but Jaques was not in the least disconcerted.

'It is too late for us to save him. The poor man's head has become so silted up with all the rubbish being talked and written that he will never disentangle himself now. Frederick Robinson, I leave you to your own little corner of misery and I weep for you with all my heart. It isn't true what they say about West Africa. I lived there for fifteen years, and some of that time I was diocesan treasurer at Nsukka. There was less rubbish talked there, but I was never able to discover whether the people were happier because God made them that way or whether it was something to do with the diet.'

'Oh really?' said Frederick. 'And now John, have you decided whether to retire honourably, or whether we must fight it out with all the squalor and publicity which that entails?'

'It's a bigger question than you seem to realise,' said Jaques, 'this matter of human happiness. What else are you worried about on earth? Food, covering, possessions, luxuries . . . all these are only the means to that most precious end, peace of mind. Perhaps sex is another thing. Is it sex which worries you, Frederick? Sexual appetites are small things nowadays in a man, when there is such abundant ease in satisfying them. The workers will never understand that it is peace of mind which they seek, and so they will never find it. One must feel sorry for them, Frederick, not add to their worries. There is a certain peace of mind to be found even in pitying those who can never find it. But for a start, I should try meditating on your own death. The Fathers of the Church always advise us to start at that point.'

'Are you going to sign these papers, John, or must I call an extraordinary general meeting?'

'I will have to think about it,' said John Robinson. 'I would be delighted to make way for a better man, but it seems to me that you have little idea as yet of the responsibility and the opportunities of a chairman. Frankly, I am a bit disappointed in you. I know that I have only been chairman for a short while, and am only now coming alive to the tremendous possibilities of the job, but your attitude seems entirely negative, and I find myself increasingly doubtful whether you are really what might be called chairman material. I shall bear in mind what you have said, but I cannot promise that my answer will be the one you most want.'

When John Robinson and Jaques had gone, Frederick buried his face in his hands and groaned: 'Oh my God, what have we done to deserve it?'

'I should have a short drink, sir,' said Mr Truefitt. 'Now we must start making arrangements for the extra-ordinary general meeting, I suppose.'

Mrs Nizam's party became noisier and more elated as the night wore on. Labour were leading by forty seats when John Robinson arrived with his daughter Rosalind, accompanied by Jaques.

They were soon surrounded by what seemed a belligerent crowd of drunks.

'I expect you're feeling rather sad at the turn things have taken, Mr Robinson,' said Tim Pardue with a nasty edge on his voice. 'Life won't be quite so easy from now on, I should imagine.'

'I don't understand . . . why not? We came to see a coloured television set,' said John Robinson.

'Mr Wilson has won a landslide victory. At long last we can start rebuilding the country. This is a great moment for the British people. For the first time our country will not be governed from the boardrooms of the big financial houses. Tonight, Mr Robinson, you have handed over the power to the people, and we're going to bury you.'

The night of March 31st 1966 was an historic occasion in Britain, when nearly everybody was talking like that. Normally obsequious people quite forgot themselves. It was a most unpleasant time to be a multi-millionaire.

'I hate politics,' said Rosalind Robinson. 'They're all in it for their own self-importance.'

'Not Mr Wilson,' cried someone.

'Nor Roy,' cried someone else. 'I honestly think he is an idealist.'

'Or Tony,' said Mrs Nizam. 'You couldn't pretend he's not intelligent. I just feel that the best people are back in charge.'

'No they're not,' said Jaques.

'You wouldn't feel like that if you had to live on fourteen pounds a week. You would want to do something about it,' said Charlie de Rothschild.

'Then you would be a fool,' said Jaques. 'Here is the colour television set we have come to see. Look at it. No, no, please. I beg you all. Look at it. Don't talk, don't say anything. Don't drink any more of that filthy champagne. Just look at it.'

'We're drinking to the future,' said Pardue grumpily. 'And I never said the champagne was any good.'

'I beg your pardon,' said Mrs Nizam, humorous but hurt.

'Good champagne can be worth drinking,' said Daniel Chamberlain, the well-connected journalist whom everybody liked. 'As a matter of fact, I am something of a specialist, although I have never met this brand before. By the way, is it true, Mr Robinson, that you may be considering changes on the board at Robsec? There are even rumours that you may be thinking of making way for someone else. Would this be anything to do with the election?'

'Please, please,' screamed Jaques above the tumult, 'do not talk for a moment. I want you all to look at the thing we have come to admire.'

The commentator's face had changed from purple to a deep puce. Occasionally, brilliant flashes of orange illuminated parts of it, while at other moments the picture reverted to black and white.

'These are early days,' said Jaques. 'We must try to imagine the ideal, of which this poor image can only be the imperfect shadow. Imagine, if you can – surely, your minds are not so fouled up by all the wretched flotsam for the moment – that this picture is perfect. We see our commentator exactly as he is. The colour is the same, nothing interferes with our enjoyment of him.'

'And now the result from Huyton,' said the commentator. 'This is the prime minister's own seat. Nothing very exciting is expected here, as it is one of the safest Labour seats in the country. Now, let me see. Here we are, Wilson, J. H. . . .'

'Labour,' said another voice.

'. . . Forty one thousand one hundred and twenty-three. Jobday, Dr T. L. . . .'

'Conservative,' said the other voice.

'. . . Twenty thousand one hundred and eighty-two. D. Sutch . . .'

'National Teenage Party,' said the voice.

'. . . Five hundred and eighty-five. A slightly increased majority for the Prime Minister, there, of twenty thousand nine hundred and forty, and a lost deposit for Screaming Lord Sutch, the pop singer. Better luck next time to the teenage candidate.'

Everybody had a good laugh at that quip. But the moment was too sentimental for laughter. 'Harold back and Oliver Twickerley back. I'm just too happy for words,' said little Mrs Pardue. 'I feel like crying.'

And cry she did. Nobody could be quite unaffected by the sight. Charlie de Rothschild blew his nose with a horrible, damp sound. Mrs Nizam hugged Danny Chamberlain, who watched the television over her shoulder.

'But my brother's a horrible person. The people in Hungerford East must have been mad to elect him,' said Orlando Twickerley.

'They all are. I've got a horrible uncle,' said Rosalind Robinson. They decided this gave them a lot in common.

'I think the party's been a great success,' said Mrs Nizam to John Robinson. 'It wouldn't be the same of course, if the other side had won. Will you drink any-thing ?'

'No thank you,' said John Robinson. 'Alcohol is one of the great mutilators. It needn't be, of course. I used to think it lovely. But there is too much mutilation. Nobody can think any more. We need an entirely new life-style, and an entirely new set of aims, an entirely new awareness of other people.'

'Here, here,' said little Mrs Pardue. 'That is why we voted Labour.'

'Too bloody right,' said Tim Pardue, who was now

very drunk indeed. 'We need to throw all this bloody trash into the refuse disposal unit.' This time there could be no doubt that he was referring to his wife, but John Robinson was unable to recognise unpleasantness.

'Why don't we all meet again tomorrow, when this horrible champagne has got out of our systems,' he said.

'I beg your pardon,' said Mrs Nizam, slightly less humorously. 'Everybody is being very rude about my champagne tonight.'

'We will discuss what we can do to become human beings again. We must shake off everything that is silting up our minds and preventing our spirits from asserting themselves. We must stop gorging ourselves with food, we must stop drinking. Even, for a time, we must stop talking.'

'Hear, hear,' said Tim Pardue unpleasantly.

'Why doesn't everyone come around to Robsec House tomorrow, after we have all had time to think,' said John Robinson. 'Come for tea.'

'A new life-style stop That is what the Labour victory means to Great Britain comma unquote said John Robinson comma chairman of the $1000 million Robinson Securities combine last night while a battle raged over his continued chairmanship of Europe's greatest single-family trust stop paragraph He expressed no uneasiness at the consequences of Labour's victory on Robsec comma the family giant which has long been the target of left-wing criticism on the grounds of its size and the monolithic secrecy which surrounds it stop' Daniel Chamberlain was talking into Mrs Nizam's telephone. Plainly, he had found peace of mind.

'Everything will be different now that Labour has come back with a decent majority,' said little Mrs Pardue. She, too, had found peace of mind. Pardue was asleep, plainly untroubled. Orlando and Rosalind were playing together, drinking in each other eyes, mindless of anything but the moment. The television set performed its inanities unregarded.

'I must say,' said Father Rasputian, 'I often think what a wonderful thing it would be if we could start everything afresh.' He had never for a moment lost his peace of mind. Only Jaques, the philosopher and financial adviser, the former Roman Catholic priest whose church had run away from him, seemed troubled.

'There is no need to start afresh. It would be quite impossible to wipe out everything that has happened, even if we wanted. History is part of the fabric of our existence. All that matters is to put a stop to what is happening now.'

'What is happening now?'

'Man is losing his reason,' cried Jaques. 'Look at that colour television set. Imagine it perfect. Can't you see what a boring and fatuous and ugly and unnecessary thing it is? Why should it be in colour? Does it make any of us any happier?'

'I thought it had been rather a success,' said Mrs Nizam tearfully. 'I thought people would like to see what the new colour television sets would be like.'

'Of course they would, and that is why they are all ill,' said Jaques. 'Can't you see the idiocy of it? This, we are told, is progress. This is faith, hope and charity. We believe in the future, we put our hope of solving every problem in creating more wealth, and we measure love in terms of ensuring that more and more people have colour television sets. It is wrong, pitifully and grotesquely wrong to suppose that we shall be happier when everyone has a colour television set.'

'What should we do, then,' said Charlie de Rothschild.

'We should learn to rejoice in our ability to think,' said Jaques.

'That is what my husband says,' said little Mrs Pardue. 'We always take the *Guardian* and the *New York Times*. Tim won't have any other newspapers in the house.'

'But first,' said Jaques, 'we must rid our minds of this pollution.'

'Please don't touch the television,' cried Mrs Nizam. 'It is on loan from the B.B.C. research unit.'

'I don't intend to hurt it,' said Jaques with quiet dignity. 'I intend to turn my back on it. It is rubbish, it is a glorification of imbecility. Can't you see how we must all fight against something which is slowly destroying the human spirit?'

'The others liked it,' said Mrs Nizam. 'I don't know why, but people seem to be criticising everything I do tonight. I only give these parties for Bill. I don't care who wins the election, and I wish somebody would say something nice about the party.'

'You've made Sophie cry,' they said. Jaques did not seem perturbed.

'It is the human spirit beginning to assert itself,' he said. 'It is just a tiny, tiny stirring, but it shows that something at least is still alive. I'll come along and cry with you, Sophie dear, and we shall see if we can build this tiny flicker into a bonfire.'

At this moment everyone decided it was time to go. Jaques carried his strange, ungainly person with its malformed leg across the room and knelt at her feet. He pushed his skinny grey head into her lap, took her hands in his, and started to cry with her.

'Goodnight, Sophie,' everybody said. 'Fantastic evening. Can't wait until we're all allowed colour TV sets. Lucky old Bill. Give him our love.'

But Sophie did not stir. She and Jaques remained huddled together, sobbing quietly, until four o'clock in the morning when Bill Nizam found them on his return from useful and important work at the Television Centre.

'Would you let me take you home?' asked Orlando.

29

'I can't,' whispered Rosalind, her lovely, velvet eyes clouding over. 'I am staying in my uncle's house and Daddy has got to drive me over before it is too late. Won't you come to this famous tea party of Daddy's tomorrow to discuss the new life-style? Please come.'

'Of course I will,' said Orlando.

'See you there, then,' said Rosalind with a jaunty little nod of her head. They kissed for quite a long time in the hall of Mrs Nizam's house, Orlando's right hand under her left breast, his left hand holding a silky, fragrant lock of hair against her tiny neck, which smelled of milk. Afterwards, she looked thoughtful and there was a sort of crazy serenity in her liquid brown eyes.

'See you at tea-time,' she said.

Frederick was still in the boardroom at Robsec House when John Robinson glided past in the noiseless lift which operated only between the chairman's private entrance in Masons' Yard and the chairman's penthouse suite on the top floor, with its magnificent views over St James's Palace, Green Park, and north to Piccadilly Circus. Only Mr Truefitt remained of Frederick's earlier court, unless one counted the stenographer who sat with her legs crossed looking prepared.

'Surely there will be no difficulty in collecting enough votes to force him out,' said Mr Truefitt, 'when we show your cousins the disastrous effect he is having on the whole organisation.'

'None of my cousins is interested in that sort of thing. The hopeful members of my family are Aunt Barbara and her sister, Auntie May. The only trouble is that they have never liked me much. For some reason, all my family have always preferred John. Even my own daughter, I sometimes think.'

Mr Truefitt looked sympathetic. If either man had been

a physiognomist he might have observed a strange expression pass over the stenographer's face which Jaques would have identified immediately, in his peculiar terminology, as 'self-think'. It was the greedy look of someone who sees a possible advantage.

'Of course, none of the Robinsons is completely normal,' continued Frederick. 'The only thing which might influence them would be if John did something to cause a scandal, something to draw attention to the family.

'Is any of us completely normal?' said Mr Truefitt. 'I mūst admit, though, that John is odder than most. Do you think that he is medically all right? Couldn't we have him declared unfit to run the organisation?'

'John is certainly a little bit touched in the head, and always has been. It takes different members of the family in different ways. Our grandfather was only interested in money. My father, as you know, was only interested in houses. My aunts are only interested in their gardens. John wants to build Jerusalem in England's green and pleasant land. I am the only completely sane member of the family. Ha, ha, ha.'

'Ha, ha, ha,' laughed Mr Truefitt.

'Ha, ha, ha,' laughed the stenographer roguishly. Roguishness was expected of her. Frederick had pushed the appropriate button.

'In any case we would need to get him certified, and for every two doctors we produced to say he was insane, he could find four to say he was not. Think of the excitement there would be in the newspapers. Neither Aunt Barbara nor Auntie May would ever forgive me.'

'But don't you think he is a little bit insane?' asked Mr Truefitt.

'Probably not quite insane enough,' said Frederick. 'We could get that extraordinary adviser of his certified tomorrow. Even by modern standards, he is a pretty extreme case. But there is an awful lot of insanity around nowadays. One sees it wherever one goes – not in the City, thank God, but nearly everywhere else.'

'Not in the big discretionary trust corporations, ha, ha, ha,' said Mr Truefitt, but his patron was in a thoughtful mood, and the laughter perished thinly, until the only noise in that hideous room came from the stenographer, who tapped a pencil against her magnificent teeth.

'I sometimes think that the businessman is the only person left in our society who is completely sane. He has his priorities worked out, of course. It is a sad prospect for the world, Harold, if I am right. Somehow, we people in business – and in politics, perhaps – must keep the rest afloat. What is it, do you think, which has suddenly afflicted the whole of our society with insanity? At this moment, of all times, when the threat of war has receded, when technology offers the promise of almost unlimited prosperity for all, why do people turn their backs on everything we have achieved?'

'Plainly, it is some form of mental illness,' said Mr Truefitt. 'We must be thankful that not everybody has been affected. We are untouched, and there is still a majority of the workers. They are not really impressed by all this talk. They know what they want – more money and more leisure to enjoy it. We can give them that, not these socialists, or these philosophers and beatniks. I don't know what has come over the rest. Perhaps it's something to do with the pollution of the environment which poisons their minds and prevents them from thinking.'

'More likely it is the fact that they no longer believe in God,' said Frederick. 'Quite frankly, I do not know what I would do if I did not believe in God. I would be a prey to any sort of false philosophy. Perhaps I would smoke marijuana and think myself beautiful until the end of my days. According to John, even the dullest minds can imagine themselves clever, beautiful and good under the influence of the drug. What more could one want?'

'To eat, of course, and to achieve something useful – to make the world a better place for everyone else,' said Mr Truefitt, sensing through his boredom that Frederick was pressing that button. He wished he could be home in his comfortable house with a swimming pool in the garden.

'One also loses all ambition, and the discomforts of the body seem less important,' said Frederick. 'John claims that only duller minds like his own need the assistance of cannabis. Intelligent minds, like that of the madman Jaques, can achieve an awareness of the beauty of existence and man's dignity within the scheme of things simply by focusing their minds away from the distractions of received thought. He believes that the worker is by definition stupider and therefore less likely to achieve this awareness by his own mental processes, most especially since the mind works best when the body is mortified, and the working classes are not capable of voluntary asceticism.'

'They live too close to real deprivation for that,' said Mr Truefitt smugly.

'No doubt,' said Frederick. 'My brother John's plan for the working classes, in his kind way, is that they should only do as much work as they need to save themselves from bodily discomfort – he says that modern technology makes this very little work indeed – and should spend the rest of the time staring at each other with glazed eyes murmuring words of love as they smoke cannabis. What do you think of that?'

Harold Truefitt wondered what he thought of it. He could sense several buttons being pressed, all ringing in his mind and prompting the correct responses, but he was tired and depressed by the General Election. 'First, I think that your brother must be mad,' he said. 'But we've already dealt with that. Unfortunately, you say there is no way we can make use of it. Secondly, I think that such a policy would be extremely harmful to the future of industry, of growth, of improved living standards, of progress for the people of the country and of the world. It would also be most harmful to the interests of Robinson Securities, which, of course, is less important. Also, it would be illegal, and the law against cannabis will never be changed – especially if it has the properties you describe – for the very good reason that our politicians make the laws and their interest is to have something big and important to preside over. So, to that extent, we are wasting our time even discussing it.'

'Of course you are right,' said Frederick. 'I doubt if many of our politicians really believe in God. John's ideas are insane as well as harmful, and we must fight them with everything in our power. But you have missed the point. What else do you think?'

Only one bell was ringing now, but it was so shrill and so persistent that for an awful moment Mr Truefitt thought that the stenographer was going to prompt him.

'It is certainly very odd that the chairman of Robinson Securities should advocate conduct which is illegal,' said Mr Truefitt slowly. 'It would undoubtedly be very bad for the organisation if it became known. I doubt whether your two aunts, for instance, would be very happy about that sort of publicity, for instance.'

'Advocate it?' said Frederick. 'Come on, come on.'

'And if it became known that he was actually given to indulging in these illegal practices, then, of course, your aunts would probably be very angry indeed.'

'Brilliant, my dear Harold. You won't have a last glass of whisky? What is the latest news of the election?' A tape machine was in the lobby of the boardroom. 'It looks like a Labour majority of about eighty-five. These will be difficult times for people in the business world, Harold.

34

We've got to work full time from now on to stay where we are. More than our own survival depends on it. For John to remain as chairman controlling the destiny of the 150,000 workers and their families, would be more than a scandal. It would almost certainly be a disaster.'

'Hear, hear,' said Truefitt. 'It wouldn't be so funny for the workers to lose their jobs.'

'That is why we must get things moving,' said Frederick. 'Neither Aunt Barbara nor Auntie May would be likely to believe me if I told them that John was a drug addict. Harold, I want you to be prepared to call an extraordinary general meeting, as laid down in our charter, for Friday week. Work with Miss Intersan and no one else. There are already too many rumours going around. Miss Intersan, could you see if my car is waiting for me downstairs? Goodnight, Harold. We will be needing a new executive vice-chairman, of course, as you have no doubt realised. Everything will depend on the smoothness of the operation to get John out.'

The button being pressed demanded that Truefitt should stammer his thanks. Truefitt opened his mouth to stammer, then shut it again. He was a human being, not a machine, was he not? To prove the point, amazed at his own childish irresponsibility, he blew a kiss at Frederick's departing back. Why should he do a thing like that? Perhaps he, too, was losing his reason. Perhaps it was some sinister nerve-weapon being released by the Russians, so that the Western World slowly lost its sanity and capitalism succumbed to the cruelties, the stupidities and the mindless futility of socialism. 'Goodnight, Frederick,' he called.

'Your driver is downstairs, Mr Robinson. Will that be all tonight, then?' Miss Intersan waited for the verdict. In bed, she called him nothing; in the office, she called him 'sir'. This was an intermediary stage. Would he be requiring her tonight? It was good fun. She approved of it.

35

Somehow, too, it brought her closer to her work, made her feel more involved.

'That will be all for tonight, I think, Stella. Get a good night's sleep.' Frederick paused as his eye travelled over her. Perhaps it would be amusing. She was a sweet girl – undemanding and convenient. No, it was too late. He was tired.

'Goodnight, sir,' she said.

CHAPTER TWO

Hospitality at John Robinson's tea-party was not nearly so copious as it had been the night before at the Nizams'. John Robinson and his financial adviser, instead of grinding caraway seed into orange cheese, had spent the day hammering out the various ideological positions they were to adopt. The only refreshment available in the boardroom of Robsec House was lime tea, with honey for flavouring and some organic scones. 'These are made,' explained Jaques, 'without the assistance of artificial fertilizer or chemical insecticides or weed killer or any of the other chemicals which are slowly transforming the degenerate, detribalised version of mankind which has survived into the urban society of the twentieth century from this, yes, from something which was recognisably human at least into a worker ant, or perhaps, a drone bee – sexless, mindless and without any conceivable claim to the dignity of self-determination let alone to the possession of an immortal soul . . .'

'. . . Yes, I think I see,' said Daniel Chamberlain thoughtfully. 'And I must say, I think these scones are first class. What I was really asking was whether you thought that Frederick, the brother, could ever muster enough voting shares to replace John Robinson as chairman.'

To Jaques, however, the most important part of this remark was that Chamberlain thought he understood what Jaques had been saying.

'Do you really see? Do you follow what I am saying?'

'I think so,' said Danny Chamberlain, with that modest, downward glance of the eyes which had made him so popular at Stowe as a junior boy. When he limped into the room, he was the first guest to arrive. Danny always limped because he was an exceptionally small person, almost a pygmy, and this somehow gave him stature – just as stupid people often need to chew gum. Unfortunately, it did not prevent Danny from being unpleasant. Anybody who was interested in other people, or sensitive to the atmosphere they created, could guess that Danny was unpleasant. Jaques could tell it immediately, and the knowledge made him sad and concerned. He could never reconcile his instincts to the knowledge, painfully acquired, that those in greatest need of help seldom profit from it much.

Nor, of course, was Danny obviously in need of help. He was successful in his career, his wife, whom people saw less and less nowadays, was beautiful and kind; in London, where very few people are interested in anyone else, he was extremely popular, and his frank blue eyes, cheery grin and yes, even his diminutive size, all made their contribution to the general popularity. Yet Jaques could see that he was damned; he sensed it in the thin white hands and in the perky air which Danny carried around with him like an uneasy smell. Danny was eaten up with selfishness. His innards were a congealed and putrid mass of modern jealousies, modern ambitions and timeless conceit.

'You really must eat more of this organic food,' said Jaques kindly. 'It is very good for you. You see we have abandoned the idea that the great mass of the workers will ever voluntarily forsake the philosophy which it has been conditioned to accept – higher production, leading to greater prosperity and greater consumption. Even if they possessed the intelligence or the imagination to comprehend an alternative, their minds have become too much polluted. When they are surfeited with everything which mass-production can produce, they will have lost the ability to identify the source of their discontent; and if something should go wrong with progress, if they were suddenly denied the various comforts and labour-saving devices which they have come to associate with the idea of happiness, progress would merely have created for them a whole new range of discontents, a heightened awareness of discomfort. That is why we have decided to withdraw.'

'From Robinson Securities?' Danny was suddenly interested.

'From contact with the rest of the world,' explained Jaques. 'We shall live a simple life, but not because we believe that simplicity is necessary, or that the comforts and the labour-saving devices of our civilisation are necessarily wrong. If everyone in Western society worked half as hard and half as efficiently as they do at present, we would still produce enough to live in reasonable comfort, and this would give us the opportunity to cultivate an awareness of creation, of our own dignity in the scheme of things. We would also see the importance of using our talents to the best possible advantage to create things of beauty and delight. Our reason for living simply will be to clear our minds of all this pollution.'

'You mean you intend to live in some sort of commune or kibbutz?' asked Danny. Clearly, the man was insane. The problem was how to say so within the absurd and restrictive laws of libel. It would be amusing enough if the whole Robinson Securities empire, employing 150,000 men, crashed – simply because the laws of libel prevented him from warning the world that the man at the centre of the financial operation was mentally unwell. It made one quite bitter, really, but Danny knew the laws of libel as well as the next man, and he doubted whether he could write a word about all this. Why, he wondered, had Frederick Robinson been so emphatic that he should come to the tea party? There was nobody else worth meeting: two aunts of the Robinson family; John Robinson's daughter, Rosalind, and his niece, Celia. The young Orlando Twickerley, a person of no importance, brother of Oliver Twickerley the Labour Member for Hungerford, who would almost certainly be given a junior post in the new Government (Danny had heard rumours of something in the Ministry of Technology). Orlando was not even smart. Danny suspected that he might take an intelligent interest in modern painting, but nothing more. Had he voted Labour? Did he know Mrs Bruce, wife of the American ambassador, by her Christian name? Had he ever been to New York? A number of the other guests were fairly dim, but none so dim as Orlando. And neither Frederick Robinson nor any of the really senior Robsec executives was present, like Bill Tiger, Stewart Harris or old Harry Truefitt. Why was Daniel Chamberlain expected to attend? Something like anger began to stir in Danny's poor, polluted little heart.

'Neither a kibbutz nor a commune. They merely prepare the way for the ant-heap.' Jaques was determined to save another soul. 'Our purpose is not to develop the community as some hybrid organism with its own rights and claims on the individual. Our purpose is to allow the development of human awareness *away* from the demands of the ant-heap. Of course, our relations with other people are part of our own awareness of the human condition. Of course there can be no happiness which does not include a love of all creation; but even words like "love" nowadays have become so polluted that they are taken to mean a desire to improve the material comfort of other people's lives by furnishing them with labour-saving devices. No, our purpose in living together will not be so much to add to each other's material comfort as to help each other towards a realisation of what used to be called God. We shall also try to keep alive something of what is in danger of being lost. Don't compare us to a kibbutz so much as to one of those monasteries which helped to keep the Christian faith and also the benefits of Greek and Roman civilisation alive throughout the Dark Ages, while barbarian hordes roamed at will over the face of the earth.'

'So you are going to preserve the Christian faith on a farm down in Somerset and learn about God that way, then.' Chamberlain tried to make his voice sound mocking, but he could not keep out the hatred. 'I thought you decided that you didn't believe in God when you gave up your career as a Roman Catholic priest and became . . . financial adviser. Is that how you describe it? And now you're going back to God and taking Mr Robinson with you? How many others?'

It was at this moment that the party was interrupted. People had been listening to the exchange uneasily, sipping lime tea and eating their organic scones. Now, there was loud hammering on the door and the boardroom of Robinson Securities suddenly filled with policemen.

They did not look at all out of place in the room. They might, indeed, have been part of the reproduction furniture. Perhaps the time will come when policemen are provided as decoration in our great boardrooms.

'Will all the ladies please go to the end of the room where there is the portrait of a gentleman with a moustache?' – this was the Robinsons' grandfather whom the police sergeant described so irreverently, a man of legendary enterprise in the City of London. 'Gents down here, please. I am afraid we are going to have to search everyone present, so we must ask the gentlemen not to put their hands in their pockets and the ladies to leave their handbags alone. For the next few minutes, I would be grateful if nobody asked to go to the toilet.'

A hubbub of anger and protest arose, but Jaques seemed too much absorbed in his conversation to notice.

'It might be, as you say, Daniel, that we shall eventually get back to God. I do not know. All I do know is that at present our minds are too polluted even to comprehend what was meant by God. I knew I was wasting my time in the priesthood when I discovered in Africa that the more educated and more prosperous my parishioners became, the less likely they were to believe in God. Our entire philosophy is so much infiltrated that learning now destroys the desire for ultimate knowledge, rather than feeding that desire. The present pope understands this, and has tried to bring his Church down to the philosophy of the age, with his talk of investment in the under-developed nations as if it could even be a kind or worthwhile thing to bring the rest of the world down to our own level of degradation. But the saddest and greatest truth of our time is that modern technological civilisation has already reduced the human race to the level of inquisitiveness and dignity which you find in a budgerigar. Open the door of its cage, and the bird voluntarily chooses to remain inside. Do you never weep for the human condition, Danny?' Jaques turned his wild, tear-stained face to the journalist.

'Please shut up. What on earth is happening?'

'You must not misunderstand me,' Jaques rounded off his peroration. 'I do not mean that there is anything wrong with technology – it is only the philosophy which has grown up around it. In order to shed the philosophy, we feel we must first shed technology. Eventually, perhaps, we will again be able to embrace the benefits of technology without being polluted by all the glib, inhuman philosophy which clings to it at present.'

'Shut up,' said Daniel. 'What on earth is happening?'

'Will you step this way, please, sir,' said a tall police-man to Danny.

In an ante-room where the tape machine still clattered out the closing prices in London and early dealings on Wall Street, Danny was asked to take off his clothes.

'Why? What is happening here?'

'We have reason to believe that there are certain substances on the premises,' explained the policeman, who was called P.C. Fender.

'What on earth makes you suppose that? In the board-room of Robinson Securities? You must be mad.' Danny was down to his underpants, now, and very athletic he looked, too, if small.

'Suffice it to say that our information came from a highly-placed source,' said Fender.

Slowly, Danny began to understand. 'Do you think you'll find any?'

'Oh, we shall find some all right. Sergeant Touchstone is with us tonight, and that can only mean one thing. Now, sir, if you wouldn't mind just lowering your drawers. That's all right. Thank you ever so much. You can put them back again now.'

'You mean, he . . .?'

'Alfie Touchstone could find cannabis resin stickin' out of the Archbishop of Canterbury's arse-hole. He's got what you might call a touch of the genius in him, when it comes to finding things if he's a mind to it. Now, sir, could you ask the next gentleman in? That rather wild-looking individual you was talking to.'

In a smaller room, almost a cupboard, which served as a place for preparing coffee, Rosalind Robinson found herself confronted by a short-haired sergeant of the women's police with a disconcertingly square jaw.

'Now, just slip off your things, dear,' said the woman

43

police sergeant, 'and we won't take up too much of your time.'

'Why must I do this?' Rosalind shivered under her thin woollen jersey. She had a beautiful, slim body, most delicate in every proportion; she suffered from no shame, and regarded herself with delight in the long mirror every time she took a bath. But something – perhaps it was pity for the policewoman, whose body was so much less well favoured – something deterred her from undressing in that awkward proximity.

'We are looking for unauthorised substances,' said the policewoman. 'Come along now, do you want me to unhook your zip?'

'No,' said Rosalind, 'I can do it.'

'Nice material you've got here,' said the policewoman. There was a mock-heartiness in her manner, but the steely, objectionable look in her eye had been replaced by something hotter and damper and more disreputable; the awakening of sexual curiosity. Policewoman Sergeant Alice Hobday was too guilt-ridden to allow this to display itself as anything more tender than a kind of bossy truculence, but Rosalind recognised the symptoms. A biology mistress at Heatherdown had been similarly affected. 'It doesn't look as if you've much room to hide anything in there, but we'd better have the bra off, just the same.' Policewoman Hobday's eyes grew steely again as they inspected Rosalind's breasts, which were a trifle on the small side, it is true, but beautifully formed. A slight flush appeared on the square, flat cheek-bones under the straight, basin-cropped hair, and her manner became brusquer.

'Now, off with your panties, dear. It's terrible where people hide things sometimes, especially cannabis. It's no good snivelling about it, dear. I'm just going to put my hand up the inside of your legs. We *could* search you much more thoroughly if we wanted, but we're going to let you off lightly this time. Don't look at me like that, dear, I'm only doing my duty you know. It's no good crying about it. Everybody's the same. We've all got to be searched some time. Cannabis is against the law, you know.'

'Why?' Caustic salt tears blinded Rosalind as she tried to climb into her panties. First she put her leg in the wrong hole, then both legs in the same hole. A tear dropped from her chin to her left breast, while her whole thin body shook with vexation, and shock.

In childhood and early womanhood, Rosalind always shared a bed with her cousin Celia, Frederick's daughter, with whom she lived. Sometimes, they would caress and fondle each other in bed, but neither attached much importance to it, nor regarded it as in any way essential to their friendship. It was a way of passing the time when one of them had been disappointed in a love affair, or when neither had anything else to do. They kept no secrets from each other and shared all they had to share. But the look in Policewoman Hobday's eyes possessed a strange, single-minded intensity which Rosalind found frightening. It was the look which Jaques described as self-think. Alice Hobday was the sort of woman who might easily commit a murder, Rosalind decided, if anybody threatened to discover her guilty secret.

Once Rosalind was dressed again, she grew calmer. Could nothing be done to save Alice Hobday? Somewhere, in that embittered and ungainly frame was a human creature, representative of the highest point in creation, with all its capacity for happiness and philosophical awareness. Even Alice Hobday's intelligence, once freed from all the pollution and clutter, might reach an acceptance of its own unassailable dignity to the extent of that supreme conceit of which only the human intelligence is capable – the assertion and belief in its own immortality.

'Why is cannabis against the law, dear? Because the

government doesn't like people to have it. That's why cannabis is against the law. Now wipe your face on my hankie. You look terrible. Anybody would think I had been assaulting you. I haven't been assaulting you, have I, dear?'

'No,' said Rosalind.

'No, just searching you,' said Woman Police Sergeant Alice Hobday. 'Don't worry about it too much. We all have to go through with these things – either searching or being searched. Otherwise, there's no knowing what people might get up to. Look, you haven't done up your hook at the back.'

Rosalind allowed Alice Hobday's hands to rest on her neck. Hard, stubby, utilitarian hands on such a beautiful, slender neck. I must be kind, she thought. We, who are the beautiful people must use our beauty to spread happiness and love throughout the world. We must not hoard ourselves. She even managed to smile at Alice Hobday, thinking how happy it would make her if she were Alice Hobday and anyone as beautiful, as young and as radiantly good as Rosalind Robinson smiled and offered her neck in the cause of world peace and understanding. But Alice Hobday only gave a hard little laugh, and said: 'You've been lucky this time. Don't think you'll be able to smile your way out of trouble next time. Will you ask the next person to come in?'

Celia was next, and Aunt Barbara behind her. Celia looked beautiful, as she always did, but rather frightened. When she came out from her search, however, her face was flushed and there was a bright, excited look in her eye. She gave Rosalind the quick, conspiratorial look which meant that she had a secret to impart. 'Can it be,' wondered Rosalind, 'that she did not mind those terrible hands pushing themselves between her legs? Perhaps I am callous towards other people, or perhaps just ticklish.'

Aunt Barbara said: 'I shall never forgive Frederick for

46

this. Celia has told me that her father told the police to come. He must have gone off his head. All the Robinsons are mad. Now I must go and be stripped naked to keep him happy. The police must be odd too, if they think I carry dangerous drugs around at my age.'

They missed about an ounce of resin which Orlando happened to have in his breast pocket, but he, too, had forgotten it was there. It was only when everyone had had their names taken down and most of the people had left that Sergeant Touchstone produced his trump card.

'Would you like to explain, Mr Robinson, how this substance came to be in the left hand top drawer of your writing desk?' He held a small pellet of grey substance, flecked with what looked like ash or charcoal. John Robinson took it between his thumb and forefinger and sniffed it disdainfully. 'I have never seen it in my life before,' he said.

'I have never seen it in my life before,' said Sergeant Touchstone, writing it down. 'Then how did it come to be in the left hand top drawer of your writing desk?'

'I very much doubt that it did,' said John Robinson. 'The left-hand top drawer of my writing desk is locked.'

'We have our methods of opening things,' said Sergeant Touchstone. 'Or perhaps it was the second drawer down.'

'There is no second drawer. If you look carefully, you will see that the lower drawers are all dummies. They open out to reveal a cupboard.'

'I suppose you are now going to accuse me of lying,' said Sergeant Touchstone.

'Yes.'

'They all do that. Funnily enough, it is usually what makes the court decide they are guilty. Innocent people never accuse a policeman of lying. They assume he must have made a mistake.'

'I am innocent and you know perfectly well that you

are lying. I suppose that what you have got in your hand is pot, but it doesn't look like anything to me.'

'Perhaps it isn't quite such high-class stuff as you're used to,' said Sergeant Touchstone. 'And perhaps I was mistaken in where I thought I found it. But I'll find a place to have found it, and none of this is going to help you in the long run.'

'Why do you do this?' asked John Robinson. 'You are behaving like a criminal, not a policeman.'

'You are wrong, sir, with the greatest respect. In Britain, nobody is a criminal until he has been convicted of a crime. That is our splendid British system of justice. You are the one who is going to be convicted of a crime, not me. Now, where shall I find this little bit of substance next? We know it's here somewhere.'

John Robinson looked angry. He tried to be one of the good people; he tried to see evil in terms of misfortune, malice in terms of unhappiness. Somewhere underneath, however, an unregenerate Robinson stirred. 'How much has Frederick paid you?' he said.

At that moment, P.C. Fender came in with a number of parcels. 'This is what we are looking for, I think. Rex sniffed it out in the bedroom. Aren't we a good dog, Rex?'

Indeed, it did seem as if the two of them somehow comprised a single good dog. Jaques, who was easily affected by the sight of happiness, hugged them both, his soft white face lined and crinkled in smiles. Even John Robinson beamed at them both.

'Jesus Christ,' said Sergeant Touchstone. 'Enough dope here to spifflicate the whole British army, and I had to go and bring my own.'

'I wondered whether you would find that,' said John Robinson. 'It was an idea I had for an office party last Christmas, but nobody in the office seemed particularly keen on the idea. Plainly, you and I have a few things to talk about, Sergeant. Perhaps the constable ought to stay, tco. Now, I must say goodbye to the other guests – you have their names, I think. Goodbye Rosalind, darling. Goodbye, Celia. Goodbye, Orlando – you're taking them home? We leave for the country tomorrow morning. Audrey goes down tonight to get the house ready. Anybody who decides to come can either take the train down to Bath, where they will be met and brought to Williams Farm, or they can join us at Robsec House at nine o'clock in the morning. I am sorry we have not been able to discuss our plans in greater detail. We must all have a good sleep tonight, and see if we can sleep out of our systems all the horror and the poison we have taken in.'

It was typical of John Robinson that he should not have asked who intended to make the journey, or how, or even whether anybody did. Since consciously deciding to become one of the good people, his greatest anxiety was not to intrude himself on others. His own path to self-realisation took him among the remote uplands of intellectual speculation, where the wilderness was too bleak and too unrewarding for there to be any pleasure or purpose in attempting to communicate it. So far as he had any social function, it was as a sounding-board for other people's ideas, and nobody could be sure how much he comprehended of what was said to him. His eyes seldom seemed to follow the train of his thoughts. There was plainly a gap between the two operations; his brain only registering what his eyes had seen after an interval of time. His face would have been handsome if it were not for a peculiarly vacant, fish-like quality in the eyes. His daughter loved him with a daughter's passion, and so did others, but the world might have decided that he was a simpleton if he had not been so extraordinarily rich. As the guests departed, wiping the crumbs of their organic scones from their mouths, nervously checking that their buttons were correctly arranged and their shoes refastened, it was to his wealth that they deferred. All were polluted.

Orlando and Rosalind had scarcely spoken to each other at the party. No sooner had they met than they looked at each other, no sooner looked, but loved, sighed, and sought the remedy. However, the remedy would have to be postponed out of respect for Celia's presence in the back of Orlando's small red car, as he drove them moodily to Frederick Robinson's residence in Campden Hill Square. He felt the warmth of Rosalind's body beside him, sensed an attitude of expectancy which emanated from her as she sat staring fixedly ahead.

'Watch out,' said Celia. 'You nearly ran over that old man on a bicycle.'

'Nobody would have minded. Nobody would have noticed, least of all himself. He lives in a bed-sitter alone. Death will only end his loneliness. Nobody will mourn him. He will not mind, he is already dead. He has ceased to think, *ergo*, he has ceased to exist.' Orlando's hand rested on the top part of Rosalind's beautiful, soft, slender leg. Unfortunately, it was now required to change gear.

'We have a philosopher at the wheel,' said Celia. She was as beautiful as Rosalind, but blonde. For some reason known only to God, her eyes could hold Orlando's without either feeling the tiniest spark travel between them, while between Orlando and Rosalind, such a current was set up as could blithely destroy every old age pensioner within the compass of the welfare state. 'You have plainly been talking to Jaques,' she added. 'Don't you find him exhausting? I could never bring myself to join Uncle John's little coterie down in Somerset while Jaques was there. Quite apart from anything else, he becomes so boring after a time. Don't you think there are more useful ways of spending your life?'

'That's what my brother, Oliver, says.' Orlando resented Celia's presence and now he had to change gear again. He did so with great bad temper. 'He proposes to improve the quality of life of the workers, he says, but all he means is that he hopes to give them all colour television sets. He won't succeed, of course, and even if he did, they would be no happier. Jaques is right.'

'He's a perfectly decent, run of the mill lunatic. You see thousands like him in every mental hospital;' said Celia. 'The shame is what he's done to poor Uncle John.'

'I must admit,' said Rosalind, who did not know whether Celia could see what Orlando's hand was doing, and would not like it to be supposed that her intellect was submerged in sensual longings, 'some of what Jaques says seems a little far-fetched to me. How does he know that the ordinary people, or anyone else for that matter, want anything different?'

The tragedy of it, the sheer numbing tragedy! Orlando nearly wept. Both these young girls, so lovely, so sweet, so clever, so infinitely desirable, so hopelessly young, were beginning to be polluted by the grotesque madness which passed for normality, in their society.

'They don't want anything different,' cried Orlando. 'And that is the blasphemy of it.'

'I am sure they don't want to go and freeze to death, eating wholemeal scones with Uncle John in Somerset. Rosalind and I are staying where we can think our thoughts in reasonable comfort.'

'I do wish Uncle Frederick had not set the police on my poor father,' said Rosalind. 'Daddy so easily gets upset.'

Even Orlando had to admit that he did not welcome the thought of life at Williams Farm. Perhaps he lacked the moral courage; perhaps he, too, was polluted. They arrived at the door of Frederick Robinson's house in Campden Hill Square.

'Are you free to come out tonight for dinner?' The

question was addressed to Rosalind, with an insolent, challenging stare. Rosalind immediately felt that Celia should have been included in the invitation, if only to preserve the decencies. Celia would have realised that she was expected to refuse, of course. Then Rosalind would have told her all about it afterwards, or next morning, perhaps. Would she, though, on this occasion? For the first time in her life, Rosalind began to feel a certain impatience towards her beautiful cousin. Nobody could have mistaken the genuine regret in Rosalind's voice when she said: 'Alas, it is so sweet of you, but Uncle Frederick told me he wanted me to stay in this evening. Apparently he has something he wishes to tell me.' She didn't dare add: 'Couldn't you ask me for another time?' She had never felt unsure of herself before. Would Orlando despise her if she ran after him too much? Would he feel hedged in, tied down?

To Orlando, her refusal was incomprehensible. It could have been that she was not attracted towards him but he knew she was. Perhaps she was playing grandmother's footsteps, reckoning to tease him a little. Perhaps she thought he was interested in her enormous fortune. He, Orlando Twickerley, of the famous radical family. Stung, he turned his back. 'Very well then. That's too bad. Perhaps I shall give you a ring, some time.'

He motored away, unaware of her frantic, waving figure behind.

John Robinson's eyes had focused themselves again. 'Well done, sergeant. I should like to congratulate you. For a moment, I thought you weren't going to find anything in your search, while you messed around with that silly little bit of plasticine you were trying to frighten me with.'

'It was proper cannabis resin,' said Sergeant Touchstone.

'Although not up to your standard, I dare say. But perhaps we can forget about that little bit, now we've found about two hundred ounces of the stuff.'

'That is very gracious of you, sergeant.'

'Not at all. Mind you, it was P.C. Fender here who really made the discovery. Now, I'm afraid I must ask you to come round to West End Central police station so that we can enter all this on the charge-sheet. It's only a formality, of course, sir, and you'll be free to come away again immediately afterwards.' There were only four people left – the sergeant, the police constable, John Robinson and Jaques. They had adjourned from the board-room to Robinson's penthouse suite on the top floor, and were all drinking tea and eating the organic scones prepared for them by Audrey. As John Robinson's house-keeper, she had always been almost insanely equable by temperament. Before they arrived, she packed her master's overnight bag with some home made scones and some honey, on the supposition that he would be spending the night in the cells.

'These formalities,' said Robinson with great sympathy in his voice. 'How troublesome you must find them. At a time when you could be doing something really useful, your life is taken up with unnecessary formalities.'

'Alas, poor policeman,' wailed Jaques, easily touched by the thought of human distress. 'Carried from cradle to grave on a sea of formalities.'

'But you mentioned that it was P.C. Fender's alertness which led to the discovery of these drugs, and I think you have a very good point there. Don't you think he should receive a reward? Of course, he never will. Our society is so unjust in that way. Only those who do not deserve them receive rewards. I should have thought that a reward of a thousand pounds would be the very least that P.C. Fender deserved for his alertness, wouldn't you, Sergeant?'

The atmosphere in John Robinson's drawing-room became suddenly tense. Only Jaques continued whimpering to himself, his mind far away on the problem of formalities.

'Perhaps he does deserve it,' said Sergeant Touchstone. 'But it would only make the others jealous as haven't got it. Now, let's get some of this down. Bein' apprehended as there was reasonable grounds for suspectin' the presence of cannabis resin.' He paused.

'C-a-n-n-a-b-i-s,' said John Robinson.

'I never was much one for spelling. Now we have to deal with words like "marijuana" creeping into the country. I would turn them away at London Airport. Now, let me see, it was cannabis resin, wasn't it?'

'R-e-s-i-n,' said John Robinson.

'Yes, of course,' said Sergeant Touchstone. 'Perhaps I wouldn't mind just another cup. Oh, you've been a very bad man, Mr Robinson. You shouldn't have had all that cannabis resin in your bedroom, you know. The government doesn't like it at all. Makes people happy, and if they're happy they don't work hard enough. If they don't work properly there's no taxes, and if there's no taxes there's no government for them to feel important about.'

'I can see that I have been most misguided,' said John Robinson.

'Misguided?'

'M-i-s-g-u-i-d-e-d. I am quite prepared to pay the fine, but I only wondered if it would not save everyone a lot of time and trouble if I paid the fine straight to you. All this entering into charge-sheets, cautioning, assembling magistrates and clerks – you yourself described it as a formality. The essential thing is to pay the fine. We must not fritter away the golden hours of life with formalities.'

'What does P.C. Fender think of all this?' asked Sergeant Touchstone with a touch of sternness.

'I don't mind what you do. It's got nothing to do with

me about the fine. Mr. Robinson mentioned a reward of a thousand pounds for finding the stuff, and, speaking for myself, I would be very grateful. The wife is always saying I should put away more of our money. We plan to buy a sweet shop when I have saved enough, but it isn't easy to save money nowadays.'

'Of course not,' said Jaques glumly. 'No doubt you spend all your money on sweets, and so confound yourself. With the money my friend is going to give you, you will be able to sell them instead and so prevent others from saving money and realising their life's dream, whatever it may be. A curious idea of happiness, putting sweet things into other people's mouths. To own a sweet shop.

> Who would true valour see,
> Let him come hither;
> One here will constant be,
> Come wind, come weather.
> There's no discouragement
> Shall make him once relent
> His first avow'd intent,
> To own a sweetshop.'

Jaques sang rather beautifully with a hopeless, haunting melancholy. His voice held a quality of desperation it is true, but even the desperation was somehow beautiful, as if it all became part of God's plan. Nobody could have been disturbed by it, although people more susceptible than either Sergeant Touchstone or P.C. Fender might easily have wept. Jaques, of course, could suck melancholy out of a song as a weasel sucks eggs.

> 'Hobgoblin, nor foul fiend
> Can daunt his spirit;
> He knows he at the end
> Shall life inherit.

Then fancies fly away,
He'll fear not what men say,
He'll labour night and day
TO OWN A SWEETSHOP.'

'It always seemed quite a pleasant life, that of a sweet-shop owner,' said P.C. Fender.

'Ah, but is it a pleasant death?' countered Jaques, quick as a viper.

'Shut up,' said John Robinson. 'I would suggest a fine of one thousand five hundred pounds.'

'What you are suggesting is most irregular,' said Sergeant Touchstone. 'And I must caution you that even to offer money to a police officer is an offence, while actually to give him money with the purpose of causing an irregularity is an extremely serious one. Are you aware of that?'

'Yes,' said John Robinson.

'Good,' said Sergeant Touchstone. 'In that case we must add a further two hundred and fifty pounds, I am afraid, for the irregularity. That will be one thousand seven hundred and fifty pounds, and I am afraid I must ask for it in cash.'

'Me, too,' said P.C. Fender.

'It saves on the formalities,' explained Sergeant Touchstone.

'Jaques will get you the money from the cashiers' department,' said John Robinson, writing on a slip of paper.

'Formality, formality,' said Jaques. 'Can't you see that money, too, is a formality? That it represents nothing any more, not happiness nor comfort nor even freedom from discomfort? You have been taught to worship it and so you do, because man requires something to worship, but can't you see that it has become an abstraction? We all need much less of it, not more, and then it might come to mean something again.'

'If you aren't going to keep your side of the bargain, the deal's off then,' said P.C. Fender, sounding hurt.

'I will settle for one thousand seven hundred and fifty bits of abstraction now, but if this gentleman goes on for much longer, I may easily require some more.' Sergeant Touchstone was angry.

'Of course I will give you the money. I only wish I could give you something more valuable,' sighed Jaques, and went to the cashiers' department on the third floor.

The clerical staff in Robsec House was paid a day late that week.

'You are not going to take away all these parcels now I have paid my fine?' asked John Robinson. 'Surely, you will have no use for it now.'

Sergeant Touchstone gave the matter some thought. 'Let us reach a compromise. Shall we say, I keep half, you keep half? It is not often we find such high-quality stuff nowadays. You would be horrified to see what they are selling the kids at twelve pounds an ounce.'

'You mean you smoke it yourself, or you sell it as a sideline?'

'I like the occasional smoke, I might as well admit. I find it settles the mind. Not all the lads back at West End Central agree with me. I suppose it is like working in a sweet factory – you eat so many the first day that you never want to eat another. Inspector Lovely – he's head of my section – finds it makes him sick. Very much against the potheads, is our Inspector Lovely. Probably have me transferred if he knew I had a weakness myself, although I don't know what he thinks we do with all the stuff we find on these raids. If he thought we sold it, he'd be demanding his cut, along with everybody else. He's very old fashioned about things like money. Everything has to be shared out, very strict, when its others as have got the money. Well, yes, perhaps I will have a little pull, if it's all the same to you, sir.'

'Will you have a pull, Constable?' John Robinson had prepared a joint with great dexterity while the police sergeant mumbled on, greedy little eyes fixed on John Robinson's fingers.

'No thank you very much, sir. Not today. I'll just take my reward money and wish you all the best; if that is the same to you. I don't really see the point in any of these things, you know. They may be quite pleasant at the time, but they don't get you anywhere, and they can land you in serious trouble.'

Jaques accompanied him to the lift, singing softly, and without a hint of mockery:

> 'Then fancies fly away
> He'll fear not what men say
> He'll labour night and day
> To own a sweetshop.'

'Goodbye, Mr Jaques, sir. It's been very nice meeting you. I hope you will come round and look in some time when the wife and me have got our sweetshop. You might wish then that you'd decided to tread the straight and narrow, too.'

'I shall certainly come,' said Jaques, beaming with pleasure, 'although I wouldn't buy any sweets. Sweets make me very sad. They deprave the whole pattern of human responses, you know. It would not be so bad if there were fewer of them, or if they were less readily available. As it is, by instantly satisfying a minor appetite, they inhibit any awareness of far greater needs within the human spirit.'

'I see,' said P.C. Fender. 'Well, that's a point of view I suppose. Thank Mr Robinson again from me for my reward.' He tapped the large packet of ten pound notes in his tunic pocket. 'It isn't often nowadays you find people who appreciate the work of the police. It's all nagging bloody criticism. Just a small gesture, like this one, when we've done a good job of work – it makes all the difference, you know. All the best.'

'All the best,' cried Jaques, quite overcome by such a demonstration of human benevolence. 'All the very, very best. For you always. And everyone. All the very, very, very best.'

'What were you talking about?' asked Touchstone, when Jaques came back to the drawing room.

'I don't know, really,' said Jaques, 'sweets, I suppose.'

'You couldn't get anything much better than this,' said Touchstone, inhaling greedily and handing the damp bundle of a cigarette to Robinson. 'You don't indulge?'

'No,' said Jaques. 'It only makes me sad, and I can be sad without it.'

'Like Inspector Lovely,' said Touchstone. 'And Constable Fender, too. He'll never make a sergeant, you know. He hasn't the necessary breadth of mind. He's always on about incentives – incentives to what, I ask? There's nothing so enjoyable as absolute peace of mind, and not all the sweetshops in the world can give you that.'

'I like you,' said John Robinson. He paused, feeling that this statement required enlargement. 'You are collected,' he said, 'together.'

'Thank you very much, sir,' said Touchstone. 'And this has been a most pleasant way to spend the afternoon. Did you know it was April Fool's Day today? Of course it is – the day after the election. Oo, are you preparing another joint? I really think I shouldn't.' Sergeant Touchstone gave a feeble giggle.

'This election,' said John Robinson, 'do you think it will make much difference?'

'Not to the likes of us,' said Touchstone, equating him-

59

self naturally enough with one of the richest men in England. 'My job is to look after your lot, and if the socialists ever succeeded in hurting what might be called the wealthier class of man, then the whole of society would collapse. The rich have got something which they think is worth defending. Take that away, and there's nothing left. You're the only thing which keeps us all going, you know, Mr Robinson.'

'It's very good of you to say so,' said John Robinson, modestly.

'Not at all. I wouldn't say anything if I didn't believe it from the bottom of my heart. Mr Wilson won't dare to touch you. He'll just make things worse for the poor, so they go on thinking how poor they are and what a shame it is that other people are richer. That way, they'll go on voting Labour, the silly buggers, and Mr Wilson will go on having his weekly tea parties at Buckingham Palace, with all the trimmings.'

'How fascinating,' said John Robinson, watching the hot, fragrant smoke rise from the end of his cigarette. 'Let me see, you work for my brother, don't you?'

'Only up to a point,' said Sergeant Touchstone. 'Inspector Lovely has some sort of understanding with him, I believe. I've never met the gentleman myself. It was Lovely who suggested I might step round this afternoon. And a very nice and profitable one it has been.'

'Yes, we must be grateful to him for that,' said John Robinson. 'I'm glad you have never met Frederick. I fear you might not like him. He is not what might be called altogether, not quite . . . collected . . . together.'

'Oh dear,' said Sergeant Touchstone. 'I'm sorry to hear that.'

'All of us nowadays, to a greater or lesser extent, suffer from a certain pollution of the mind, which prevents us from seeing things freshly . . . as they are . . . we only see things as other people have seen them before us, at thousandth hand . . . often cruelly distorted . . . like a game of Russian whispers.'

'That is quite true,' said Sergeant Touchstone, taking the cigarette from him. He was in the process of making a great discovery. 'You are absolutely bloody right there, squire. Fancy that. Like a game of Russian whispers. Makes you laugh to think about it, when you realise.' Sergeant Touchstone giggled happily.

'Well some of us, some of the time, try to fight against this pollution,' continued John Robinson. 'We try to clear away the debris and see things as they really are, not as people have decided that they should be, for the sake of convention. Then you understand that so much of the conventional wisdom of our time is raving lunacy.'

'I've often had my doubts about some of the things going on nowadays,' said Touchstone. 'Are you going to prepare a third joint? I really don't think you should. Ah well, why not?'

'For instance, I am always being asked either to fly to New York myself or to send other people across to attend conferences. But there is nothing which they could possibly want to say which cannot be written on the back of a postcard. They are all mad.'

'With postcards, you can even have a pretty picture on the back, as well.'

'Right on. I knew you would understand. You see, the trouble with Frederick is that he's different from us. Instead of trying to rid his mind of the debris which fouls up the pure flow of thought, he collects and purifies the debris, as if it were what mattered most, an alternative and greater truth than the truth it hides. He uses this debris – to build ever more fantastical edifices of infinitely intricate and subtle design, each more marvellously fragile than the last, all rubbish. Look at colour television, look at the money we are spending on supersonic airliners, or on getting to the moon, or at what has come of

61

the whole idea of money itself, of scientific progress and its relation to material benefit. It is all mad, and Frederick, I am afraid, is part of it.'

'Oh dear,' said Sergeant Touchstone. 'I am sorry you feel like that about him.'

'Ah yes,' said John Robinson. 'And I could tell you other things about him, too . . . about how he used to behave in the nursery at home when we were children . . . about the lies he used to tell, and the very serious emotional harm he might have caused once to an impressionable young nanny . . . we grew up, together, you know . . . I've known him all my life . . . the main thing about him is that he's not quite . . . altogether . . . not quite gathered together.'

'Oh dear,' said Sergeant Touchstone. 'A bit scattered around the place, is he?'

'Poor Frederick,' said Jaques, with tears starting in his eyes. 'He has never tried to look up and see the stars, or look at his feet where a flower may be opening its face to heaven.'

'The fact is,' said John Robinson, 'I would not recommend Frederick to be chairman of our little family concern, you know. I do not think he has got . . . quite the right ideas. It must be terrible for you and Inspector Lovely to work for someone who is . . . not quite altogether.'

'It does add to the difficulties,' said Sergeant Touchstone. 'I must say. Perhaps I will have a last cup of tea. I feel unaccountably thirsty.'

'Perhaps you would both prefer to work for someone whose . . . vibrations are slightly less . . . discordant with the way things were planned . . . I mean . . . the way God intended us to be . . . together?'

'I should of thought so, sir, wouldn't you? Certainly it is an idea which would be worth mentioning to the Inspector, when I see him next.'

CHAPTER THREE

Neither Celia nor her cousin Rosalind enjoyed their dinner that evening. Delicious course after delicious course slipped down their slender young throats to disappear into those dark, regions of the stomach which mysteriously nourish and sustain the rest, but neither girl paused to wonder at the process on this occasion. In their stomachs the miracle proceeded, watched only by God.

'Why on earth did you have to go to John's gathering in the first place?' Frederick Robinson had not had a successful day: no charges had been laid against his brother for possession of dangerous drugs; he had suffered nearly an hour of abuse on the telephone from two crucial aunts who had been searched by the police; he had been betrayed by his daughter; the Labour government had been returned with a huge majority; a raving lunatic seemed more firmly ensconced in the chairmanship of Robinson Securities than ever before.

'Because we were asked,' said Celia.

'Daddy particularly wanted us to go,' said Rosalind. The sound of his niece's voice made him wince all the more.

'The fact that Rosalind had to go does not mean that you had to go too, Celia,' he said in a petulant grinding tone. 'You should be grown up enough to be able to do a few things apart. It is high time you split up. Quite honestly, I think it is time Rosalind found somewhere else to live. Daniel Chamberlain tells me you have been seen fooling around with the young Twickerley boy. You cannot expect me to put up with you for the rest of your life just because you've got a crush on my daughter. Now you have found someone else, I think it would be as good a time as any for you to leave.' His ugly, brutal words frightened both the girls. They stared at each other with wide, wet eyes, blushing. 'I've been meaning to say this for some time, Rosalind, and after what has happened today, I really can't feel safe with you in the house. Would tomorrow be too early for you to move?'

The servant who waited at table heard this and sighed. He was called Giovanni, and loved Rosalind with a spaniel-like devotion, often flirting with her when he spoke, holding her hand and caressing her with his beautiful brown eyes. Once she had kissed him in the hall, her slender white arms around his neck, her lovely young breasts pressed into his chest – only in affection, of course, and bantering encouragement, and because she knew they would both like it. He would die for her, if asked to do so, but at the moment he had more pressing business, as soon as there was a lapse in the conversation.

'In that case,' said Celia, 'I shall go with her. You know I love her as well as she loves me. We have always been brought up as sisters—'

'Oh, shut up,' said Frederick. 'Yes, Giovanni?'

'Two gentlemen to see you, sir,' said Giovanni.

'Tell them I am at table. In any case, I wasn't expecting anybody. Who are they?'

'Yes, sir. Two policemen,' said Giovanni.

Orlando's brother, Oliver, was not improved by success. The night after the election, Downing Street had still not issued its list of junior government appointments, and Oliver had no way of knowing whether he would be included. Something in the Ministry of Overseas Development, or anything connected with Africa, was what he really hoped for. Oliver very much wanted to see the entire world organised sensibly, but experience had taught him that tribal Africans were the only people left who were polite enough, or vulnerable enough, to acquiesce in his schemes. As a teacher, once, in Kenya he had persuaded the whole school to adopt the binary system of mathematics, and the Zeuss-Hoppner method of reading, with the result that none of the pupils in his school passed a single examination for two years.

'Perhaps Harold thinks I was criticising his fatstock subsidy review in the talk I gave to the Hungerford Young Farmers,' said Oliver.

'I shouldn't think Mr Wilson cares very much what you said to the Hungerford Young Farmers,' said Orlando. Relations with his brother had never been very cordial. Their father, on his death, had mistakenly specified in his will that Oliver should be Orlando's guardian, controlling all the money until Orlando's twenty-fifth birthday. Oliver's disapproval of unearned income was particularly intense where it applied to the unearned income of other people; the notion that Orlando, at the age of twenty, should enjoy an independent, unearned income was more than Oliver's tender social conscience could endure.

'What I meant, of course, was that our fatstock subsidies would have been more generous last year if the Conservative government had not left the economy in such a mess when we took over in 1964. As soon as we can restore prosperity again, the fatstock subsidy will be restored as a matter of first priority.'

'For God's sake,' said Orlando, 'I am not the Prime Minister, and I couldn't care less about the fatstock subsidy. But I wish you would give me something better than this protein powder to eat.'

'It has all the nutritive qualities which the human body requires. Added to pig-swill, it can facilitate the breaking down of nutritive elements within the digestive system by a ratio of fifteen per cent. Nothing is wasted. Of course, you couldn't care a farthing about agricultural problems. You are all right, Jack.'

'No, I'm not,' said Orlando. 'You feed me on pig-swill and give me no money.' A sympathetic snuffle behind told him that Adam, their ancient family servant, agreed. Adam, too, had been bequeathed to Oliver in their father's will, in a manner of speaking, and Oliver disapproved of him equally.

'You couldn't care about anything, of course, except yourself. Look at that protein powder which you are eating. When we have solved a few problems of production technique – at present it costs two pounds a meal, which is, of course, uneconomic – we shall be able to present all the nations of Asia and Africa with a final solution to their nutritional problems. There are a few other matters to be ironed out first. Side effects include diarrhoea and a propensity to lose hair.'

'Thank you very much. I know about the diarrhoea,' said Orlando.

'But think what a break-through it will be. As soon as Harold has got our economy straight, he is going to arrange for the distribution of this protein powder throughout the whole underdeveloped world, as a matter of first priority.' Oliver's eyes were shining with that inner light which, in the Middle Ages, would have identified him as a man touched by God. At the present time it merely identified him as a bright young Labour back-bencher who was hoping for a job in the new government.

'I thought you said that fatstock subsidies would be Mr Wilson's first priority.'

'You could never hope to understand anyone as fundamentally different from yourself as Harold Wilson. For him, everything has first priority. Good heavens, man,

66

can't you understand how much needs to be done? Did you know that here in England there are a million children who are seriously undernourished, living on the breadline? That is the extent of the problem we have inherited.'

'I don't believe it,' said Orlando. 'Why don't you give them this pig-swill?'

'Of course you don't believe it. You don't *want* to believe it. As a matter of fact, it appears in a Report produced by the *government*.'

'The Labour government,' said Orlando. 'I have heard that over-feeding and obesity are much greater problems in England.'

'Perhaps they are,' said Oliver. 'There is quite literally no end to the problems we have inherited. Some people eat too much, some people eat too little. We in the Labour government somehow have to make sense of it all.'

Adam came into the dining room again.

'Mr Twickerley is wanted on the telephone,' he said. Orlando was always referred to as 'Mr Orlando', while Oliver, ever since his father's death, had been 'Mr Twickerley'.

If Oliver was ever unaware of the rebuke contained in this subtle distinction, he was certainly in no mood to think about it now. He nearly knocked old Adam down in his excitement, as he ran from the room with a yelp.

'The young master seems very excited tonight. People did not behave like that when his father was alive — running out of dinner to answer the telephone.' O good old man! How well in him appeared the constant service of the antique world. He was not for the fashion of these times.

'I fear,' said Orlando, 'my days here may be numbered. I will be sad to miss you, Adam.'

'Sad days indeed, Master Orlando, when a son of the

house is made to eat pig-swill, and I, who have worked for the family these last twenty-five years, must be rebuked because my master wants to answer the telephone.'

When Oliver came back, his eyes were shining. 'Under Secretary of State at the Commonwealth Office;' he shouted. 'I must go round to Downing Street at ten-thirty. What's the time? For God's sake, what's the time, Orlando? Adam, will you go and put out my light grey suit? It always looks slightly better in photographs. And a plain-coloured tie. The orange one, I think. That is Harold's colour. A light blue shirt. For heaven's sake hurry up.'

'It is only nine o'clock. You have an hour and a half to get from Ebury Street to Downing Street, which should require about eight minutes at this time of night.'

Oliver sat down, suddenly deflated. The implications of his new responsibility began to suggest themselves. It would do his image in the party no good if it became common knowledge that he kept a butler. To have a playboy brother living with him was even worse. Without them his house in Ebury Street could soon become a meeting place of the new government. Problems of world significance would be hammered out into the small hours of the morning. The Foreign Secretary would be there; the Commonwealth Secretary; the Prime Minister would come in after dinner; protein powder would be handed round with the cheese-straws and olives, as Oliver and his friends discussed new and fearless initiatives in the under-developed world. But not with Orlando there. Would Harold want to have an idle playboy listening to their conversations? Orlando was a menace. He was preventing so much from happening in the world that was really necessary, really progressive, really for the good of all mankind. As a junior minister at the Commonwealth Office, he must show that he really cared, that he was sincerely committed to the exciting adventure ahead, by repudiating this unwelcome souvenir from the past.

'Orlando, do you remember telling me that you had never held a national insurance card, never paid insurance stamps?'

'Of course. You never gave me any money to pay for them.'

'There are more ways of gaining money than being given it by your brother. Has it never occurred to you, Orlando, quite how irresponsibly you are behaving? The money paid on national insurance stamps not only covers your own insurance – for health, old age, supplementary benefit and everything else. It also covers the insurance of other people, too handicapped or too unfortunate to compete in our "never-had-it-so-good" society.'

'No doubt, but I can't very well buy them if I have no money.'

'It has never occurred to you, I suppose, that most people of your age are working for their livelihood?'

'Why do they want to do that?'

'Orlando, you owe three years of stamps, plus the penalty for non-payment – about two hundred and twenty pounds. It is thanks to people like you that the national health service is running down. Old people in my constituency often have to wait ten years for an operation if they have varicose veins, or piles.'

Adam had plainly suffered from both in his time. He coughed sympathetically.

'Don't blame me. I'm not stopping them from having operations on their varicose veins or their piles. I have never had either.' Orlando loved old people, and would have done anything within reason to save an old person from discomfort or pain, but he could not accept responsibility for the sorrows of Oliver's old age pensioners in Hungerford, sixty-five miles away. These discomforts were merely part of old age, a preparation for death, something to be welcomed after a good life, seeing life renewed in one's children and grandchildren. 'Piles are not the ultimate evil. They are merely a nuisance,' he said. Society was doomed to failure if it approached the problem of nuisances by trying to remove them all. Others would assuredly arise to take their place. After consumption, cancer of the lungs. After deprivation, poisoning by excess. The correct and only hopeful way to approach the problem of nuisances was from the opposite end – to concentrate on not being made unhappy by them. For most people, who lacked the necessary mental agility and self-discipline, this could only be achieved through drugs, and the important thing was to find the right drugs. Orlando was almost positive that cannabis was the one, or some derivative of it. Every generation would produce its quota of people like Jaques who could achieve the same peace of mind without recourse to drugs, and they would give meaning and beauty to the world, directing such desultory efforts as people chose to make for their own accommodation. Perhaps these few people would slowly find their way back to the meaning of God, and they would slowly awake the world from its drugged slumber and take it back to the society envisaged in the Sermon on the Mount, where all God's creatures would find their true dignity and forget about colour television, moon travel, supersonic airliners and every other substitute religion of our time. 'We must all try to bear our nuisances,' said Orlando.

This was the moment when Oliver finally realised that the situation had become impossible. 'I should strongly advise you, Orlando, to go to the ministry of Pensions and National Insurance tomorrow morning, down the road in Ebury Street, and make a clean breast of everything. They will expect you to pay a penalty, of course, on top of the two hundred and fifty pounds you owe.'

'I won't make a clean breast of anything,' said Orlando, thinking, despite himself, of Rosalind's lovely young

70

breasts, which he had never yet even seen. He had felt them, though, through her slip . . . 'In any case, I haven't got the money.'

'You leave me no alternative. I will go myself and make a statement about you in the morning. It would risk bringing the whole government into disrepute if it became known that a minister was giving shelter and protection to someone who is a parasite on the welfare state.'

Oliver left the room looking like the noblest Roman of them all. Quite plainly, he intended to do everything he said. Orlando swore most foully.

'Please, Mr Orlando, I have about four hundred pounds in Post Office Savings. They are all I've got, but I'm sure you can have them.'

Why did Adam always behave predictably? Perhaps it was a characteristic of his class. Even if Orlando accepted the offer, he would need to buy insurance stamps every week until his sixty-fifth birthday. Thus the welfare state makes a slave of its citizens.

'No, Adam. I am going away. This place has become too uncomfortable. I'll take the money, in case I need it. Thank you very much.'

'I'll accompany you, sir, if I may. I'd sooner join the monkeys in the London Zoo than stay here any longer. The common man is trying to score off his betters again, and no good ever comes of that. Your brother's a bad man, to give encouragement. Perhaps I can be of some help, wherever you are going.'

Orlando had always felt the most peculiar detestation towards polishing his own shoes. 'All right,' he said.

'Because I have reasonable grounds for suspecting that there may be dangerous drugs on the premises, that is why,' said Sergeant Touchstone severely. 'I must ask you to submit to a search.'

'Who gave you these reasonable grounds? Does Inspector Lovely know what you are doing?'

'Information was received from a highly placed source, and the warrant was issued by City of Westminster magistrates on Inspector Lovely's application. Now, I must ask you to co-operate, sir. We are only doing our duty, as you must know. If we don't find anything of an illegal nature, that will be the end of the matter so far as we are concerned.'

'Not as far as I am concerned,' said Frederick. 'Come into the study.'

'There will be no need to search the girls again,' said Touchstone, giving Celia and Rosalind an avuncular wink. 'They have already been searched once this afternoon. If you can look around this room, P.C. Fender, and keep an eye on the girls at the same time, I shall deal with Mr Robinson in the study.'

The girls were left alone with Constable Fender. Both thought he looked rather handsome, in a functional sort of way. 'You're sure you don't want to search us?' asked Celia, while both girls giggled into their plate of cold grouse, which Giovanni had laid reverently in front of them.

'No thank you, miss. I am a married man, as it happens,' replied Fender stiffly.

'Won't you have Uncle Frederick's grouse, then? He seems to have left the table. At least have a glass of wine – burgundy, or claret, or whatever it is, while we are waiting,' said Rosalind.

'No thank you, miss. Not while on duty. It's against regulations, you know.'

'They always say the British police force is the best in the world,' said Celia, her eyes wide in admiration.

'As a matter of fact, I expect the wife will have my

supper ready for me when I get home.' Constable Fender allowed himself to thaw a little. With much cajoling, he was persuaded to sit down in Frederick's seat, take off his helmet, and even nibble at Frederick's grouse.

'Does your wife cook well?'

'What will you be having for dinner?'

'If she blonde or dark?'

'Do you prefer them like that?'

'I expect you must spend a long time away from home. You must be terribly lonely, sometimes. What does your wife do all the time you are away? Are you *sure* you can trust her? She must get terribly bored, too, you know.'

'As a matter of fact, my wife works in a frozen vegetable process factory,' said P.C. Fender. 'We are saving up for retirement, when I hope to buy a sweetshop.'

'Now you can just drop your drawers for a minute please, sir.'

'Why must I do that?'

'We have to make sure you haven't anything hidden between your legs, as it were. Don't let it worry you. We're all the same. Everybody has to be searched nowadays, in case they're carrying this drug called cannabis. The government's very much against cannabis, even a Labour government, you know.'

'I know all about that,' said Frederick. 'What makes you suppose that I've got any? I've never taken it in my life. I *support* the government in this matter. My friend Charles Lovely knows perfectly well where I stand. So does the Home Secretary. I am appalled by the thought of young people wasting all their opportunities to get on in the world. I would never allow the stuff in my house.'

'You wouldn't be likely to say anything different, under the circumstances, now would you, sir? All this talking isn't getting us nowhere. Just lower your drawers for a moment, so I can have a look. There we are. Nothing to be ashamed of, is there, sir? You can pull them up again now. I'll just go through your pockets as I hand your clothes back to you.'

Sergeant Touchstone's hand was in Frederick's neat blue trouser pocket when he let out a low wolf-whistle. 'What have we got here? Oh, you naughty man. Constable Fender, will you step this way please? I think I'm finding something nasty in Mr Robinson's trouser pocket. Look at this. What do you think this is, Mr Fender?' It was the same jaded, grey lump of resinous material which Touchstone found wherever he looked.

Fender sniffed it carefully. 'It smells like cannabis resin to me.'

'That's what it looks like to me.'

Frederick's manner changed. 'Give me that, please.'

'I am sorry, sir. We have to put it in an envelope and seal it up for analysis in the police laboratories. Now, if you will sign your name across the seal, here . . . thank you very much, sir. And I'll sign my name, and Mr Fender will sign his. I'll write something above our signatures to show what it is. Now, let me see. Substance found in left hand trouser pocket of Mr Frederick Robinson when apprehended and searched on the night of April 1st 1966 at his residence in Campden Hill Square. Apprehended is the right word, I think.'

'A-p-p-r-e-h-e-n-d-e-d,' said Rosalind. The two girls had followed P.C. Fender, who resumed his helmet.

'You should know that, Sergeant,' said Fender roguishly.

'Residence is, I suppose, how you would describe this house,' said Touchstone.

'R-e-s-i-d-e-n-c-e,' said Rosalind.

'Will you all sit down,' said Frederick quietly. He rummaged in his drawer for a while. 'I do not know how much money you want from me, but I find that I haven't got any in the house . . . at any rate not nearly enough for you. You were the two policemen who searched my brother John's house earlier this afternoon, I suppose. You didn't find anything?'

'No, sir. Clean as a whistle, I'm pleased to say.'

'How much did he pay you?'

'Well, really, sir, I'm not sure what you're talking about.'

'Really, Uncle Frederick. These are policemen in the best police force in the world. You cannot talk to them like that.'

'Rosalind, I have already ordered you out of the house by tomorrow morning. If, as I suspect, you and your father are behind this attempt to lay false charges against me by bribing the police, you will be in a lot more trouble before you are through.'

'Tut, tut, sir,' said Sergeant Touchstone. 'You shouldn't be found in possession of cannabis resin if you're going to take that attitude. Now I must ask you to come along with me to Notting Hill police station, so we can get the details jotted down in the charge sheet. It's not too far to go, just across the road, and we'll probably be able to lay on a station car to bring you back.'

'Just a minute, please. First, I would like to know how much my brother John paid you.'

'Why would you want to know a thing like that?' Something in Frederick's manner disturbed Touchstone. He had no personal animus against either brother. Business was business, and he had a job to do, just like everyone else. Inspector Lovely had been most receptive to the idea that John Robinson should become the section's patron in place of his younger brother. Other stations and other inspectors accepted Greeks, Cypriots, Italians, even Irishmen as their patrons, but Inspector Lovely had his standards: no tarts and no foreigners. If the tarts paid their fifteen pound a week, that was all right so far as the inspector was concerned, but he didn't want to know any more about it. Frederick Robinson had never been a par-

75

ticularly generous patron, but he had not been a demanding one, either, and Touchstone expected the evening to end as amicably as such evenings usually did.

'I should have thought it quite obvious why I wanted to know,' said Frederick. Again, there was an unpleasant ring to his voice which Touchstone did not like. The man must be aware of the current tariffs.

'Surely, you cannot hope to get away with accusing the police of perjury, or planting evidence against you,' said Touchstone. 'If the British courts were to accept that sort of suggestion, not a single criminal in the land would ever be committed. Besides, the courts trust us. They have got to, or they could never trust anyone. We in the police force have over a hundred years of tradition behind us. Impartiality, integrity, cheerfulness . . . Nobody would believe you, Mr. Robinson. Take a friendly word of advice, and forget about that side of things. Nobody's guilty of an offence until they've been found guilty in a court of Law, and you're going to be found guilty, so you might just as well decide you're guilty and say you're sorry.'

'I want to know how much my brother paid you.'

'And I can't see why I should tell you.'

'So you admit that he paid you something?'

'Of course, I'm admitting nothing of the sort. It's you who's admitting things.' Sergeant Touchstone took out his notebook again. 'On being cautioned, Robinson said: "I apologise most profusely, officer. I can see I have been extremely silly. I would like you to take seventy-six other offences of a similar nature into consideration, so that I can start again with a clear conscience, after I have repaid my debt to society." Touchstone paused.

'A-p-o-l-o-g-i-s-e,' said Rosalind.

'I never said, "I apologise," ' shouted Frederick.

'You've just this minute said it,' said Touchstone.

'Oh, Daddy, what's the use?' said Celia.

76

'It sounded like an apology to me,' said P.C. Fender. 'Of course, you can always withdraw it.'

'Later, Robinson said that on reflexion he wished to withdraw his apology. He believed that the laws against cannabis were immoral in principle, unenforceable in practice, and he wished to make a public statement to that effect.'

'How much did my brother pay you?'

It may have been that P.C. Fender was bored by the repetition of that question. More likely, perhaps, he was thinking of his sweetshop, and frightened that Touchstone had forgotten it. At any rate, disregarding a pained look from his sergeant, he told the truth: 'I received a thousand pounds reward for actually finding the stuff. Sergeant Touchstone took the fine – I think it was about one thousand five hundred pounds. Of course, if you think that is rather a lot – and I suppose it is rather a lot – you must bear in mind we found much more hash at John Robinson's house.'

'Hash?'

'Cannabis resin. You probably wouldn't need to pay quite so much, would he, Sergeant?'

'You mean to say, Constable . . . ?'

'Fender, P.C. Barny Fender.'

'Constable Fender, that you and the sergeant found a large amount of cannabis at my brother's flat; that in exchange for a sum of money you agreed to keep quiet about it, and then he persuaded you to come here and plant some on me instead?'

'It wasn't a very large sum of money,' said P.C. Fender. 'You musn't expect that we'll let you off with very much less.'

'Good,' said Frederick. 'Now perhaps you will listen to this.' He pressed a button on his desk. After a short time a voice answered as if from nowhere: "I received a thousand pounds reward for actually finding the stuff, Sergeant Touchstone . . .'

77

'You bloody fool,' said Sergeant Touchstone. 'That's torn it.' The tape played out to its end.

'. . . It wasn't a very large sum of money. You mustn't expect that we'll let you off with very much less.'

'All right, all right, Mr. Robinson. I could ask you for those tapes, of course, but it might only lead to unpleasantness,' said Touchstone. 'We'll forget about the whole episode, then.'

'No we won't' said Frederick disagreeably. 'I intend to take these tapes round to Scotland Yard immediately.'

'What's the purpose of that? Why do you want to make unpleasantness?' said Touchstone.

'Because I don't like being ratted on,' said Frederick.

'And what about me?' Police Constable Fender saw his dreams of a sweetshop receding forever. 'It wasn't my idea. Touchstone merely brought me round with him.'

'You will come to no harm', said Frederick, stern but just, 'provided you tell the truth about Sergeant Touchstone's activities.'

'Thank you very much, sir. Of course I will tell the truth about the sergeant. It's a good job someone's caught up with him, too. He had a bad influence on the whole section. Ask the inspector.'

'I intend to ask him. And I have a feeling that Charlie Lovely will agree with me on this occasion.'

Touchstone looked from face to face around the heavy, mahogany-furnitured room. Fender was dog-like and self-righteous. Frederick looked like the Lord Chief Justice asking for his black cap. Giovanni, uncomprehending, stared at Rosalind. Rosalind and Celia, oblivious of everyone, appeared to be playing some game together.

'That seems to leave me rather on my own,' the sergeant said.

Three people in the room began to think of John Robinson's invitation to start a new life-style in Williams Farm.

PART TWO

CHAPTER FOUR

Williams Farm, near the village of Combe Mendip, appeared on the rent books of Robinson Estates as being unoccupied. John Robinson had only visited it once, on a tour of his organisation's agricultural holdings in the West Country, and then it was empty, the hilly fields slowly but perceptibly being allowed to fall into a state of neglect.

It was bought with a resident family of tenants called Williams by John Robinson's father shortly after the second European war – a very good time to buy land in England. The land around Williams farm had been farmed by a family called Williams for as long as records had been kept, although whether it was always the same family, or whether different families merely adopted the surname of Williams on assuming the tenancy, nobody knew. Nor is it a matter of the smallest importance.

But the recent history of Williams Farm and of its tenant is essential to an understanding of what happened after John Robinson's arrival, on the night of April 2nd 1966.

When the Robinsons bought the property in 1946, the ninety odd acres around Williams Farm were farmed by old Mr Williams called Wee Willie, and his son, also called Willie Williams. In addition, there was a daughter, called Esther who never married. Old Willie Williams took to drink in later life, and let the farm fall into disrepair. There was talk of evicting him – not from the landlords, needless to say. They dealt only through an agent, a local man called Partridge who would never have dreamt of evicting a Williams from Williams Farm. No, the threat of eviction came from something called the War Agriculture Commission Board, known as the War-Ag, a menace to all farmers at the time. On the day before he died, old Wee Willie Williams took thirty two hundred-weight bags of fertiliser, a present from the War-Ag, and emptied them out over Monk's Cleeve, a field so steep that no one had ever been able to plough it, in the shape of his initials. W.W. For many years, the grass was bright blue where he had scattered the fertiliser and neither cows nor sheep would eat it. Twenty-five years after the old man's death, it was still possible to make out his initials where the grass was higher and richer. Old Willie died the night after committing this outrage. Nobody ever knew how he died. Twenty five years later, it was still a subject of speculation in the countryside around.

When the old man was buried, young Willie inherited the tenancy and lived on in the farm with his sister as housekeeper. And so the matter might have remained – Patridge felt so sentimental about the Williams family that he did not even raise the rent, as he was perfectly entitled to do, on the old man's death – if Willie had not bought a horse called Kirstie from his friend and neighbour, Charlie Winter, down at Hatch Bottom. Charlie laughed at the time because Kirstie was a useless horse.

Kirstie was not only useless as a horse, she also had a very mean nature. Eventually Willie Williams tied her to the brake van of the Bridgwater train while it was waiting in Combe Mendip station. There were four trains a day, then, between Bridgwater and Glastonbury, through to Wincanton and beyond. Now the line has been closed, of course.

The train left to a cheer from the Railway Arms, where

Willie sat drinking with his friends. Kirstie reluctantly trotted behind until forced into a canter, then a gallop as the train gathered speed and turned away towards West Hay, Edington Burtle and Huntspill Level.

'Good riddance to 'un, har, har,' said Willie to his friends at the Railway Arms, and they ordered more of the sour, brown local cider in high humour. A signalman at West Hay saw Kirstie galloping behind the 12.32 in a lather of sweat, and laughed himself sick. But by the time the train reached Huntspill Level, Kirstie's mean nature had finally been purged.

'Boi the time un reached Huntspill Level, down Baron's Bridge way, she were dead,' explained Willie to himself, in the high-pitched, sexless voice of the West Mendips. 'Har, har, har.'

Everybody in Combe Mendip had a good laugh over the story, but then some meddling woman in Bridgwater came to hear of it, and in no time at all the cruelty people from Taunton were round, asking aggravating questions and trying to make trouble. It was thought that Mrs. Winchcombe, at the post office, told them the story. Willie had to go to prison for six months.

It was while Willie was in prison that his sister, Esther, died of cancer. He took the news philosophically. 'She were a most aggravating woman,' he explained to his cell-mate, a scrap-dealer from Norton Fitzwarren who stole the lead from church roofs. It was while Willie was in prison, also, that John Robinson chose to make his tour of Robinson Estates in the West Country, and saw Williams Farm for the first time.

Partridge, seeing that he had received no rent, that the land was untouched and the house empty, took fright at the impending visit and applied for a County Court order ending the tenancy. He redistributed such land as was useful among the neighbouring farms, all of which belonged to Robinson Estates, and left Williams Farm empty and desolate among thirty-seven more or less useless acres. Nobody told him that Willie's stock had been moved across to Charlie Winter's farm, at Hatch Bottom. Charlie wasn't going to tell anyone, as he received twelve acres of good arable land in the share-out.

Monk's Cleeve remained with Williams Farm, the ghostly initials W.W. still standing out on the hill-side; there was a wood, an orchard, a small pond and a stream in the valley between the uncultivable hills. This was what John Robinson saw on his tour of inspection in May 1965, and he lost his heart to it from that moment. The farm-house, which was empty at the time, but kept in a reasonable state of repair by Partridge, might have been built at any moment since man first learned to pile one stone upon another and seal the gaps with mortar. Probably the existing structure dated from the mid-nineteenth century, but a building had stood there since time immemorial and a team from the Somerset Archaeological Society, which visited the place, declared that the cellars were of mid-fifteenth century origin and the well, now sealed by an iron cover, even older.

The farm buildings were unspoiled, largely owing to the scepticism with which the Williams family had always greeted innovations in agriculture. John Robinson thought about the place night and day, as he dreamed of creating new life styles in the Somerset countryside. Somehow, Williams Farm seemed to contain the seed of a greater and more enduring Truth than could be found in the executive suite on top of Robsec House.

But in the intervening period, Young Willie Williams came out of prison. Obviously, he went straight back to the only home he knew, at Williams Farm. When he stepped off the train at Combe Mendip Station – the same train, as it happened that Kirstie had spent her mean and evil nature in trying to follow – he was greeted as a hero home from the wars. The West Mendips had been remarkably sceptical about both European wars, as it happened, and Willie was accorded the nearest thing to a civic reception that Combe Mendip is ever likely to see. Farmers collected from miles around to pat him on the back, and chuckle anew over the tale of how he had put paid to Kirstie. The Railway Arms stayed open for an extra two hours, and Charlie Winter, from Hatch Bottom, fell into his own silo on the way home and spent the night there, while the green fodder rotted and steamed around him: "It were a better smell than you get from Mrs Winter most nights of the year,' he told them afterwards.

Willie slept the night in his own bedroom at Williams Farm, and did not open his eyes until the afternoon of the next day. He was happy to be home among the familiar smells and sights of the farm he had never left for more than a week in his life before, but as soon as he woke up, he knew something was wrong. It was not that his sister Esther was missing. They told him in prison that she had died of the cancer, and Willie just nodded his head in agreement. The two used to scream at each other night after night, when they got in each other's way. He would have to peel his own potatoes now, and boil up his own onions in the huge, cast-iron pot that sat on the hob, but it was a small price to pay for being spared so much aggravation.

Willie climbed out of bed, decided not to shave, and poured some paraffin over the damp logs in the grate. He always slept in his clothes, and seldom bothered to shave. Without Esther, there would not be so much unnecessary washing and sweeping, either. It never failed to get on his nerves. But something was wrong.

'Yern bin people snooping their noses round these parts,' he piped, when the fire was lit. He often spoke to himself, even when other people were present. The habit dated from the time when a small white dog used to follow him around wherever he went. It was called Titch, and some people might have described it as a form of terrier. It never did anything at all but follow Willie Williams, and when it stood still, it shivered. Originally, all Willie's conversation had been directed at the dog, but one day it wandered down a badger hole where it stayed. Willie waited a short while for it to come out, then he said: 'If yew wants to stay down there, that do be yourn decision,' and from that moment his observations had no audience but the rushes and the heavy black mud which stretched from his farmhouse to the beginning of the marsh at the far end of the valley. Now, as he looked over the sodden landscape, nothing stirred but a jacksnipe flitting through the bracken and a curlew cried hopelessly into the wind. It was nearly dark when Willie first saw movement in the paraffin house next to the tractor shed under the hayloft.

'Ung yer be people in un,' he shrilled to himself excitedly. 'Ern have no business in barn.' With no very clear idea of what he intended to do, Willie collected a tin of paraffin, some matches, a pitchfork and a knotted tangle of binder-twine, then he crept down to the deserted chicken house behind the paraffin store.

There were two of them, moving around and talking. Willie settled behind an empty TVO drum and began to listen. Two of them were definitely there, and from the way they talked, one of them might have been a boy, the other a girl, but quite honestly Willie was not prepared to say which was which.

'Now that we've arrived,' said the voice which was probably a man's – 'we must guard against any feeling of regret. This is where it is all going to happen – the last judgment, the Four Horses of the Apocalypse. This is where the spring point enters Aquarius. Can you feel the vibrations?'

'Yes,' said the girl. She had a soft, musical voice. 'It makes me so tired, all this activity. Everything is happening all around us. I just find it so exhausting.'

'Do you remember when we arrived at the farm?'

'No,' said the girl. 'No, I can't remember that.'

'Neither can I. It is wrong to remember things like that. We never arrived here, of course, in the sense of movement and destination. We were always here, or rather, the farm was always in us.'

'Yes, yes,' said the girl gently. 'Like it was growing in us, you know, until we suddenly realised this amazing thing. Oh my God, I'm so tired.'

This conversation set Willie thinking. She must suppose it was a very small farm to be able to fit inside her. No wonder she was tired, with trying.

'The farm were being inside of they,' he reasoned to himself. He had forgotten he was not alone, and his voice sang out shrill and peculiar, in the silence.

'Hullo,' said the one with a man's voice.

'Ung, whom be you, an howm you come here?' Willie's voice when he was surprised or slightly frightened climbed several octaves higher.

'We walked,' said the man.

'Walked, did 'ee? Ung, yewm can walk right back again, then, or Oi'll set the paraffin to 'ee, an' light um, tew, just see if Oi won't. Can't stay the night here, yew can't.'

'Why not?' said the man. He said it pleasantly, as if he was quite interested in the answer. For the life of him, Willie couldn't think of what to say. It would have been different if the girl had answered. Willie was not used to being rude to men.

'Wull, if you baint up to of doing no harm,' he said doubtfully.

'We won't do any harm,' said the man.

'That's not our thing at all,' said the girl. 'We're actually into *desperately trying* to do the opposite, like we were mending the harm which other people do, kind of restoring it, you know . . .'

'That's all right, then,' said Willie. Then, feeling that

87

he had been bettered in argument, he returned to the attack. 'Ung, whom be yew, then?' He glared at the girl, daring her to answer.

'I'm called Buttercup,' she said.

He stared at her uncomprehendingly for a moment, then his great red face split into a grin. 'Yewm telling Oi yewm called Buttercup? Har, har, that's a funny name, Oi'll say. What does us think of that, Oi'd like to know.' But the dog Titch, to whom this remark was addressed, had been dead for ten years, and its ghost did not answer.

Buttercup smiled, and with her smile a sweetness and a gentleness lit up her whole face. 'Yes, I'm called Buttercup,' she said. Years ago – so long ago that the mind recoiled from any memory of it – she had been called something else. Laboriously, she had washed away the name like a stain on her character; now she was clean, unpolluted Buttercup, as God made her, and she probably could not remember her original name, even if she tried.

'And what be yewm called? Cow parsley or something?'

'I'm called Strong Arm,' said the man.

This was less successful. Willie regarded him doubtfully, not so sure who was being mocked. 'Strong Arm? That's not English, is it? Be yewm an American, then?' Terrible wartime memories stirred Willie's breast. During the American occupation, loud, incomprehensible strangers had driven around his own beloved country-side in jeeps, throwing oranges at the women and candies at the children. Those were the days when his father had started drinking heavily, and the War-Ag was always trying to interfere. Willie was not much given to patriotic excesses, but rather than see another American invasion he would enlist in the army, pour paraffin over every one of them and set it alight. He might even vote in a parliamentary election, if someone would tell him which way to do it. Americans were worse than a swarm of horseflies.

'No, I'm not an American,' said Strong Arm.

'And yewm be called Strong Arm? Ung, yourn arm don't look too over-strong to me. Here's an arm for 'ee, yere.' Willie waved his own arm in the young man's face.

'He is called Strong Arm,' said Buttercup. 'It's his name.'

'Uf it's his name, then, 'ee can't help it. I'm called Willie William, and this is my barn.'

'It's beautiful,' said Buttercup.

'It's all right,' said Willie, rather pleased. 'But don't go getting up to any mischief. Goodnight to 'ee, un.'

'I am so tired,' said Buttercup. 'Goodnight, Mr. Williams.'

Later that night, Willie sat alone before the dying fire in his large, wet kitchen. The old barrel of cider had gone so sour it was scarcely drinkable, but Willie had much to think about and the brown, cloudy liquid helped him.

'They tinkers do have queer names,' he mused to himself, and his piping voice sent a rat scurrying to its refuge under the sink. 'That talk on carrying other people's varms in their belly were plain daft,' he said. In some distant part of the house there was a crash. Probably one of the farm cats, mean and skinny creatures, which bred in the old dairy and were never given a plate of food or a bowl of milk until the day they died. But suddenly, Willie was suspicious. What were the two tinkers up to? Perhaps they were going at each other to have babies, like the cats did, the sheep did, the pigs did, the cows did (and Willie even had to help them). His cell-mate in the prison had spoken a great deal about fucking, but Willie had never rightly been much interested in the idea, to tell the truth. Perhaps he ought to go and have a look.

Stealthily, Willie collected his tin of paraffin, his pitchfork and his binder-twine. With the matches between his teeth, he crept down to the barn. Not a sound, but soft breathing. He lit a match, and held it trembling. The two were asleep, Buttercup's head pillowed on Strong Arm's shoulder. For the life of him, Willie could see no harm in it. He collected some sacks from the potato room, and covered the pair of them. Neither stirred.

'Un ern't doing no 'arm,' he muttered as he stumbled through the puddles in the rutted, manure soaked yard.

Next morning, Willie was to collect three sows (two with their litters) from Charlie Winter at Hatch Bottom, where they had been taken in after Esther went to hospital. There were also nine head of young stock and some heifers to put in Monk's Cleeve. Suddenly, Willie had problems. He almost forgot about the tinkers, until the man came into the kitchen with an empty tin.

'Can we have some water, please?' said Strong Arm.

'No. Not 'til you've put up they fences round the back 'n' helped Oi wi' yer litters on pigs,' said Willie.

Buttercup was much affected by the piglets. 'But they're beautiful,' she said.

'Ung, ur eat noicely when ur will have been a little bigger,' said Willie.

Buttercup clapped her hands in delight. 'Do you mean we're going to be able to eat them? How wonderful. I don't think I've ever eaten baby pigs before.'

'Oi didn't say as how yew was going to ate un,' said Willie meanly. He had given water and sacking; that was quite enough. 'Them is my piglets, and if anyone be going to ate of them, that person be Oi.'

But Buttercup didn't care. She and Strong Arm busied themselves about the farm by day, in the evening they sat staring at each other wordlessly, awaiting, no doubt, the Day of Judgment or the spring point's moment of entry into Aquarius at the end of the 2,000 year Piscean Cycle. If Buttercup peeled his potatoes, Willie would let her keep the peelings. Occasionally, he gave them milk, or even an onion. Once, Strong Arm caught a frog, and presented it to her.

'It is so precious, so beautiful. Do you think I can eat it?'

'Of course, that is what it is for.'

Buttercup lowered the frog, dangling by one leg, into her mouth. She swallowed it whole, taking infinite care not to crush the little creature in her mouth. She could not bear the thought of cruelty, or of pain.

'Now it is inside me. How funny it must feel,' said Buttercup.

'It must be happy now,' said Strong Arm. 'It has existed and it has fulfilled its purpose. Its happiness now resides in your happiness, and you make the world happy, by your beauty and your gentle goodness.'

'I can feel it jumping around inside my tummy,' said Buttercup. 'I am so glad you taught me about eating it.'

'They was eating frogs – live uns, tew. I couldn't believe my eyes,' squeaked Willie in the Railway Arms.

'I've heard as how yern tinkers did that. Same as hedgehogs and worms. We none of us knows how many worms we eats in the 'taters,' said Charlie Winter. 'Like Mrs Winter says, it's all meat.'

'But they baint going of ating none of my piglets,' said Willie. 'I've seed them looking kind of greedy-like over the sty sometimes. They'll take the mash, too, if you don't watch them. They pigs would be bloody starving if Oi didn't keep my eyes open.'

'They do some work, though, sometime, do they?' said Charlie. 'What do you pay them? Mrs Winchcombe down post office, were asking.'

'Nothing, of course,' said Willie. 'And it aren't no business to 'er. Her be after making trouble.'

'I expect she be after thinking you ought to be paying

Insurance Stamps for yourn tinkers,' said Charlie, who had himself suggested this line of inquiry to Mrs Winchcombe that morning.

'They tinkers doan' pay Insurance Stamps,' said Willie, 'interfering old bitch.'

'She were wondering how yew managed, now they took all the land away from yew up Williams.'

Willie suspected that his old friend was curious about this himself, and gave a noncommittal reply. In point of fact, his sister Esther had been sitting on a tidy sum of money all this time, unknown to anyone but herself. If Willie had guessed it at any moment in the past nineteen years, he would have had it off her for farm improvements, but as it was he found himself unexpectedly with nearly £6,000 in the bank, in a private account. His farm account was overdrawn as always, but the bank manager in Glastonbury did not know he had lost his land, and allowed the overdraft to continue. A man can live very well on the sort of overdraft farmers are allowed. And the free labour of Strong Arm and Buttercup helped, too, so long as he could prevent them eating food intended for the pigs. It was a pity, he reflected, that human beings could not be turned into a field to graze like other animals. Then they would be no trouble at all. Today, he had bought himself a nice shoulder of mutton on the butcher's van which came from Glastonbury every Thursday. He was planning to give his tinkers some of the tatty bits, at the end, and he had even bought them a few scraps from the neck, four pigs' trotters and two pounds of bones, although the butcher had given these last to him as a present when he said they were for some poor people with no money.

'Faggots is cheap, only they must go and ate tew darn many of un,' he said. 'It's not loike they was pigs, where yer be some purpose on fattening them up.'

*   *   *

Willie pretended not to notice when four weeks later the two tinkers were joined by another two. They introduced themselves as Ruby Wednesday and Macbeth. Macbeth had wild red hair and side whiskers. Ruby Wednesday would have looked very slim and pretty but her skin was grey and blotchy and her eyes had a listless look to them. They said they were searching for the Holy Grail, which they knew to be hidden somewhere near Glastonbury, probably not more than a day and a half's walk from the site of the old Abbey. They were reasonably sure that their path would be north-west from the old High Altar, towards the Bristol Channel. The only way to find out was to live in a place until you absorbed its vibrations. If its vibrations were encouraging, you were on the right road. A preliminary survey suggested that the vibrations at Williams Farm were excellent.

Willie put out no extra food for them, but Macbeth, unlike Strong Arm, seemed to have resources of his own. Sometimes he would walk the two miles of cart track and lane into Combe Mendip returning with tins of luncheon meat, Cornish pilchards in tomato sauce, Frankfurter sausages and other delicacies which he'd bought from Mrs Winchcombe. At other times he would trek into Bridgwater or Glastonbury, spending the night in a hedge, and returning with fresh herrings, boiler fowls, a goldfish in a glass bowl, a blue budgerigar, some drinking glasses with the picture of a huntsman on them (these he gave to Willie) and various other purchases.

On one occasion, he returned from a trip to Glastonbury with four friends, immediately identified by Willie as tinkers. By this time, the tinkers were sleeping in various unused bedrooms in the farmhouse. They did everything for Willie: dug the garden, prepared the food, swept the house, mended an overflow pipe which was dripping (Williams Farm, like all the farms in the area, was on mains water supply. It could also have been on mains electricity, but Willie preferred to use an old dynamo machine, powered by a paraffin engine and batteries, which worked only occasionally). However, the new invasion might have proved too much for Willie if it had not been followed soon afterwards by the arrival of quite a different sort of person – Walt Izzard, who had shared a cell in Exeter Gaol with Willie, and promised to look him up on his release. Walt was put in charge of the tinkers and made to see they worked properly. He also introduced the community to the wonders of Supplementary Benefit, unemployment pay and the National Health, all of which he understood profoundly, and from that moment there was no food shortage. Thereafter Willie and Walt had their meals brought to them by Beauty, one of the new girls, in a separate room on the farm.

The four newcomers were introduced as Rock (he was also sometimes called Black Stone), Snowman, Beauty and Dumpling. There were many like them around Glastonbury in those days, long-haired, listless creatures who congregated there on some whim or other. Rock explained that by a careful study of ancient records, he had come to the conclusion that Glastonbury was the point of the earth's equipoise, that it marked the gravitational and magnetic centre of the earth. He never explained why this made it important that he should stay at Williams Farm. In fact, he said that he would much prefer to live on the top of Glastonbury Tor, which was the point, he said, at which all the ancient lines of primeval energy met, the dragon lines, the serpent lines, the leys and all the ancient alignments from the Pyramids, Stonehenge, Old Sarum, St Michael and St George. 'I just can't approach the Great Tor. The power is too great. It withers me,' he said. Apparently it had the same effect on Snowman, Beauty and Dumpling. So they followed the Dragon Path to Williams Farm, where they seemed to settle quite happily.

94

Rock and Beauty had brought some hashish, which they called 'shit', and this was fallen upon with quiet cries of delight by Snowman, Dumpling, Macbeth, Ruby Wednesday, Strong Arm and Buttercup.

'You got this shit from London, Black Stone? That's really incredible. I mean, what did you think of the place?'

Rock thought for a long time before delivering his judgment.

'What did we think of the place? Well, the food struck me as fucking terrible. There were a few things that were really nice – Red Currant Mountain Ice Cream sandwiches which are this really nice-tasting ice cream with three big red-currant wafers on top. Apart from food, well I thought the young people in some places were very strange. Very strange. The freaks were heavily into this political thing. There was an election coming up, and all the straight guys had to be getting up and shouting like 'Shit', 'Bull', 'Codswallop', you know, and the heads just stood there staring at them. It was all very strange.'

'Oi heard there was an election, tew,' said Willie. He sometimes ate with the tinkers in the old front room of the farm, to learn what they had to say, 'Ung, yern send me nothing threw post, this time, so Oi can't rightly vote for any on us, can't Oi?' In fact, he had only once voted in a parliamentary election, against Mr Churchill after the war, in protest against the war and the American occupation.

Willie's remarks were always greeted politely – almost sycophantically at this stage.

'True, man, true. That's very good,' said Snowman.

'He's kind of cool, isn't he?' said Beauty. 'I think he must have the most wonderful brain working there. All his ideas are like so collected together.'

'It's the simplicity,' said Strong Arm. 'None of us can be really good until we've learned to be simple. Like, I can't really understand half of what he says, but I can see how good it is . . . I mean, I can really see it.'

'He has nice vibes. I mean they're really nice' said Ruby Wednesday. 'People do have these ectoplasms.'

It was only when they persuaded him to share one of their joints that discussion became franker. After much preliminary coughing, Willie really entered into the spirit of it.

'Oi doan rightly know how anyone of yous is called,' he said. 'If Oi call one on you Buttercup, you next one moight be called Marigold or Cow Parsley or bloody Nasturtium Leaves for all Oi care, har, har, har.' After a time, his voice drifted into complete incomprehensibility, from which occasional phrases could be disentangled. 'Mistress Cabbage Patch, Oi'll say, har, har, har.'

'Mr Lettuce-Leaf yer, hoo, har, har.'

'Mrs Strong-foot an' us be called Big Bum, heh, heh.'

'Who,' said Beauty – this was the evening of their arrival – 'is this *strange man?*'

'He lives here,' said Macbeth. 'He is the farmer.'

'Does he own the place?' asked Rock, who was also called Black Stone, or Blackie.

'I don't think so,' said Strong Arm. 'He sometimes talks about a landlord who owns all the land for miles around. Somebody who lives far away, and recently took some of his fields. He may have mentioned the name of Robinson.'

Black Stone perked up at this, and became very knowledgeable. 'There was a farmer called Stone Killer Robinson in the middle of the eighteenth century who made it his business to destroy as many as possible of the Great Stones of Avebury. You see a picture in Dr Stukeley's book, showing how he did it. First, he heated the stones by lighting a woodfire underneath them, then, when they were red-hot, he poured a great jug of stone water over them, so that they split.'

'What a horrible, really evil sort of thing to do,' said Beauty. 'He must have some kind of hang-up against stones. Is he really evil, this man Robinson? I mean, he sounds so fucking violent.'

'Ung, yern be called Mistress Potato Flower, Oi be thinking,' gurgled Willie, 'har, har, har, Oi be laughing so much moi face hurts now.'

'Potato Flower, that's really cool.'

'Any sort of violence just turns me over. I am that excited, like I'm shaking all over. Who is this guy Stone Killer Robinson?'

'He's not the landlord,' said Buttercup. 'I think it must be some sort of Duke, he owns that much land.'

'A Duke. That kind of bundles me. I mean, where do we move from there?'

'Mistress Cucumber Frame, oh dear, her said Oi was cool. Oi haven't laughed so much since my Father died, and that weren't no laughing matter.'

'He's really incredible, this guy,' said Macbeth. 'I mean he's a really natural head, like he takes to shit as if he'd been born with a black bomber sticking out of his arse. I mean do you hear what he's saying? This is a really magical cat, really far out . . .'

So it was that when Audrey arrived at Williams Farm to arrange it for John Robinson's arrival, the house was not empty, as she had supposed. Partridge, the agent, who accompanied her to the farm, knew perfectly well that Willie Williams had returned there after coming out of prison, although he pretended to be taken by surprise. He had not been able to think of any explanation by the time they reached the farm, beyond the fact that the property was entered as unoccupied in the estate books, and no rent had been paid.

Both were equally surprised, however, to meet in addition to Willie Williams, who received them courteously enough: Buttercup and Strong Arm, Ruby

Wednesday and Macbeth, Rock (also called Black Stone) Beauty, Walt Izzard, Snowman and Dumpling. Audrey left the matter for her master to decide, merely ordering them out of two bedrooms.

'Like, I help with the cooking,' explained Dumpling, a plump girl with bad skin and frizzy hair, on being introduced as Mistress Artichoke by the cackling figure of Wee Willie Williams.

'Good,' said Audrey, who recognized an immediate sympathy in Dumpling's vibrations. 'Let's get started then.'

CHAPTER FIVE

John Robinson was not in the least bit upset to find Williams Farm already occupied. He even seemed to expect it, although Partridge was incomprehensibly obtuse during the drive from the station. 'I can't think how they got there, sir. These most extraordinary people have moved in, like a colony of monkeys. The house is crowded from floor to rafters. I don't know what they think they are doing there.'

'Probably trying to create a new life-style, I should imagine,' said John Robinson.

'Two of them said they were searching for the Holy Grail,' said Partridge. 'Of all unlikely stories.'

'Aren't we all, in one way or another?' said John Robinson.

'I suppose we are, if you look at it that way,' said Partridge, although plainly he was unhappy at the idea.

'Not all of us,' said Jaques. 'That is the tragedy of it. I don't think you have ever had a Grail in view, Mr Partridge. First, we must recognize the need for the search; then we must identify the quarry; after that, of course, we must start searching for it, although very few people can entertain the hope that they will find it on this earth. Your Mr Partridge, have not even begun to recognise the need for a search.'

'I suppose not,' said Partridge. 'If you look at it like that. I don't really even know quite what I'd do with this Holy Grail if I found it. There's not much point in searching for something you don't want. It would make quite an interesting souvenir for the family, I suppose, but they'd probably take it away from you and put it in the local museum. Very few people visit the museum at Glastonbury nowadays, but it is quite a good one, I believe.'

'We have betrayed the past and therefore do not want to be reminded of it,' said Jaques. 'Do you smoke pot?'

'Good gracious me, no,' said Partridge. 'Although I sometimes watch television in the evening. I suppose we *have* betrayed the past, if you look at it that way. The Americans were here during the war, you know, and the place has never been quite the same since. But we made all the farmers pull down their ugly tin Dutch barns, like Mr Robinson said last time he was down here. And we haven't allowed any building in concrete breeze blocks. Particularly against concrete breeze-blocks, Mr Robinson was, I seem to remember.'

'The purpose is to try and create a little corner of the world which is not contaminated,' said John Robinson.

'Scarcely that,' said Jaques. 'There are vast areas of the Himalayas which are not contaminated and probably never will be. Or the Sahara. Or even my own beloved West Africa. Tin barns and concrete breeze blocks are a symptom, not the cause. The garden we must cultivate is inside us, now. Outside the wolves howl and the devil holds dominion. The pollution which has overtaken our environment, and the imbecility which has clouded men's minds, are unconquerable. The purpose now is to learn to disregard them.'

'Well, here we are at the farm,' said Partridge. 'I'm sure I wish you both luck in whatever you are trying to do.'

When he was safely home, Partridge reflected on what a shame it was that John Robinson should be mad. 'We're all of us working down here, just so that he can have a good time. You might almost say that the whole modern world was geared to giving Mr Robinson a good time.

Instead, he has to make himself miserable worrying about pollution and suchlike. We can live with it. Why can't he?'

'Now, don't go getting yourself in trouble at work,' said Mrs Partridge. 'No good ever comes of asking questions.'

'You must be the Duke,' said Beauty, when she was introduced. 'Are you by any chance a relation to this Stone Killer Robinson, who used to burn up all the stones at Avebury?'

'The Robinsons are quite an old family. I think we come from Norfolk,' said John Robinson, a trifle stiffly.

'I don't mind at all if he is something to do with you,' said Beauty earnestly. 'I know it sounds kind of violent and evil, but violence and evil sometimes do things to one. I mean, I don't mind them at all, and sometimes they really turn me on.'

'It's like violent and evil things really turn her on sometimes,' explained Rock, or Black Stone. 'Not as a rule, though. Just when she is in the mood.'

What a sad and terrible thing,' said John Robinson. 'Have you ever tried smoking pot?'

'Tried smoking it? Let me tell you, Duke, I just can't have too much of that like magical substance. Have you brought some with you? Tell all the others. I think the Duke has brought us something that is sweet and fragrant and drops from heaven.'

The Duke, as he now became known, was taken on a tour of his dominion. Willie Williams became quite obsequious, as the blood of some forty generations of tenant farmers asserted itself. He saw the attic where Dumpling slept with Audrey, the housekeeper. There was a window-less cupboard next door where either Rock (Black Stone) or Snowman slept alone depending upon which one was keeping Beauty company in the cold, dark hours of night when she would often wake up in terror and need comforting with soft, nonsensical words about flying saucers, the Apocalypse, the Holy Grail, the Pyramids, Glastonbury Tor and a few other approved subjects from her strange but restricted list of interests. The next attic was Beauty's and the next, which had no door on the landing, was shared by Ruby Wednesday and Macbeth, although it could not have been very comfortable, lacking two panes of glass in the window and a bed. On the first floor – magnificent black oak floors, which would never need replacing in five hundred years – there was a huge bedroom where Willie's sister used to sleep. Walt Izzard had been turned out of this to make way for the Duke; he now slept on a sort of stool at the end of Willie's bed, but not without complaining. Jaques was given a small, cell-like room off the master bedroom, where the window was an iron grill nine feet from the floor. The theory was that salt pork had been hung there throughout the winter, to keep it from farm dogs and the rats which swarmed out of the corn-ricks at threshing time. Buttercup and Strong Arm retired to their original tractor shed when Walt Izzard arrived. There were two other rooms which might have been used as bedrooms on the first floor. One was full of rotten applies, laid out in rows by the dead hands of Willie's aggravating, unmourned sister. The other was full of the clutter of ages.

Downstairs was more of a mess. Apart from the huge kitchen, where everybody lived most of the time, there was only a small parlour, where Wee Willie and Walt Izzard had been in the habit of eating, waited upon by Beauty – talkative, voluptuous, incomprehensible Beauty with her strange urges and soft, slender eyes. Otherwise there was a dairy, now disused, a laundry room, with huge copper cauldron still intact, a still room where the vats of scalded milk once stood for buttermaking, a harness room, a garden room, where the strings of onions hung from a beam almost to the floor, a huge larder and a sort of scullery which also served as entrance hall.

'We must build a community, based on selflessness and love,' declared the Duke. 'There will be no private property, no selfishness, no greed. If there is want, we shall all suffer it, if there is surfeit, we will share it out among ourselves.'

'What about the other people, outside our community? Shouldn't we share it with them?' asked Jaques.

'No,' said the Duke. 'Unfortunately, that is not practicable. Our purpose is to create a little island of purity in an impure, surfeited world. There is nothing to be gained by adding to the material comfort of those outside our little island, since they are already stifled by a surfeit of comfort.'

'There's no surfeit of comfort where I was,' said Jaques. 'I could show you villages along the Cross River and in Calabar Province where it is still normal for one child in three to die of malnutrition before it is two years old.'

'How perfectly terrible. Did you hear that, Dumpling?' Beauty clung to Dumpling, and they hugged each other. Macbeth merely shook his head in disbelief: 'Three babies out of four die like that? I mean, why doesn't somebody give them like something to eat? That seems crazy. I mean just think of all those little dead babies.'

All twelve of them sat round the kitchen table thinking of those dead babies, while Audrey prepared some tea. Occasionally, one of them would give a little whoop of astonishment as realisation dawned anew. Buttercup wept openly, her tears splashing from her chin to Snowman's arm as he tried to comfort her by rubbing her stomach in a circular motion, as boxers are sometimes rubbed before a match.

'But we can't sit around weeping for all the babies who die in Nigeria,' cried the Duke.

'Why not?' asked Jaques. 'It is as good a way as any other of passing the time.'

'Because we can't do anything about the Nigerian babies; even if we could, there would be other babies dying in Chad, in the Upper Niger and the Congo. We try and create a new life-style for ourselves here, in the parish of Combe Mendip. You yourself told me how the most important thing was to establish an awareness of human dignity and the beauty of creation.'

'Any awareness which does not take into account that babies are dying in the Congo is not awareness, it is wilful ignorance,' said Jaques. 'Of course we can do nothing for them. In the last century, when man was full of hope, we might have tried. I myself went out there as a missionary priest, hoping, pathetically, that where I led, others would follow. But selfishness and despair have reasserted themselves in the twentieth century. We can do nothing about the situation, but we must still be aware of it and feel sorry for its victims. First think of the babies, then think of their mothers.' Jaques threw back his head and gave a pitiful howl, in which all the others soon joined, except the Duke and Ruby Wednesday, who had fallen asleep. Macbeth tore his bright red hair and Beauty pulled at her clothing in a frenzy of grief.

'And what good is this doing to the Nigerians?'

'None, of course. Don't you understand that the time is past for that? Where our own discomforts are concerned, the dirt, the vulgarity, the tawdriness and appalling pain of our contemporary society, the thing is not to try and improve anything, but to concentrate on trying to live with it, either with the help of drugs or, better, by exercising the will. Where other people's suffering is concerned, one must make it part of our awareness, and offer our sympathy, our compassion, even our whole-hearted concentration. The time has come to accept what optimists of the last century could never accept, that there will always be suffering in the world. The proper response is not to try and abolish it, which is impossible, or alleviate it, which is pointless, but merely to carry a sympathetic awareness around at all times, as persons of quality used to carry a pomander around with them during the Great Plague.' Jaques climbed on the kitchen table, and imitated a dandy sniffing at his pomander during the Great Plague of 1665. For all its sorrow about the babies of Nigeria, the company could not help laughing.

'I think I must have a smoke while I think about your remarks," said the Duke.

'Yes, yes,' cried everyone. 'A smoke, a smoke.'

An hour later, when discussion of this important and emotionally-charged matter was resumed, the Duke appeared to have been won round. Only Jaques, who did not smoke, was unaffected. His bright eyes darted birdlike from speaker to speaker as he sat on the kitchen table and the others sat or sprawled around on chairs. Occasionally he would break into the conversation, brighter, cleverer than the rest, and retire with the worm dangling from his beak which the others had been clumsily mutilating.

'You mean,' said the Duke, 'we should retain an awareness of the world's suffering in our minds, just for our own entertainment, as it were, without trying to do anything about it?'

'It is the same thing as praying,' said Jaques. 'The only alternative is to shut it out of your mind, and that is very wicked.'

'But couldn't we – couldn't I – do something? I mean, I have certain advantages, you know. I may even have business interests in Nigeria, for all I know. Couldn't I help these starving babies in Nigeria?'

'I spent six years there,' said Jaques, 'hoping that by education and by example I could lead them along until none of them would ever need to starve. But through education they only learned greed. Of course, you could adopt and save one, two or even three children. It would be a most beautiful thing to do, I suppose, watching them grow fatter and more competitive every day, but it would not alter the fact that others were starving.'

'Oh God, don't let's get boring,' said Macbeth. 'I just think that it's the most terrible and beautiful thing, all those babies out there. I mean, think of the sheer, fucking uselessness of it.'

'Why did they ever bother to get born?' asked Ruby.

'Perhaps so that we could have something to think about,' said Macbeth, after a long pause.

'Oh no,' said Buttercup. 'You are being very sick. Who on earth would go through all the business of being born just so that some people – thousands of millions of miles away – people they've never even heard of, mostly – could think about them?'

'It's like Raquel Welch taking all her clothes off in a film so that people thousands of miles away can, you know, do their own thing when they see her naked.' Macbeth was sticking to his own point of view.

'I am sorry,' said the Duke, who with his charming, old-world courtesy was trying to following everything that was said, 'what do you mean by "doing your own thing" in this context?'

'He means like masturbate, you know,' said Beauty. 'Macbeth's always on about it. He thinks it's terrific.'

'Or look at Marilyn Monroe,' said Macbeth. 'People still turn on when they see her nude in some film although they couldn't possibly hope to meet her personally because she was like dead before they were even born. That's what I call real immortality, making people turn on long after you're dead.'

Macbeth, moved to sit beside Beauty. If everybody present had not been in such a gentle mood, they might have noticed that this manoeuvre put him in line for an extra pull at the cigarette which he had just passed to Black Stone on his left. They all took the charitable view, if they noticed it at all, and decided that Beauty had started to turn him on again. Only Jaques noticed what he had done, and stored the information somewhere within his sharp, birdlike brain.

'I think she was buried at sea,' said Buttercup. 'With nothing on at all, but naked as she will always be remembered; without a coffin or anything else to confine her, thrown into the deep.'

Beauty gave a sort of groan, at this beautiful thought, or perhaps it was because Macbeth was gently massaging her through her faded blue jeans. Dumpling said:

'Unless they put weights on her, she would have floated.'

'That was the idea, that she should float naked and unfettered through the seven seas for all eternity,' said Buttercup. She had been keeping the cigarette for longer than was generally considered polite, but the convention was that nobody should notice.

'It wouldn't be very pleasant for a swimmer who happened to meet her after she had been in the water for a few weeks,' said Dumpling.

Beauty and Macbeth got up and left the room together. Ruby Wednesday had fallen asleep again, her head pillowed in Snowman's lap. Snowman rather sweetly refused to move for fear of waking her, so he missed the rest of the cigarette.

'Now wait a minute, wait a minute,' said the Duke. 'There seems to me an essential difference between these Nigerian babies and watching old films about Marilyn Monroe.'

'What is it?' everybody asked.

'The difference is this,' said the Duke speaking very slowly. 'Those babies are still alive.'

107

'So is Raquel Welch.'

'And anybody who can think of those babies dying without being moved to do something for them must be a very evil man,' said the Duke.

'Mr Jaques has just explained,' said Buttercup patiently. 'It's the same as fucking Raquel Welch. You can think about it, but you can't do it. I mean, the difficulties would be like so enormous. First you'd have to find out where she lives, then you'd have to make like an appointment to see her, saying you were from a newspaper or something like that, then, when you'd actually met her, you'd have to put it over to her pretty strong saying, you know, like Raquel, this is your serious duty, I mean I've been watching your films so long now this is really getting to be a serious thing, you know, so how about getting out of those like crinoline pants and coming across because I feel that would be really nice to do, you know, and would be really like appreciated if you could possibly get round to doing such a really nice thing etc. etc. But you can't do it, I mean, you can only think about it and it's the same with these Nigerian babies.'

'But that is the counsel of despair,' said the Duke.

'Not at all,' said Jaques. 'It is the voice of hope.'

'He's really fantastic, this guy Jaques,' said Snowman. 'Just listen to him.'

'You mean to say,' said the Duke, 'you think that the purpose which these unfortunate children fulfil is to give us all something to think about, so that we can enjoy indulging in compassionate thoughts. It seems to me that your reasoning is erroneous there, Jaques.'

Jaques did a little dance of vexation in front of him. 'It will take too long to explain. You would stop listening before I was half way through. Must I spend my whole life trying to explain things to a mind dulled by cannabis? I am not saying you are wrong, of course. For most people, cannabis is the only way of blotting out the futility, hideousness and appalling pain of our world. But it makes it harder for me to explain things to you. It is not so bad. You put your minds into a gentle sleep, rather than murder them as it is the conventional thing to do.'

'No doubt,' said the Duke, but there was a level quality to his voice which did not support Jaques's contention that his mind was affected. 'Now perhaps you'll explain what you said.'

'In the course of the next year, I shall explain what I meant about hope," said Jaques. 'For the moment, learn this. The main point about those Nigerian babies is that for a moment, at least, they exist. So do we all, for a greater or lesser period of time, exist. In the perspective of eternity there is no distinction between the longer and the shorter period of time."

'Why must we always see everything in the perspective of eternity?' demanded Macbeth, who had come back into the room with Beauty, and now sat down next to the person with the cigarette. 'It gets kind of depressing.'

'Maybe, of course, we all exist for ever, as the Christian religion used to teach.'

'Still does,' said the Duke.

'It no longer teaches, merely repeats, parrotwise, a number of propositions in which it no longer believes in order to justify . . .'

'I am sorry I interrupted,' said the Duke.

'But even if we don't live for ever, it is better to have existed even for a thousandth of a second than not to have existed at all.'

'Better?'

'Anything is surely better than nothing.'

'I think it is time I started another joint.'

'Hear, hear. Good old Duke. You just keep talking, Jaques. Nobody minds. Get it off your chest. Have a good cry, if you feel like it.'

'Thank you, Strong Arm,' said Jaques sadly. 'Of course,

it doesn't make any difference whether people understand what I am saying or not. It seems terribly selfish not to try and explain. My great point is that there would be no harm in trying to improve the lot of those Nigerian families – it would be as engagingly fatuous as any other human occupation nowadays – if I did not know perfectly well, from my own bitter experience, that in trying to do good one invariably does harm. By changing one destroys, and the powers of destruction are infinitely greater nowadays than the powers of creation. A hundred years ago, it was all different. There was room for optimism, then. Now we must all learn to hope again, before we can even begin to wonder about faith or charity, the state of love which nobody can hope to attain on cannabis. That is why we have all come to live at Williams Farm.'

'So that we can amuse ourselves by thinking about the Nigerian babies?' asked the Duke.

'To stop us from doing any worse harm by trying to change things,' said Jaques. 'Why do you suppose we are here?'

'We come to Williams Farm for various reasons,' said the Duke.

'Like Macbeth and me were searching for this Holy Grail,' said Ruby Wednesday.

'Good,' said Jaques.

'Mr Williams said we could sleep in his barn,' said Strong Arm.

'I suppose so,' said Jaques.

'I met Willie in Exeter Jail,' said Walter Izzard self-righteously.

'Snowman and Dumpling joined up with Black Stone and I when we were following the Dragon Path out of Glaston, along these strange and wonderful ways,' said Beauty. 'The vibrations were so fucking powerful when we got here that it was like predestined we *had* to stay. These voices kept saying to me, Beauty, you know, like this is the end of the road, you aren't going to take any more powders, this is Peace, perfect peace.'

'No doubt,' said Jaques.

'Ung Oi live here, though yewm moight not think it,' said Willie.

'Why did you come here, Duke?'

Jaques had fallen into the habit of calling John Robinson this name. So, for that matter, did Audrey, the beloved housekeeper. There was almost nothing she could not take in her stride.

'I came down here,' said the Duke, speaking very slowly, now, 'in order to escape from the evils of modern technology.'

'Oh, yes?' said Jaques.

'The whole idea that happiness can be secured by the acquisition of labour-saving gadgets must be a product of chemical poisoning,' said the Duke. 'First we must testify to our rejection of the process which has led to the brutalisation of our species. We must refuse the benefits of electricity. We must let no petrol engine or paraffin engine burn at Williams Farm. We will grow our own food, burn our own wood, draw our own water . . .'

'Import our own hashish from Afghanistan,' said Macbeth, a trifle sarcastically.

'Stop taking the pill and just have babies,' said Beauty. 'Or I suppose Snowman could improvise something nice and primitive, using a pig's gall-bladder tissue.'

'When we get ill, of course, we will just die. Then we can dig graves for each other, using a cow's horn for a spade. Our sheets and clothes are the products of modern technology, so we must wear cowskin, having first eaten the cow. But how do we set about killing the cow? Do we creep up to it from behind and stun it with a large stone, or do we throttle it with our bare hands in open combat?' Strong Arm was quite interested in the Duke's idea.

The Duke had always hoped that they would not eat

meat, believing it to degrade the intelligence, until Jaques pointed out that cows were vegetarian, and their intellectual vitality was disappointingly low.

'We could have the cow struck by lightning, I suppose,' said Ruby Wednesday. 'That would save us the awful confrontation at death. Have you ever seen the look in the eye of a dying cow?'

This idea appealed to the company even more. 'Really nice, that, Susan,' said Walt Izzard, who never bothered much with the tinkers' names.

'Far out.'

'Fantastic. I mean the eyes would be really kind of lumpy, don't you think? Perhaps we'd have to blindfold them first.'

'Or blindfold ourselves.'

'Oh, that's too much. Just think of it. All of us groping around blindfold with you know knives and things while somewhere in the middle is this unbelievable cow with like huge gentle tender eyes only no one can see them like mooing away to himself little knowing – I mean having no fucking idea whatever on earth about what we were like into doing to him until zonk crash some cats' knife has suddenly buried itself up to the hilt and the cow's last thoughts as he like sinks into oblivion lifting his gentle, droopy eyes heavenwards . . .'

Beauty prattled on, while the Duke, even through the effects of the marijuana began to feel something of the hopelessness of the situation. At least, he thought to himself, like we are here. The thing has started. But how does anyone set about killing a cow?

Wee Willie William came to his rescue. 'Killing a cow?' he said. 'Why there is nothing tew it. The difficult thing as to keep them alive. Ung, you can dew ut with anything that comes to hand – a sledgehammer, an old wooden mallet, a pair of scissors. It doesn't matter what you use, because cows don't put up no resistance.'

'Of course,' said the Duke. 'Everybody shall contribute his special abilities. Willie William will be our slaughterman.'

'What is my special ability?' said Beauty.

'Fucking, of course,' said everybody with a certain impatience. She was always fishing for compliments.

'Absolute simplicity will be the keynote of our alternative culture,' said the Duke. 'Cannabis is only a means of escaping from the lies and confusion of our consumer society. After a time, we will not need it. Nor will we need doctors and medicines, because nearly all the most prevalent diseases are the result of our urban culture. The others are a risk we must accept, knowing that the price of the remedy is higher than that of the disease. Contraception is of course a more difficult problem, but when we have cultivated the peace of mind and the simplicity which go with the other things, we will mind having babies much less.'

'Thank you very much,' said Beauty.

'In any case, it must be our duty in the alternative culture to have as many babies as possible, so we will not be taking any more pills.'

'The banquet of life,' murmured Jaques.

'Exactly. The fact of existence is supreme, not that a limited number of people should have washing machines and frozen fish cakes,' said the Duke.

Walt Izzard cleared his throat and looked important.

'Yes, Walt?'

'As a matter of fact, sir,' he said, with the cheeky diffidence of the expert, 'I believe there are ways of avoiding having babies without recourse to contraceptives. I wouldn't like to explain exactly what you have to do, because it has a Latin name and some people might not be able to follow me, but if the young lady would like a word with me in private I think I could show her that it is by no means necessary to rely on these things.'

'Thank you, Walt.' Once again, the Duke felt that things were slipping away from him. 'The purpose of our life here, as I have said, is to teach the world that there *is* an alternative.'

The company took kindly to this. 'Of course there is,' said Ruby Wednesday.

'*Vive la différence*,' said Walt Izzard.

'No, you are quite wrong,' said Jaques. 'Our purpose is not to teach anybody anything. Most people already have what they want in the modern world; practically nobody would voluntarily choose the sort of life you describe. If you wish to reduce us to the level of pre-industrial peasantry, you should appoint Willie Williams your leader, not me. Our purpose is quite different. It is to withdraw from what is happening so that every one of us can at least be sure that we are no longer doing any harm. As soon as you start teaching people things, you are telling people what you think they ought to want to do. All the misery in the world is caused by those who wish to make people think and behave differently. Our purpose in coming here is simply to be out of harm's way. Now we must make the best of it.'

'Hear, hear,' said Ruby Wednesday. 'It's not such a bad life, when you get used to it.'

'It is no good pretending that the world outside does not exist,' said Jaques. 'On the contrary, we should carry it in our awareness, and grieve about it. We should even look at it, from time to time, on television. It is no good trying to pretend that nothing has happened – that is what the modern people would like us to do. You cannot un-invent things which have been invented. Perhaps it would be a better, cleaner place without the hydrogen bomb, the pill, the petrol engine, but nobody knows. We are bound to be parasites on modern society, but we are none the worse for that. It is perhaps the main justification of capitalism – or at any rate the one which makes its absurdities and injustices less abhorrent than those of socialism – that it can afford to maintain any number of parasites, it offers the alternative of dropping out and adding nothing to the things it holds sacred – greater productivity, greater wealth for all and ambition within the system. Of course we must have petrol engines and hot water and everything else, if we can get them. The great point is that we are doing nothing in return. Discomfort has no particular virtue, it is only the glorification of comfort which is a vice. It is a waste of time to think about such things, when there are so many more important matters to worry about.'

'Exactly,' said Ruby Wednesday. 'We must do our own thing.' She looked hard at Black Stone, who walked across the kitchen to join her.

Conversation was interrupted at this point by a new arrival. Three hard knocks sounded on the front door. Beauty said: 'Christ the fuzz.'

Macbeth said, 'We can't get a bust put on us here unless they have a search warrant.'

Strong Arm said: 'You must wake up, Buttercup, my sweet. We think the Pigs have arrived. It is an intrusion.'

Buttercup rubbed her eyes and said: 'I was having such a beautiful dream, playing with the rabbits down by the marsh where the dragonflies are.'

Under normal circumstances, everyone would now have gathered round and discussed the symbolism of Buttercup's dream, its implications for the future, what it revealed about her character and the nature of her sexual desires, its correlation with the astrological season, her birthday, the conjunction of various planets and everything else not omitting the Great Pyramid of Cheops, the ground plan of Glastonbury Abbey and the proximity of the Holy Grail. On this occasion, however, there was greater concern about the new arrival.

'Audrey, go and open the door,' said the Duke. 'We have

nothing to hide. If it is a policeman, we will bribe him to go away again. Money, after all, is the sacred token of the society he wishes to protect. If injustice can be measured by money, so can justice, and by this token I am one of the most just men alive.'

'Quite right, Dukey,' said Walt Izzard nervously. 'I always said you were one of the best.'

But it was only Orlando who had arrived at the door, wet and exhausted after two miles walk across country.

'Who is this amazing man?'. cried Beauty.

Everybody took stock of Orlando's swaying figure by the light of the wood fire. 'He's beautiful.'

'Do you think he's a messenger from Heaven?'

Orlando walked up to the Duke, who sprawled on an old oak farm chair, his heavy lids half closed against the heat of the fire.

'Where's Rosalind?' he asked.

'Rosalind? He wants to know where Rosalind is. Look, man, like you can say I'm Rosalind if you want,' said Beauty.

'I'm Rosalind,' cried Ruby Wednesday. 'Come to me.'

'Rosalind,' said Buttercup. 'What a *strange* name. What *can* he be looking for?'

The Duke, of course, had recognised Orlando immediately. 'My daughter is not here,' he said. 'I think she is staying with my brother Frederick, in London. If you have come all this way just to find her, you had better stay the night at least. You look completely exhausted.'

'My poor boy,' chirruped Beauty. 'Come with me and I'll show you a bed where you can spend the night. Don't worry about this Rosalind any more. She's happy where she is. We'll make you comfortable.'

'My bed is bigger,' said Ruby Wednesday. 'There is plenty of room for two.'

'This place is beginning to get a little bit crowded,' said Macbeth.

116

'Come with me,' cried Beauty. 'I'll be your Rosalind. Ask anybody here. Beauty is best. We all have our special capabilities at Williams Farm. Dumpling does the cooking, like, and I'm the best for taking people to bed.'

Orlando's face had lit up every time he heard Rosalind's name, but as he searched the room without finding any trace of her it settled again into weariness and dejection.

'There's an old man outside who is too tired to walk any further. I would be grateful if you could bring him in. Has none of you seen Rosalind?'

Adam was carried in by Strong Arm and Black Stone, while Macbeth complained loudly that Williams Farm was not to be regarded as a District Cottage Hospital. 'Ruby and I came here in our search for the Holy Grail, which we were promised, in a dream, to find in a valley where the ground slopes up to form a quiet hillside, and this will be the only place left in England where man is at peace with his environment.'

'That's right, sir,' said Adam, who was propped up on an old sofa, and now prepared to bore them all. 'There's no civility at all around nowadays. Men are only interested in one thing – money. In my day we were proud to work for someone, and if ever he acknowledged our help with some wages, or a kind word, we was suitably grateful. It would never have occurred to us to demand anything. We took pride in service, in those days. Look at Mr Orlando's father, sir. There was a real gentleman. He never paid me a penny's wages for the last five years of his life, and I never said a thing. Then, when he died – everything had to be left to the oldest brother, Mr Oliver Twickerley, a most terrible gentleman; no doubt you've heard of him – they said I could keep Sir Roland's old morning coat and the riding boots he used to wear out hunting when he was a young man. I was that touched I nearly sat down and cried. I had been cleaning those boots of his for the last thirty-five years, and all that time I never dreamed I would be allowed to keep them. It goes to show I was right never to mention the little matter of the wages. He was that forgetful, old Sir Roland, towards the end of his life . . .'

'Like, we just had to find this Holy Grail. I mean, it must be somewhere, because matter is indestructible, you know, so we came to Williams Farm sort of following these old paths of magic power.'

'No good for cleaning silver. No good at all. If you'd found this Holy Grail in the old days, I would have kept it clean for you and polished it up with a mixture of meths and chalk powder. Nowadays they'd put all these new fangled chemicals on it, and ruin it before they'd started. It used to be one of the world's wonders how I kept my silver in the old days. "Adam," Sir Roland would say to me, "you are a *stupor mundi*." Do you know what that means?'

'Yes,' said Jaques.

'No doubt God loves him,' said the Duke. He enjoyed seeing Jaques wince whenever he mentioned God. 'He has a place in the scheme of things.'

'One thing I always knew in life was my own place,' said Adam. 'There's only unhappiness comes from pretending anything else. Nowadays, these young people haven't any idea about what's what. They think they've already inherited the earth, like Sir Roland always said I would after we were all gone. But they haven't of course, and it gets them into much more trouble than it's worth. And nowadays there's people giving them encouragement. Look at Mr Twickerley, always encouraging them to think they're better than they are. Mr Twickerley ought to know better.'

'You're right of course,' said the Duke, 'but you are not speaking in the fashion of these times.'

'He's already dead,' said Jaques, in extreme irritation. 'He has not a thought in his head. Teach him to sing songs. That is the most useful thing he can do now.'

They laid Orlando down in Ruby's bed but Beauty undressed him and sponged his poor tired limbs. He was asleep before they left him, and when Ruby came to bed later in the evening, she did not have the heart to wake him up. Instead, she went and slept with Beauty, while Black Stone slept on the floor and Macbeth sat up with Willie Williams in the kitchen underneath.

Willie was nearly asleep, what with the pot, and the cider, and the incomprehensible conversation, when Orlando came down. Orlando was naked, except for a sheet wrapped around him, and he shivered. When he walked, a long, thin, beautifully formed, almost feminine leg broke out of the sheet in front of him. Macbeth regarded it sourly.

'I could not sleep. I was worrying about Rosalind,' Orlando explained.

'That's funny,' said Willie. 'I can't scarcely stay awake. Which is Rosalind, then? I can't keep up with all they names. Would she be Miss Cabbage Patch with the big eyes or Miss Onion Leaves with the big bum?'

'She is the pretty one, with a kind, velvety look to her eyes, and a funny way of turning her mouth down when she smiles. Her hands are quite small, although with long fingers' and her wrists are the sweetest, most fragile things you have every seen,' explained Orlando.

'Oh ur, ar, ung,' said Willie. 'Do yew be looking for that one? I wouldn't rightly know which way she might have gone.' Suddenly he became very angry and vehement. 'But I do know one thing, and that's I'm going to bed,' he shouted. 'All the bloody rubbish you talk about Holy bloody Grail. Oi'd expect ung yew'd have more bloody intelligence still to talk about this toime on night. Yew keep your bloody mouths shut the pair on ee or oi'll knock your bloody heads together ung oi'll hang 'ee up on the ham hooks same as bloody tinkers should be hung up,' he said. 'All this bloody talk. Talk, talk, talk. Yewm trying to drive Oi mad same as the rest of you is all mad. Stark bloody cuckoo, with all your talk.'

He left the room muttering and raving to himself.

'He is a most violent and unpleasant man, that one,' said Macbeth. 'Could he be the keeper of the Holy Grail, just as ancient treasures had a dragon to guard them? Do you think Willie William suspects, in some unexplored corner of his understanding, that we have come to destroy, or at any rate to take away, what he and his family have been protecting for generations?' In his excitement at the idea, Macbeth quite forgot how much he mistrusted Orlando.

'Perhaps,' said Orlando. 'Did he also say that he had seen Rosalind?'

'I think he mentioned it,' said Macbeth. 'If I am right, then we really are at the spot where the Holy Grail has been hidden all these centuries since it disappeared from Glastonbury.'

'If he has seen Rosalind, she must be here somewhere. Have you seen her?'

'No. Do shut up about your Rosalind. There are plenty of other girls around. You are upsetting the vibrations I keep receiving. The end of my quest is very close. It is like a wireless station, you know, broadcasting very loud on an unknown wavelength. Now you come sending out these distress signals of your own, jamming every hope of reception for miles around. Go and pick Beauty. She's dying for the touch of your tender white hand.'

'Is she?' said Orlando vaguely. 'But I thought he said he had seen Rosalind here.'

'Perhaps it's Ruby you're after,' said Macbeth nastily.

He was too vain to say that Ruby was his girl. 'She took a powerful kind of fancy to you, I noticed. I wouldn't touch her, if I was you. She's mean and stupid and she has a terrible smell. We set out looking for this Grail thing together and I nearly had to give it up after a time, I found her so heavy. She's another example of this living death thing which Jaques was talking about. You're not interested in her, are you? I mean if she comes running after you again, you'll give her a kick up the arse and tell her to get a deodorant, won't you?'

'No,' said Orlando. 'But anyway, I'm looking for Rosalind.'

Macbeth thought about this long and hard, rubbing the bright red whiskers which grew from his face and even from the front of his neck. 'This Rosalind,' he said, 'I mean she does exist, doesn't she? I mean, she's not just your name for Miss Right? You wouldn't tell me, anyway, of course. But why was Ruby telling you that her name was Rosalind?' He was talking to himself, but each time he mentioned Rosalind's name, Orlando looked hopeful again. 'There can be no doubt that Ruby fancies you. I mean, she really did start scratching between her legs the minute you came into the room. What have you got to say to that.'

'If Rosalind was there, I am sure I would have seen her,' said Orlando.

Slowly, a very mean idea began to form in Macbeth's mind. It was so mean, he found it almost incredible, himself. He scratched his head to make sure that he was the person he thought he was, shook his head hard several times, perhaps to see if the idea would fall out. No, the thought remained. He had come too far on his quest to abandon it now. The Grail was beckoning to them, calling, shouting from very close, and this stranger seemed to be getting in the way, threatening to take away Ruby and leave him alone.

'I think I can give you something which will help you to see things,' said Macbeth taking a small glass phial from his pocket.

'What's that?'

'Acid. Really good and there's enough in this little cap to send everybody in this house on a trip from here to the moon and back. No, further than the moon. From here to the furthest reaches of the universe. Have you ever dropped acid?'

'No,' said Orlando. 'I think I am rather frightened of it. How can it help me find Rosalind?'

'If you are upset about something, it will help you see through the problem. You will see Rosalind as you have never seen her before. You will learn self-knowledge and peace of mind.'

Was it Satan who spoke through Macbeth's mouth? Would it have been possible to disbelieve in the existence of a personal Devil if one had sat in the kitchen of Williams Farm on the night of April 3rd 1966, and heard Macbeth tempt Orlando, taunt him, cajole him along the path to destruction? Normally, Jaques kept a watchful eye, but Jaques was upstairs in his bedroom. Perhaps he stirred in his sleep, in that tiny cupboard-like cell where salt pork used to be kept, away from the rats and cockroaches. If he did, there was nobody to see him, except perhaps the eye of God, if there is a God which bothers to record such unimportant details.

'All right,' said Orlando, 'I'll join you.'

'You won't regret that decision,' said Macbeth. 'After tonight, you'll never be the same again. Wait a minute.' He fetched two lumps of sugar. Into one, he poured the entire contents of the phial, making it so wet it could scarcely hold together. Finding his fingers wet with the acid, he cursed and rubbed them on his clothes.

'Here you are, Orlando. Happy travels.'

Macbeth put the treated lump of sugar on the tip of

Orlando's tongue with great ceremony. 'Suck it gently. Can you taste the acid, now? Let it trickle down your throat. That's the way, sonny boy. Now, just let things happen to you. That's the way. We don't want to go intruding in other people's holy quests do we? We just want to be left alone to think about Rosalind. That's what I'm going to do to you, sonny boy. I'm leaving you alone. From now on, you're on your own. Rosalind has gone away, I think. You're too late. Goodbye.'

Macbeth tiptoed out of the room. The summons which he constantly received from the Holy Grail seemed particularly strong tonight. No matter where he was – alone, trudging a field or moor, by the seaside or in a crowd at the cinema, the messages kept falling upon his mind. Tonight, they came as a triumphant shout.

Orlando sat and watched the extraordinary way the fire was behaving. At first, he managed to preserve his detachment. The orange of the flame, with its strange blue edges, seemed more vivid, more immediate, more personal than was usual. Perhaps, in some previous existence, he had seen such colours on a lantern in his father's palace outside Peking. Certainly, the colour was familiar, reminding him of candy and other childish delights. Moreover, it was obviously a benign phenomenon, something for his delectation. When the fire drew nearer and settled immediately in front of his face, it still seemed to present no threat. Even when Orlando closed his eyes and found that the fire had crept behind his eyelids, he still judged it, on balance, a pleasant diversion rather than a rude intrusion.

It was only after the novelty wore off that Orlando began to resent what was happening. The fire started dancing around, threatening to leave the grate altogether (although it never did) and Orlando realised that the entertainment was getting out of hand, that he was losing control of the revels.

'Now, don't be silly,' he said, but his voice sounded oddly thin and querulous in the deserted kitchen. He was not even sure that he had enunciated the words properly. Perhaps he had only made a hopeless, squeaky noise. The fire, rather like the Holy Ghost at Pentecost, collected in a ball only thinly connected to the logs underneath and swayed towards him.

It was when Orlando allowed his glance to drop that he understood the full horror of the situation he was in. One of the logs underneath the fire had unmistakably turned into a crocodile. Moreover it was a crocodile which kept him fixed in its eyes, with an occasional angry twitch of its tail to show its intentions. Dragging his eyes from it, Orlando saw that another log was also in the process of changing into a crocodile, while he could not quite make out whether a third had changed, was changing, or remained a log. Its shape was indeterminate but undoubtedly menacing. Every time he moved his eyes from the first crocodile, it had advanced a few steps towards him, with the light of the fire glowing redly from its snout and the tip of its tail flicking ever faster. But if Orlando kept his eyes on the first crocodile, the second one advanced, like a hideous game of Grandmother's Footsteps, and the third log had now resolved itself into a monstrous, giant slow-worm. Orlando realised that if ever he took his eyes off them for long enough, or if ever the fire were to part company from the grate, they would all three be upon him. His chief horror was of the slow-worm. In some part of his mind totally unconnected with his nose or other olfactory organs he smelled a most disgusting smell, and he was sure that this came from the burning slow-worm.

The fire danced and waved above the logs, always connected by a thin and tenuous link. Sometimes tongues of flame would break off and dangle luminously in the air.

Some would even lick around Orlando's cheek, infusing him with temporary confidence. But then Orlando suddenly knew that the fire was collecting itself to break away from the grate, releasing the logs, whether crocodile or slow-worm, from their bondage. Some malign force had taken control of the fire, and soon – very soon, any moment now – Orlando would find the crocodiles at his throat, the slow-worm curling itself around his face.

Even as he thought these things, he knew they were an hallucination, but the knowledge did not in any way detract from his terror. His brain received orders from the poisonous drug to be terrified, and even the tiny corner of his mind which remained independent and detached, as God has designed it, could do nothing against the spasms of terror which seized every other faculty. His scream, which ran like a needle through the draughty, unfeeling old house, was a curiously dispassionate one. He was not personally involved in the scream at all. The time had come to scream, so he screamed, like a small child drawing attention to some imperfection in the day's arrangements. So far as the walls of the house were concerned, he might have been a cow in labour, a pig being slaughtered incompetently, a female servant who had caught her fingers in the mincing machine – all these things had happened within the house before, and no doubt many worse things as well. Orlando's agony was something peculiarly his own; there was no reason why the environment should share it. It is only when two or more people are involved in some tragedy or moment of heightened passion that a house will sometimes absorb the event into its atmosphere.

But Orlando's scream brought the other occupants of the house running to the kitchen in three waves. The first – Buttercup, the Duke, Strong Arm, and Snowman – came in response to an urgent summons for help. They knew nothing, except that there was somewhere some pain to be relieved, some danger averted, some wrong righted. The second wave, after a pause of about three minutes, came out of curiosity, to see what was happening. These included Ruby Wednesday, Black Stone and Audrey. Finally, after another ten minutes, came those who did not want to help and were not even curious to know what had happened, but were frightened to be left alone. These were Beauty, Dumpling and Adam. With them came the brutal, guilty Macbeth. Walt Izzard remained in his bed, too terrified even to blink. Willie Williams snored his way through the entire commotion and Jaques, Jaques the philosopher was nowhere to be seen. Perhaps he was praying, or focusing his mind, in the pork cupboard where he lay.

Orlando seemed unaware of their arrival. He lay collapsed in the great armchair, uttering stupid, choking sounds and constantly moving his arms as if to protect his face from some imagined attack. Once he sat up and said quite lucidly: 'Must we take our football boots with us this time, sir?' At other times, he merely shouted, 'No, no,' and other incomprehensible words. Sweat trickled down his face, and sometimes his eyes seemed to bulge in his head, before they glazed again and his mind clearly wandered away.

'Do you think it is appendicitis?' said Buttercup. 'Should we get a doctor to look at him?'

'It is a surgeon you want,' said Ruby Wednesday, suddenly the schoolteacher again. She would probably have answered to the name Fiona, then. 'Ask Macbeth. He used to be a medical student.'

Macbeth looked shifty. 'It looks to me as if he has really blown his mind this time.' He hadn't seen anything like it since he was at University College and one of the Nigerian students got it into his head that he had been changed into a dog.

'Poor man,' said Beauty. 'If it is appendicitis, we will

have to operate ourselves. There probably is not a surgeon for miles around. Can you do the operation, Macbeth?'

'No,' said Macbeth. 'Somebody else will have to do it.'

'Black Stone?'

'No, sorry. It's just not my kind of scene at all. I don't like operations. Even childbirth, you know, doesn't really turn me on. Of course I can see it's something very beautiful, and all that, but not for me.'

'It's just as beautiful to save life. Is nobody going to do anything to help?'

Orlando's sheet had slipped off and he lay on the floor, naked and beautiful by the light of the fire and a solitary electric bulb which hung from the ceiling. He was unconscious. Only a fast flickering under his eyelids, and an occasional spasm of his limbs revealed that he was still alive.

Strong Arm cleared his throat. He had plainly not yet had time to descend from the high level of public spiritedness which brought him out of bed in the first place.

'Well done, Strong Arm, what do you need?' Beauty was dancing around the room in a state of extreme distress. 'Boiling water, of course. A sharp knife; some scissors; a needle and some thread. Hurry up, hurry up, I think he's going to die.'

Under Beauty's agitated directions, Snowman and Rock lifted Orlando upon the kitchen table where he lay, much more beautiful than Shelley on his slab, warm, breathing and most provocatively defenceless.

'Ah, I am not absolutely certain about where to make the – ah – incision,' said Strong Arm. Everybody agreed that he spoke exactly like a surgeon.

'Here, here,' shouted Beauty, lifting up her night dress to show her own appendix scar. Everybody examined it carefully.

Suddenly, Orlando stirred, and lashed around with his arms. Beauty, who had been sponging his poor, damp forehead, while she held up her night dress for the world to inspect her appendix scar, received a nasty scratch down the inside of her arm.

'Dirty brute,' said Macbeth. 'As a matter of fact, an appendicectomy is one of the simplest surgical operations imaginable.'

'There you are,' said Beauty. 'I told you so. I don't mind what he does to me, poor man.' She licked the inside of her arm like a cat licking its kitten.

The Duke had been walking up and down the kitchen, ignoring all that was happening. 'Of course Jaques was right,' he said. 'We should have a first-aid box here, and a car, in case of emergencies. Perhaps we should even have a telephone. It is absurd to take serious risks like this just because we don't like some of the things nowadays. What on earth are you doing with that knife, Strong Arm?'

'It has – ah – been suggested that I should perform an appendicectomy,' said Strong Arm, with a nonchalance he did not quite feel. He kept looking from Beauty's stomach to Orlando's, trying to find exactly the right place for his incision.

'I am the nurse,' said Buttercup, drawing attention to the small white enamel bowl she held. No doubt it would take an appendix, when extracted.

Suddenly the Duke felt unaccountably tired. Where was Jaques? He should be present to analyse and explain. It was thanks to him that twelve people were gathered together around a seriously sick boy lying naked on a kitchen table somewhere in the middle of Somerset. Why couldn't they just lead ordinary lives and risk a little pollution, like everyone else?

'There's no time for an operation tonight,' he said. 'In any case, I dare say that there is nothing wrong with his appendix. Perhaps it is indigestion, or a tumour on the brain.'

'We were only planning an exploratory operation,' said

Macbeth with a mean look. He licked his lips greedily. 'Strong Arm was prepared to go ahead with it.'

Who were these people? What on earth were they all doing here? Beauty dropped the bottom of her night dress and Strong Arm thankfully laid down the small red kitchen knife which Macbeth had sharpened for him. Dully, the Duke realised that whoever they were, and whatever they were all doing, at three o'clock in the morning standing around the kitchen table of a dilapidated Somerset farmhouse, they were his responsibility.

'Put Orlando to bed,' he said. 'Everybody else should go to bed, too. We shall have the doctor come to see the boy in the morning.'

As they carried Orlando back to his bedroom, again wrapped in the sheet, he suffered a convulsive attack, in the course of which he was sick. Beauty mopped him up and sat by his bedside, wrapped in his blanket, until the morning.

When Rosalind and Celia arrived after breakfast, accompanied by Mr Albert Touchstone, sometime sergeant of the Metropolitan Police, Orlando did not recognise any of them. He continued to call Rosalind by name, however long after Beauty had slipped away, tired and white-faced, to make way for the real Rosalind, who sat beside his bed and sponged his poor tortured face, while tears ran silently down her own.

CHAPTER SIX

'Our purpose,' said the Duke, 'is to create the sort of community where the human spirit can take root again and thrive. The technological consumer orientated society is gradually dehumanising the human race.'

'Dearie me, now,' said Touchstone. 'Is that what is happening?'

'Yes,' said the Duke. 'One can argue, of course, about the extent to which this degradation is the result of chemical poisoning, or the result of fitting humanity into a scheme of things basically designed for the machine. The automated human animal loses his powers of independent thought; independent action is treated as lunacy, which, of course, within the conventions and imperatives of the social order, it is. One must always bear in mind the inverse of Descartes's proposition, *I think, therefore I am.*'

'What would that be?' said Touchstone.

'*It does not think, therefore it does not exist.*' The Duke was rather proud of this little conceit, which he had learned from Jaques. 'The danger facing the world today is that through immersing his intellect in the requirements and accommodations of social existence, mankind will lose his soul. An ant will emerge in his place. Already you see him bombarded with falsehood and prepackaged opinions, his reflexes conditioned until thought only becomes possible within the parallel lines on which he is permitted to advance.'

'I see,' said Touchstone. 'You mean this rock here,' – he kicked it – 'has no existence because it is unable to think.'

'Up to a point, I suppose it has none,' said the Duke.

They were walking over the field in front of Williams Farm, a steep hillside where the grass was scanty and poor. 'At any rate, it is scarcely in a position to convince itself of its own existence.'

'Sounds an odd reason to want to come and live in this God-forsaken spot,' said Touchstone. 'Perhaps people can't think properly in London, like you say. I don't know. Now I am in Somerset, but three days ago I was in London and it seemed a better place.'

'You have not yet evacuated your mind and body of all the poison they have absorbed,' said the Duke. 'If you come with me, I will show you where our organic food is being grown.'

'A sorry enough sight,' said Touchstone, when they reached the spot. Black Stone was raking over a bit of the field which he had already dug. 'You won't be able to feed yourselves very nicely on this.'

'We catch rabbits, too, you know. Snowman turns out to be our huntsman. We all do whatever we are good at. Some of us, like Dumpling and Audrey, are good in the kitchen. Willie William knows when to plant things. Strong Arm can handle horses, so we may have to get a few horses. They will be very useful for the manure, too. Ruby Wednesday knows how to make beer. Beauty is very good at – you know – fucking, and all that sort of thing. Jaques is our philosopher and guide. Macbeth is good at rolling cigarettes. Buttercup helps everybody and gives good advice. We are a happy little community.'

'What are you good at?' said Touchstone.

'They call me the Duke. I don't know why. I am not really a Duke you know.'

'You mean you pay for all this little corner of fairy-land,' said Touchstone. 'Very kind of you, I'm sure. The only pity is that you don't bother to make it a little bit more comfortable. When winter comes round, this place is going to be awful, you know. Why can't we have central

131

heating, a proper hot water system, draught excluders, television and everything else?'

'That is what Jaques was saying,' said the Duke. 'My feeling is that we are trying to get away from that sort of thing. We might grow to attach too much importance to them.'

'In that case we are trying to be a proper set of bloody fools,' said Touchstone. 'Make it more comfortable and you might get a higher class of person staying here. I can't say I think much of your present selection.'

'We are no more than a collection of people trying to find our way,' said the Duke. 'What can you contribute to our welfare?'

'It is not a question of what I can contribute. It is a question of what I can get out of you. I can direct traffic, conduct an investigation into any crimes which may be committed and keep the peace. I know all the rules of evidence and can be relied upon to conduct myself with dignity in the witness box. Why, I have even had jurors crying when defence counsel accused me of deliberate falsehood. I can play the mouth organ and have a pretty turn of voice when it comes to singing. I know some card tricks, like the Lady Vanishes. Oh, I am a man of parts, which is more than you can say for most of the idlers and freaks and weirdoes you have collected. All I want is a little peace and quiet. There's no need to make us uncomfortable as well.'

'Well, I shall see what can be done,' said the Duke. But he was not happy about it at all. His original dream was bound to be modified. That was in the nature of things. But modification of so radical a description was another matter. As he often did in moments of stress, the Duke sucked his thumb and thought of something else.

Dr Mogg visited Orlando that morning, took his temperature, felt his pulse and produced a bottle of something labelled 'The Mixture'.

'There's nothing basically wrong with him which shouldn't cure itself in the course of the next few days,' he said. 'If he doesn't get any better, give me a call and we'll come and have another look at him. It isn't appendix, as you feared. I notice that these agitated states of mind often come upon people in the spring – something to do with the change of the seasons, you know. The other time, of course, is after harvest. Don't worry too much. We have plenty of rather odd people round here, and they seldom come to much harm.'

'Thank you, doctor,' said Rosalind. 'Can I give him a bath, now, or should I wait until he's better?'

'Shouldn't do much harm,' said Dr Mogg, who had taken rather a fancy to Rosalind. 'Careful he doesn't hit his head on the side, though. Now, there's no one else in the – um – family who needs any help? Good oh. Righty ho. There you are then. That's it. Absolutely lovely. Cheerioh. Goodbye.'

'Goodbye, doctor,' everyone said.

'I take it nobody's unwell then,' said the doctor. He seemed strangely reluctant to go.

'Beauty's got an appendix scar you can look at, if you like,' said Macbeth, trying to be helpful. He felt rather ashamed of his behaviour the day before.

'Not if it's only a scar,' said the doctor.

'No, you really can see it. Show him your scar, Beauty.'

Beauty, who was wearing trousers, pulled out her shirt, undid her belt and started to expose her appendix scar.

'No, that'll be all right then. Righty-ho. Goodbye for now.'

'Goodbye, Doctor.'

Doctor Mogg drove off. His next task was to sign the death certificate for Elsie Bender – the aunt, as it happened, of Charlie Winter, down at Hatch, who had died in the night.

Orlando had moments of almost complete lucidity between the hours of sleeping and the more troublesome times, when his mind would cloud over and find itself in some terrible struggle against imagined adversaries. At these moments he would talk to Rosalind seriously and articulately. She never left the side of his bed, except to fetch something for him, or to assist him to the lavatory or the bath. His conversation was always about Rosalind, or about the idea of her which he carried in his poor, muddled head. Even at his most lucid, he never realised that he was talking to the object of his passions. Orlando seemed to think she was a boy, and talked to her as if she were one.

Under other circumstances, Rosalind might have been flattered to hear herself described in such anatomical detail. 'She has these long, thin legs, which I like especially, and a flat tummy, you know, but you have to kind of climb up the legs and she's tingling with this electric current. Then you look into her eyes and you see all the kindness, all the *concentration* on loving you. Do you know what I mean?'

'I think so,' said Rosalind. 'Have you made love to her often?'

'No, never. In fact, I have only met her a few times, then she left London. But do you know what it is when you see some girl from a distance, and feel attracted to her, you know, then you move closer and talk to her, and suddenly your eyes meet and you realise that she *knows* what you're thinking, and she agrees, and as far as she is concerned you are the one person she's been wanting for all her life, I mean, she just *lives* in your mild and magnificent eye – do you know that sort of feeling?'

'Yes, I do,' said Rosalind, with a catch in her voice.

'Has it happened often to you?'

'No, only once,' said Rosalind.

'Oh dear, I'm sorry,' said Orlando.

'That's all right.'

'But isn't it a most fantastic, unbelievable feeling?' said Orlando. 'One minute you just walk into a room, same as ever, and a minute later your entire world has been turned inside out. If only I could explain about this girl to you. She's called Rosalind Robinson – the daughter, you know, of the man they call the Duke. It is not a very lovely name, I agree, until you learn to attach it to her face, to the way she talks, the way her legs seem to electrify your fingers, you know, if you happen to be sitting next to her say in a car and pretending to look out of the window because you're driving. Her legs seem to guide your hands along, up and along, come and be with me, they say, I'm yours for ever. Oh my God, I think I've got the horrors coming on me again. Help me again, whoever you are. Hold my hand.'

Rosalind lifted his hand to her face. Already some nameless shapeless horror had taken control of his mind. The irises of his eyes rolled up into his eyelids. His left arm flayed the air, although his right arm, whose hand was held in Rosalind's, was as relaxed as that of a sleeping child. Beauty appeared in answer to the shout, and started sponging his face which had broken out into sweat.

'My poor Orlando,' murmured Rosalind. The tears from her eyes fell on Orlando's weak, trusting hand. 'Try to imagine that I am your Rosalind. I know you think I am only a boy, but treat me like your Rosalind. Make love to me as if I were your Rosalind. Together, we'll find our way back to her.'

With an angry noise, Orlando pulled his hand away. Rosalind went to fetch Dr Mogg's medicine, which was marked: *two teaspoonfuls every four hours or more if required*. Every four hours throughout the night an alarm clock rang beside her bed, and shivering she took Orlando the precious medicine – a placebo prepared by Dr Mogg which had no medical properties whatever, but at least tasted nice. His other medicine, also labelled 'The Mixture' but green in colour, was much nastier, and reserved for the more persistent invalids.

Nobody else in the farmhouse paid the slightest attention to the various dramas which enacted themselves around Orlando's bed. Through constant repetition, they had acquired monotony. But sometimes Macbeth crept in, to see how the invalid fared. Nobody suspected his guilty secret, but this did little to reduce the burden of guilt. Sometimes he would bring some soup, or some mushrooms, or a bunch of spring flowers which he had picked and Ruby Wednesday arranged. Macbeth had grown to love the helpless, prostrate Orlando, and was bitterly ashamed of having poisoned him. Sometimes he played with the idea of a public confession, to be followed by a dramatic self-poisoning. However, in quieter moments, this did not seem such a good idea; in one such he threw away his remaining phial of LSD, thus removing all temptation. He poured it down a well in the scullery, first lifting the huge iron plate which covered it. Immediately afterwards he was attacked by further agonies of shame and guilt, in case anybody ever drank from the well. What worried him most was the certainty that until he could purge all the wickedness in his soul, his quest for the Holy Grail was lost. When he confided his doubts to Ruby Wednesday, she hugged him in silent sympathy and said she had never believed in the Holy Grail, anyway.

Jaques was seen less and less in the communal rooms of the farm as the days progressed, and spring made way for summer, with the rich scent of wild mint and crushed reeds from the marshy area on both sides of the stream.

At meals, he listened without comment to the various suggestions, squabbles, theories of the universe and wild, meandering explanations of the day's events. More and more he seemed to miss his life in West Africa. When he spoke at all, more often than not it was to describe some village child in Eastern Nigeria he had befriended, or some sermon he had given in the Catholic cathedral of Owerri, urging the townspeople not to make a god of sophistication; not to suppose that education, or possession of a superior intelligence made them in any way more admirable or important in the perspective of the infinite. It was this point which troubled him most. 'Perhaps I was wrong,' he muttered to himself from time to time. But he could scarcely return to Owerri and publish a correction. News from West Africa filtered through from time to time, either on the television, which, having once been installed, was watched by the family in an astounded, uncomprehending half-circle every evening, or in long letters which reached Jaques from the man who used to be his religious superior in Port Harcourt. Perhaps Jaques needed something on which to focus his mind during the long hours he spent alone in his cell, where pigs' quarters used to be stored. He followed the dramas and agonies of Nigeria to the exclusion of everything else, and sometimes made them the subject of strange, incomprehensible harangues to the family.

Nobody minded this at all. It was even expected of him. Communication inside the family usually took the form of uninterrupted monologues. There was no heckling, no attempt to connect one monologue with another. In any case, everybody always agreed. If it was already certain that one agreed, there was no purpose in making the effort to listen. Sometimes it was a lecture by Macbeth on the ancient leys or dragon paths connecting Stonehenge, Avebury, the Pyramid of Cheops, Glastonbury and everywhere else in the world with Williams Farm. Sometimes it was a dissertation by Beauty on the importance of sex. Sometimes they watched television. On one memorable occasion, on television, a young man taught them how to cook kidneys in a manner which, he said, had been invented in New Zealand.

'First, you put a little oil in your pan, then some mustard,' he said. Suddenly, Black Stone (or Rock) who had been watching the programme up to that moment with his mouth hanging open and a look of bland incomprehension on his long, sensitive face, let out a cry of excitement: 'Oh my Christ, look *what he's doing*. He must be stoned out of his mind. He says, "let's put in some mustard", and now he's put in the whole fucking pot.'

Murmurs of amazement were heard around the room. It was quite true, the young man had put the whole pot of mustard into his frying pan.

'What a really incredible guy,' said Ruby Wednesday. 'That mustard must turn him on. He'll simply freak out there and then, I mean he'll simply blow in when he starts eating those kidneys.

'How can he do it? I mean, how can anybody be so cool as to just pour all that mustard into one like *cooking utensil* without even turning a hair?'

Thereafter, everything the young man did was endowed with a fourth dimension. 'Oh my God, look he's putting salt in now. When will he ever stop?'

'Now he's going to put some pepper in, just watch him. No he isn't. *I don't believe it. He's putting in some flour*. On top of all that mustard! People are going to be ringing up the television centre in their thousands, asking what on earth has happened. Have Martians landed, they will ask, and taken control of all transmitting bases and major train terminals?'

'Venusians, more likely,' said Black Stone, a trifle abruptly. He was the resident expert on flying saucers and had, in fact, once been taken for a ride on one by some people who came from a planet which was unknown to Western astronomers (the Russians had guessed its existence) because transparent. The family had been treated to a long account of his adventures some time previously; but more probably than not, the family had neglected to listen.

Further merriment was caused by the young man on television describing the kidneys as 'kiddlies'. He was introduced as 'The Galloping Gourmet', and could have had no idea what a sensation this pleasantry caused down in Somerset. When the programme was over, the family settled down to discuss its significance.

'He was just too unbelievably wonderful,' said Beauty. 'What can it mean?'

'In St John's writings, there is a reference to four horses,' said Macbeth.

'You mean those might have been their kidneys?' said Ruby. 'That might explain why he wanted all the mustard, but it can scarcely explain why he called them kiddlies. What *can* he have meant by saying kiddlies?'

'Children,' said Snowman the Hunter. 'Of course, we're all God's children, if you look at it like that.'

'He seemed very full of compassion,' agreed Ruby Wednesday.

It was Strong Arm who called them to order. 'I think we may have seen something very important and very significant indeed,' he said. 'It could mean one of two things. The first is that they're beginning to realise we're right. We all agree that the man we've just seen was stoned out of his mind. Alternatively, he was one of those who don't need it; but in either case, he might have been one of us. And there he was, allowed to appear on television. Something must be happening. Either the message is getting across, or alternatively, the second possibility, they've got their eyes on us down here and they're beaming special programmes down to Williams Farm, which nobody else can watch, just to put us off the scent. I think this is too important a matter for us to discuss between ourselves. I think we ought to ask Jaques in here to discuss it with us.'

So Dumpling went to Jaques's cell and brought him back to the kitchen. He listened to an excited and confused account of what they had seen on television, but his mind was distracted. 'I expect they're more interested in what is happening elsewhere at the moment,' he said. 'There was a change of government in Lagos last January, but it won't solve anything. There are too many problems out there, too much hatred, ever since easterners started leaving home to work in the north. Soon, there will be the most terrible killings. It was bound to come. I always told them not to go, but they were only interested in the money. We missionaries weren't allowed to accompany them to the north, you know, because everybody was supposed to be Muslim there. As a result, our children forgot everything we taught them and became hard and arrogant. They thought that because they were better educated and cleverer they must be more admirable in every way. No wonder they became un-popular. If we had taught them that to be more educated and cleverer *does* make you more admirable, but it also imposes greater obligations, perhaps none of this would have happened. But they should never have left their villages and their families in the first place. Those with families should always stay in them. Those without families should try to create one. A man without family or village is already halfway insane – look at America. There is going to be no end to the bloodshed in Nigeria now, just because those men left their families and went to live in the north for money.'

A moment's silence followed Jaques's speech. They were back again, in the old routine. Black Stone nodded his head wisely. 'Right on,' he said absently, and began thinking about Beauty without any of her clothes on.

Strong Arm said: 'I think that's it. I think it may be what the Galloping Gourmet was trying to say. Symbolically, of course.'

'Or he might have been telling us that Mars was moving into opposition with Uranus. A lot of people say: so what? – but, of course, I care because I'm Gemini. Black Stone is a Scorpion. It's us two who are in the most danger. I think we had better get together and join forces.'

'So do I,' said Black Stone, getting off his seat. They left the room together.

'I must go and pick some flowers,' said Ruby Wednesday.

Jaques went back to his cell.

After the first violent attack, which only lasted eight hours, Orlando slowly returned to normal, subject to occasional relapses when he could feel reality slipping away like sand between his fingers. On these occasions there was nothing he could do but sit and suffer. He never experienced any hallucination which could be described as enjoyable. For a week afterwards, he was extremely feeble in his limbs, feeling as if he had swum ten miles. After that, he was taken for walks by Rosalind and the Duke; sometimes by Beauty, who once tempted him to make love to her under a beech tree about two miles from the farm. But his only conversation was of Rosalind, and the only apparently ineradicable scar left by the poison which Macbeth had given him was his inability to recognise the object of all his affections and desires. Beauty and the others soon tired of hearing him talk about Rosalind, but Rosalind herself never did so, nor did her father.

The Duke was rather relieved, in a way, that Orlando should mistake his daughter for a boy. He had none of that vicarious, gloating pleasure in his daughter's sex life which is so common among parents of a certain age; nor was he upset, particularly, to think of his daughter coupling unmarried, with a strange man, outside the family. He was merely embarrassed by the whole thing, feeling that he had no business to know about it. His daughter's sex life was something extraneous to his affection for her, or hers for him; he did not want to be bothered with it, unless she decided to marry, when he would have to take an interest. But Orlando, whom he liked, had decided that she was a boy, and on that basis a warm friendship seemed to have developed between the two. There were a few quarrels at the beginning, when Rosalind started to protest her true sex and identity; Orlando at once became extremely angry. After that, nobody bothered; Rosalind was quite happy to hear her sexual delights extolled. In moments of great intimacy, she advised Orlando on how best to set about seducing his Rosalind, when next he met her. The Duke, too, was always prepared to listen, and even give advice.

With the absence of Jaques in his cell, these walks with Orlando and Rosalind were probably the only thing which kept the Duke in Somerset. It would not be true to say that he was disillusioned. But he needed great refreshing draughts of Jaques's wisdom to keep him set in his purpose. He had changed his life-style, as Jaques advised that he should; he now lived closer to the earth; his food was less poisoned by chemicals than previously; he never heard people utter the sort of inanities which had been commonplace in the London of April 1966, when he left it. Perhaps an entirely new set of inanities was now commonplace, three months later. Perhaps Mr Wilson's Labour government had transformed everybody – people were now only concerned with truth and kindness, they had seen through the shallow materialism of the capitalist ethos. Whenever he mentioned such things to Touchstone, the clown replied: 'Ah yes, of course, you are in a position to understand the shallow materialism of the capitalist ethos aren't you, sir? It must be wonderful to have your understanding of the world.'

Touchstone's relentless cynicism began to depress him. Bit by bit, the world outside began to seem not such a dreadful place as he had originally supposed. The disadvantages of life in a small community were increasingly apparent, more especially since few of its members seemed entirely sane. Perhaps the Duke would have left all his followers and returned to London if it had not been for an incident which occurred on one of his walks with Orlando and Rosalind.

They were coming out of the wood above the farm. The day was extremely hot, but they could nevertheless smell wood-smoke from the farm's chimney. No outside warmth ever penetrated the thick walls of the kitchen, and in any case the fire was necessary for cooking and for hot water. They stopped to admire the tranquillity of the scene, when Rosalind drew their attention to a rabbit sitting under a sycamore tree about twenty yards from where they stood.

'If we caught him, we could eat him with the pigeons Snowman trapped yesterday,' said Orlando. Rosalind, who could not bear the thought of animals being killed (although she ate them happily enough) begged him to leave it alone. It was an unusual time of day to see a rabbit; when they walked towards it, they noticed something odd in its behaviour. Instead of running away, it waddled a few paces and then sat still. Orlando realised what was wrong before he had seen its disfigured head and tiny, popping eyes. 'I'm afraid it looks as if we've got another outbreak of myxomatosis,' he said.

This news had an alarming effect on the Duke. He always carried a heavy walking stick with him on their walks; he used it now to club the rabbit to death, swearing and shouting violently. When the creature was dead he continued battering it for a while, then instructed that nobody should touch it; it should be burned. Afterwards, he sat on the ground, trembling with shock. 'Why do people do it? Why must they try to murder an entire species of animal in the cruellest most useless way imaginable? Nobody sees that the man who spreads myxomatosis is a criminal, guilty of something nearly as disgusting as genocide. What has happened to the human race that they are prepared to inflict this sort of thing on their fellow creatures?'

At that moment, the Duke knew that he had been right all along. There need be no further looking back. The rest of the world was insane; the inmates of Williams Farm were those trying to rediscover their sanity.

Three days later, Orlando and Rosalind found themselves alone on the same walk. The Duke had stayed behind, saying that he wanted to collect his thoughts on the situations in Nigeria and Vietnam. He had also been quite interested of late in the subject of poverty in Britain: while acknowledging that it was only comparative poverty, and therefore involving none of the moral imperatives created by the spectacle of absolute poverty, such as existed in the under-developed world, comparative poverty also created distress. Nobody could deny that absolute poverty – the shortage of food, warmth and shelter – still existed in Britain, but it was too small to be a matter of general concern. If one met it, of course, one must do one's best to alleviate it. But where comparative poverty was concerned, distress arose from the resentment of some people at being poorer than others, and it would flourish at whatever level of prosperity existed, until such time as everyone was materially equal. The only way to remove the resentment and distress which were created by inequalities of wealth was to abolish inequalities of wealth; yet to do so would create further resentment and distress;

possibly more, possibly less; nobody knew. Was it one's duty to minimize resentment and distress by imposing whichever system caused less? Or was there some moral distinction between the aspiration of those who, having already everything they needed, wanted more, and those who, having already more than they needed wanted to keep what they had?

'Of course not,' said Jaques. 'The great thing is to do nothing but to remain aware. That is why we are all here.'

'I think the answer is for everybody to concentrate his mind on not resenting that some people should have more, or minding that others have less,' said the Duke.

'A very convenient philosophy, of course, for those as has more than most,' said Touchstone. 'And coming from one who has more than almost anybody else in the kingdom, I should say it was ideal. But I shouldn't worry your poor head about philosophies, sir. As long as there's a police force, there's no need for the rich to have philosophies and suchlike. What's wrong with the Church of England, for God's sake? It was invented for the likes of you. Think of all those poor parsons slaving away night and day to convince the rich they needn't worry, then you have to go thinking up philosophies of your own, all independent and on the quiet. We used to see some really nasty characters in West End Central, you know, sir. Burglars, protection gangs, rapists, the lot. It was no good telling them to concentrate their minds on purging the envy and resentment from their hearts. They had their hands full twenty-four hours a day trying to keep a safe distance between themselves and the fuzz.'

'Poor men,' said Beauty. 'Rapists must be so unhappy.'

'They only have to steal and rape because they can't get what they want any other way,' said the Duke.

'Don't you believe it,' said Touchstone. 'They do it because they've got a nasty turn of mind.'

'You mean they're evil. They're really absolutely evil,'

145

breathed Beauty. 'How fantastic, I mean, just to be an evil man, you know, and to go around looking out of your eyes, knowing like I'm an evil cat, really evil, thinking bad thoughts, doing suddenly the most incredibly mean and hateful things,' Beauty's eyes were shining. 'I think I'd like to meet some of those really heavy, nasty people. I mean, of course, I wouldn't want to meet them, but, you know what I mean like they might teach me something.'

Beauty's breath was coming fast and she stroked herself in an agitated manner. The Duke retired to his bedroom to think about everything which had been said.

'I think the Duke was wrong,' said Orlando, when he and Rosalind were pacing the reed-scented slopes about a quarter of a mile from the farm. 'Why should we concern ourselves with people who are unhappy merely because they are greedy? I agree there are some people who really suffer through their poverty, and we should always try to bear them in mind.' Orlando looked down at the valley. An ancient apple tree stood a few yards to their left, behind them stood another. Across the valley an unbelievably ancient oak gnarled its way to the sky, assuring them of the earth's integrity and the timelessness of the English countryside. A pair of jays squabbled in the wood behind them. The sun beat down indiscriminately, a universal benediction from above.

'Ah yes, the poor,' said Rosalind. 'We must always think about the poor.' She wondered why they had to think about the poor. She could only think about her own beautiful young body, dressed in a thin, tight jersey, faded blue jeans, short socks, gym shoes and nothing else. No underwear. No stockings. So free, and so close to her beloved. Orlando, she knew, was wearing a rather absurd pair of underpants – she knew, because she had helped him to dress. Every morning she took into his bedroom a

146

basin of warm water, a sponge and a towel. It dated from the time when he was ill, and neither saw any particular reason to end the tradition. Once, when she was sponging his secret parts, she noticed a quickening excitement in them, and gazed lovingly, longingly into his face for some sign of answering awareness. But he referred to the matter in some coarse, masculine expression – although making no effort to impede her ministrations – and she let the moment pass.

They came to the place where the rabbit had been killed, three days before. Nobody, of course, had removed the body, let alone burnt it. 'Poor rabbit,' said Orlando. 'Uselessly, joylessly done to death. Aren't we men pigs?'

Rosalind could only think of his body's proximity to her own. 'No, I don't think so,' she said. 'I love being with you. Tell me again that I remind you of Rosalind.'

'You do,' he said. 'Oddly enough, when you were giving me my blanket bath this morning, I suddenly thought you were Rosalind. If you were a girl, I might almost be taken in.'

'I know you thought I was your Rosalind this morning. I could tell by the way you reacted.' She rejoiced in the blush which appeared on his fine, manly cheek. 'Now you're blushing just like a girl yourself. But you do love me, don't you, Orlando, even though you think I am a boy.'

Orlando looked at her steadily. 'Oddly enough, I think I do. I don't quite know what you're trying to say or do to me, but the answer to your question is yes, I do love you. Not in the same way as I love Rosalind, of course. That wouldn't be possible. Or at least, I don't think it would.' A feeling of generous exasperation overcame Rosalind. She stood, inches from Orlando, melting for a touch from his hand, while he soliloquized endlessly and fatuously to himself. 'After all, you are a boy, and, of course, that is bound to make a difference.'

'Do you really think I am a boy, or are you merely ask-

ing me to expose myself?' screamed Rosalind. Orlando
looked startled. She seized his hand and held it against her
breasts, first the left one, then the right. 'Do they feel like
a boy's breasts?' she yelled. 'Now feel your own.' She
undid the button of his shirt and pushed his hand inside.

Orlando collected himself with an effort. 'I know perfectly well what I feel like,' he said in a quiet, dignified
voice. 'I also know that different people develop in different ways. It is well known that they do. There is
nothing to be worried about – there is nothing *unnatural* –
in having well-developed breasts . . .'

Rosalind took his hand inside her jumper to where her
breasts – not large, but perfectly formed – stood out to
greet them. She took his hand and put it between her legs,
holding it there tenderly and staring into his eyes. He
gasped slightly. 'You see, Orlando, my sweet, there really
are differences between us,' she said. 'Look.' She undid
her belt and let her jeans fall to the ground, entangled
about her ankles. She held Orlando's hand to her crutch and
asked him to look at the whiteness of her skin, at the soft
and delightful curve of her thighs, at the thin, round
length of her leg. She undid his own belt and unzipped the
front of his trousers, pulling them down impatiently.
'Look,' she said, pointing to the shape inside his absurd,
rather dirty underpants. 'Boys have those things. Girls
have these.' She pulled down his underpants and cupped
her hands, 'Do you see the difference? It is a wonderful and
amazing thing. Now do you see then I am your Rosalind?
Look what is happening to you now, Orlando. That is
because I am your Rosalind.' She held his angry, exigent
person in her hands under the open sky, while the sun
smiled on them from above and a small, dead rabbit lay at
their feet. At that moment she suspected that his madness
had been a pose, or at best an exercise in self-indulgence.
This is what he had been wanting all along – an act of total
humiliation from her. It was as he himself had said, that

men were greedy pigs. But Rosalind, the eternal woman, was quite prepared to humiliate herself. She started to take off her jersey so that he could really appreciate the difference, as they stood facing each other, their trousers around their ankles, in the glorious warmth of an early summer's afternoon.

It was thus that Jaques found them, on his stroll, muttering to himself about all the sorrows of mankind. The sight gladdened his heart. He beamed at them affectionately. 'Such a beautiful day to be up and about,' he said. 'I see you are getting to know each other at last. I am sorry to interrupt you so rudely. There are moments, of course, where a third person's arrival can be most upsetting, but you have a lifetime ahead of you both, and one moment's delay will only prolong the rapture. It seldom lasts for very long. Perhaps, when you are old, you will thank me for breaking it up this afternoon. It will give you one more memory to smile about as you sit in front of the fire on a winter's evening, your weak but kindly old eyes searching each other's face for a sign of the youth you once knew. Ah well, perhaps nobody will be allowed to grow old together in the new world, with all its divorce and other exciting, wonderful things. But seeing you both caressing each other, naked, in a wood, suddenly made me wish that I had once known what it was to be young. So few people ever know. It was lovely to see you both.'

Orlando plainly resented his intrusion. There was an exasperation in his movements as he retrieved his slightly absurd, off-white underpants from around his ankles, hitched them up, bend down again for his trousers strapped his belt, and buttoned up his shirt. Rosalind, by contrast, who had never succeeded in removing her jersey, dressed herself with a quiet, contented, dreamy sort of dignity; her eyes, velvety and soft with remembered pleasure, never left Orlando, but Jaques felt that her benevolence embraced him as well.

Orlando never glanced at her. 'I suppose it was lovely for you to see us both. Many men of your age often spend much of their time watching young couples, I believe.'

'So I have heard,' said Jaques.

'Well, I wish you would not come to try your perversions out on us,' said Orlando.

'Oh dear,' said Jaques. 'You know perfectly well I had no reason to expect you. But the devil gets into a man when his rod is stiff. I often think that the easiest way to accept the existence of God is to study the activity of the devil. One sees him everywhere nowadays. In Belsen and Auchswitz, of course – there is no other explanation for them – in Soviet Russia, in the futility and stupidity of the arms race, the moon race, coloured television. But above all, one feels him working in one's own heart. Do you feel the devil working in your own heart at the moment, Orlando?'

'Perhaps I do,' he said.

'I don't,' said Rosalind. 'I feel rather heavenly.'

'Well, bless you both,' said Jaques. 'Don't spend too much time thinking about this dead rabbit. There's nothing but gloom in it. There's nothing we can do for that rabbit now, nor any of the others. Save such thoughts up for your old age. You can dance on its grave while you're young, and it is probably the best thing to do.' Jaques capered ridiculously around the body of the dead rabbit, looking, no doubt, rather like Nijinsky in his last performance of Petrouchka. When he led them back to the farm, his face was streaming with tears.

After tea – a most important meal in Williams Farm – Rosalind told Orlando that he needed a rest. She brought a blanket bath to his bedroom – just a basin of warm water and a sponge. This time, as she sponged his secret parts, it was he who reached up and fondled her breasts.

150

'Who am I?' she asked, as he fumbled at her belt. 'Rosalind of course,' he said. She stood naked for his inspection. 'My darling, sweet Rosalind, I am so sorry.'

She stood proudly in front of him. 'You have nothing to be sorry for,' she said. 'You are the most beautiful man alive.' Her huge brown eyes were misty and serious.

If Jaques had come in at that moment to pronounce the marriage blessing over them, he would not have caused them a moment's embarrassment or pain.

It was some time after supper that the television set played a very nasty trick on them. Several members of the family declared that they would not watch it again, that it had betrayed their trust. They had been watching a play about a young married couple who did not seem to get on very well together.

The man starts flirting with a girl in the office; to punish him, his wife goes out with a married man and gets involved in a tragic situation when it appears that his child, who suffered from an incurable disease, is about to die; husband and wife come together in the end, both fortified by draughts of newly acquired self-knowledge, and discuss plans to start a family.

This poignant drama was received with almost total incomprehension, despite occasional efforts to explain it to each other.

'Why can't his wife look after the child? She hasn't got anything to do when he's out all day balling this other chick.'

'She's all up tight because she wants him to lay *her*,' explained Ruby.

'Nobody seems to be getting laid, if you ask me,' said Buttercup. 'They're all just talking about it.'

'Why can't he lay both of them?' said Macbeth. 'They don't look too bad, really.'

'Macbeth is always on about how people look,' said Celia. She constantly resisted his clumsy, tentative advances. It seemed to her most unfair that nobody ever made advances to Dumpling, whose life and bed she now shared. 'Anyway, what's the child got to do with it? It seems a very silly play to me.'

'Right on, there,' said Macbeth. 'It's the most crazy fucking ridiculous play I've ever seen. So some people want to go balling and there's a sick child which hasn't got anything to do with it. That's not a play. It's not even a bloody anagram.'

'Hush, hush,' said Snowman the Hunter. 'I think that she doesn't even like fucking. That's what they're not allowed to say on television, of course. If ever they realised, out there, that none of them really like fucking any more, the whole of their society would collapse. They've *got* to go on believing it, you see. Otherwise they wouldn't be able to buy newspapers, or catch a train, clean their teeth, or do anything at all. Their life would have no purpose.'

'You mean, it's another of these coded messages they send to us from London.' The Duke frowned. 'You may be right, but I'm not too happy about it. It seems to me that it's just a very bad television play, demonstrating how the vitality is fading out of our culture. It may be that television has introduced playwrights to an undiscriminating captive audience, and the mass market determines its own level of mediocrity in entertainment. I would prefer to think, however, that our culture has become one in which the creative imagination can no longer flourish. It is therefore moribund. We, at Williams Farm, are witnessing the birth of a new culture.'

Black Stone argued from this that the culture of Williams Farm was essentially pre-Ptolemaic, not a birth but a rebirth. The Duke was their pharaoh, who also sat in for God. Jaques was the high priest. Soon, they would have to start making sacrifices to discover where the Duke's tomb should be sited. Everybody agreed that Beauty was the one to be sacrificed. She had been making rather a nuisance of herself lately. What the play had been saying was that the fair lady, who obviously symbolised the moon, must be laid before our dying culture, represented by the sick child, succeeded, by its death agonies, in frustrating the quest.

'But how,' said Macbeth, who was by now most agreeably stoned: 'do we set about laying the moon?'

'Easy,' said Willie Williams in the silence which followed. 'Just give Oi some binder twine and a little bit of paraffin. There's nothing to it.'

'Or you walk out at night in your white cotton night dress – nothing else – and meet the moon, alone, on a hill,' said Celia. Opinion seemed to agree that hers was the best way. 'You can hunt the moon, of course, with dogs and things, but it gets very cold,' said Snowman.

'Often the moon comes into my bedroom, and I feel like ice inside,' said Beauty.

'Anybody can lay the moon in two lines of verse, or even in a single pretty thought,' said Strong Arm, looking steadily at Macbeth. 'Those who ask how they would set about the job have no business to be at Williams Farm.'

'I still say it was a rotten play,' said Macbeth. Further conversation was forestalled by the arrival of the advertisements, always greeted by calls of delighted recognition from the girls.

'How can anything be whiter than white?' said Jaques despondently. 'They have nothing to say to each other, so they utter nonsense. Nobody need worry about his sanity if the whole world is shown to be insane. That is the function of television. It establishes the new idea of normality. Nobody dares question it. But we are right to have television in the farm. We must surround ourselves with these reminders of the outside world's depravity.'

It was too late in the evening for anyone to pay any attention to Jaques. Nor did anyone pay any attention when Black Stone piped up sleepily: 'Isn't that exactly what Tutenkhamen was trying to say?'

Instead, with fascinated incomprehension, they watched the news. It started reasonably enough, giving no hint of the shock that was in store. The Chancellor of the Exchequer, a Mr Callaghan, had made a speech in Exeter, saying that his July austerity measures were working well, and the country should soon be out of its economic difficulties. He apologised to those who were feeling the pinch, but could give no clear indication of when the present curb on domestic credit and public spending would be lifted.

'What on earth is he doing in Exeter? That is quite near here.'

'The Rougemont of Exeter is directly on the Ley of St Michael, linking Land's End with Glaston,' said Rock. 'If he follows the Dragon Line back to Glaston, he will arrive at Williams Farm.'

They locked the front door and piled chairs against it, in case a strange, wild-eyed Chancellor of the Exchequer should be tempted to catch them unawares.

The next news item concerned a report which the government was planning on the organisation of the foreign and diplomatic service. A third news item described how Mrs Elsie Peartree, an old age pensioner, had tackled two gunmen robbing the pay office of the co-operative dairy, in Worcester.

'Must be mad,' said Touchstone. 'The things some people will do to get their silly faces on television.'

Next, it was said that the M4 motorway had been blocked for three hours by a pile-up. 'Perhaps,' said the Duke in his humorous voice, 'this is what Marx meant by a crisis of over-production.' Only Walt Izzard laughed.

'Skimming the cream off the economy,' said Strong

Arm. 'That is the secret of the pyramids, the moon programme, the Vietnamese war and nearly everything else. The only alternative is to eat it all ourselves. We should die of surfeit.'

'Worse,' said Jaques. 'We should lose our appetite for consumption. Then the whole house of cards collapses.'

'I'm sleepy,' said Beauty. 'Who wants to go to bed?'

Beauty practically never slept alone. She was terrified of the dark, and her poor, gentle little mind shrank from the effort of thinking. Several of the men might have gone with her, whether for company or for the sensual delights of her body; sometimes, when she wanted a rest, one of the girls would accompany her, or she would go and sleep with Audrey. But it was at that moment that the television chose to take its revenge.

'Hey, look at this,' cried Black Stone.

Quite suddenly, the screen had filled with running, screaming Negroes. There was a noise of shots and further screams. The camera showed bodies and parts of bodies, hideously mutilated, lying on the ground.

Jaques covered his eyes. 'It's Kaduna,' he said, 'Jos, Kano. Oh my God.'

'What is going on?' said Beauty. 'Is this some sort of tribal custom? Why do they suddenly have to get so completely out of hand?'

'It *is* a tribal custom,' said Black Stone, who knew everything. 'Some sort of harvest festival. They're celebrating the fertility goddess.'

'Rubbish,' said Jaques. 'They're massacring all my friends from the Eastern region.'

Silence fell after that announcement. They saw further pictures of mutilated bodies, some piled up in heaps. A train was shown arriving at a station, full of wounded refugees. Then there were roads, blocked with swarms and swarms of people walking, pushing bicycles, carrying children and household possessions. Over two million Easterners were making the long trek home from all parts of Nigeria after the third and most violent outbreak of massacres. They no longer felt safe in any other part of the Federation. Observers waited to see whether the young country could hold together. Its young leader, Colonel 'Jack' Gowon, recently come to power himself after a military coup, had appealed for calm. Meanwhile the massacres continued, especially in the North. It was as if the rest of Nigeria had decided to tell the Easterners for the last time to keep to their own region or take the consequences, said the commentator, rather oddly. He was an expert on West Africa, called Aubrey La Touche. Almost condescendingly, he showed them a few more photographs of terrified black faces running along a country road.

'Whether or not Nigeria will be able to hold together, of course, remains to be seen. Opinion in Whitehall tonight was that it probably will, and no effort is being spared to assure the government in Lagos that it will continue to receive the support and assistance of the British government. The position in Enugu, capital of the Eastern region, is somewhat different, since they have never recognised Colonel Gowon's régime in Lagos, despite its recognition two months ago by Britain, the United States and all other countries. However, British government sources made it plain that they could give no support whatever to any secessionist movement on the part of the Eastern regional government, but would instead give whatever aid was necessary to the central government to preserve the integrity of the Federation.

'No figures are available for the number of casualties in the present upheaval, although they are not thought to be less than 15,000. However, in the light of the British government's uncompromising stand,' said Mr La Touche, the merest hint of smugness in his winning smile, 'it seems unlikely that the Nigeria we know will be allowed to disintegrate. Perhaps what we have just seen,' the smile was unmistakable now – cruel and conspiratorial, yet somehow superior at the same time – 'will prove to be no more than an example of what happens in modern Africa to any tribe which tries to get just that little bit above itself. Goodnight, Aubrey La Touche, ITN African Service.'

His smile, like that of the Cheshire cat, faded slowly, to be replaced by the picture of a mutilated corpse.

'Oh my God, why do they have to show us such disgusting things?' said Beauty.

'Because it's what the world's all about,' said Walt Izzard. 'If you can't bear the sight of blood, you shouldn't eat meat.'

'It's not the blood I mind,' said Beauty. 'It's that perfectly disgusting young man. Why do they have to bring such, I mean unspeakable, horror into our drawing rooms? Can't they see we might be sick or something?'

'They showed us the young man because that is the sort of person who is running things nowadays,' said Jaques. Tears were streaming down his face. 'God alone knows what my poor children over there have done to deserve Aubrey La Touche. Now there will be no end to the misery they have to suffer. Did you see, two million of them have been driven out of their homes?'

Soon Beauty was weeping, and Celia, Buttercup, Ruby Wednesday, Dumpling; then Walt Izzard started to snivel. The Duke again began to feel at a loss. 'Yes, but are we achieving anything?' he asked. 'What can we do for the unfortunate people of the Eastern region of Nigeria? Perhaps we should send them some blankets, we have more than we need, surely.'

'Not since Mr Orlando arrived with Adam and then Miss Rosalind and Celia came with Mr Touchstone,' said Audrey. 'We scarcely have enough.'

'Oh dear,' sobbed Beauty. 'We can't even send them a blanket, because we haven't got enough.'

'It would make no difference if we did send them blankets,' said Strong Arm. 'There would certainly be others in other parts of the world who need them more. The great thing is to thank the Lord that we have enough blankets ourselves, or at any rate to be aware of how lucky we are. No, the only thing we can do for Jaques's friends in West Africa is to think about them.'

'I know,' said Beauty. 'That is what I am doing, thinking about them.'

So it was that in a farmhouse kitchen at the bottom of the Mendip Hills in North Somerset, on the night of September 30th 1966, fifteen people sat and thought, with varying degrees of concentration and varying degrees of accuracy, about events in West Africa.

PART THREE

CHAPTER SEVEN

Mr Titus Burns-Oates enjoyed the most cordial relations with his political master, the Secretary of State for Commonwealth Affairs, but he found the parliamentary under-secretaries less congenial. As his rank in the Commonwealth Relations Office was only that of counsellor, it might be thought that he saw the Secretary of State very seldom. In fact, he somehow managed to see him more often than many functionaries of twice his seniority. By some oversight – probably it was due to an error in the Foreign Office computer which dealt with these things – he had also been made a Companion of the Most Distinguished Order of St Michael and George, while still a first secretary in the Ottawa High Commission. True, he was older than most people of equivalent rank, and his fine white hair and slight limp made him look fairly distinguished. Only the extreme dinginess of his office gave him away. The smart notice outside: TITUS BURNS-OATES, C.M.G., WEST AFRICA, could not disguise the fact that his career had been less distinguished than his neighbours in Weybridge, Surrey, might have supposed. Yet he regularly saw the Secretary of State; on one occasion, recently, he had spent an hour with him, in the presence of the permanent under-secretary, their personal assistants and one assistant under-secretary on the intelligence side, from the Foreign Office. Next year – in October, 1968 – it was planned that the Foreign and Commonwealth Offices should merge, but for the moment they kept their independence, making a big business of closer liaison. Mr Burns-Oates was nothing if not good at liaising.

There were those among his Surrey neighbours who wondered if he did not find it difficult to be his robust and charming self with Labour ministers. In fact, Mr Burns-Oates got on very well indeed with the Labour team. Perhaps it was because they respected his greater experience; perhaps it was because a lifetime of dealing with Africans had taught him a certain bluff savoir-faire: he knew when to look serious about problems like South Africa; when to make jokes about the black man's general incompetence and backwardness; when to show appreciation of the educated Africans' extreme cunning in extorting money from gullible, philanthropic white governments. Above all (he would admit it to his Surrey neighbours but never in Downing Street) he despised all Africans: humble, half-witted peasant and arrogant, élitist politician; earnest, frightened intellectual and corrupt hereditary leader. It was this secret feeling about Africa which communicated itself to his political masters and somehow, secretly, matched their own. Whenever they spoke together of a successful African politician, it was always in terms of great respect, to say that he had enormous charm. What Mr Burns-Oates meant, of course, was that he had enormous charm himself.

And so he had. He was also extraordinarily handsome. If he held his head in a particular way, it made him look like a film star, or an elder statesman. It distressed him when people failed to respond to his charm. Women invariably responded. If he had not been a compulsive adulterer, he might have advanced further in his career. But then, as he thought whimsically to himself, he would not have had such an enjoyable life, either. One of the best things about Africa was the women. There was quite literally nothing they would not do, if you asked them. Nobody could ever accuse Titus Burns-Oates of colour prejudice. Rather the reverse, in fact – it made it less embarrassing, less complicated, somehow, if your partner on these occasions was a black lady.

Mr Burns-Oates sat back in his scruffy little office (nose up, chin in, eyes narrowed, spectacles off – twiddle, polish and suck the frame – frown slightly) and wondered what to say next. He did not particularly relish having to talk to junior ministers. They were too keen, somehow, and unwilling to take into account those things that were always better left unsaid. He was unable quite to gauge the measure of the new parliamentary under-secretary. Why was he so interested in Africa? With Conservatives, it was always because they had some family business there – nothing wrong with that, either. Was it the women Mr Oliver Twickerley was interested in, or did he see Africans as children, to be taught about State planning and filled with contraceptives? A lot of these Labour people were basically school-teachers, and dealing with Africans made them feel self-important and generally superior, in the nicest possible way. 'I think we've covered all possible supplementaries,' he said.

Twickerley had been referred to him by the Information Department, whose responsibility it normally was to prepare answers to parliamentary questions. In addition to an answer, the information department provides intelligence which might be required for supplementary questions – nobody ever knows what the supplementary question will be. This is one of the wonders of British democracy: backbenchers are able to ask anything they like and ministers must somehow have an answer. Hence the need for background briefing.

And, of course, Twickerley could not have come to a better person. It was Titus Burns-Oates, as a matter of fact, who had formulated recent British policy in Nigeria. Outside the carefully guarded corridors of the Commonwealth Relations Office, in Downing Street, people might have been surprised that a policy involving the future of some fifty-five million people would be formulated at such a low level. This policy, which would later encompass the death of about two million civilians, mostly children, in the most ferocious and appalling civil war which Africa had ever known, came to him after luncheon one day in the canteen. Later, of course, it would have to be defended passionately in the House of Commons by a Foreign and Commonwealth Secretary reduced to all the symptoms of a nervous breakdown; the Prime Minister would be booed and spattered with red ink by demonstrators in Germany and Canada, a British trade week would have to be cancelled in Switzerland after numerous protests. At the time however, it seemed both statesmanlike and obvious. Mr Burns-Oates remembered the occasion well. He had been adding his own memorandum to the reports which came in from the High Commission in Lagos and the deputy High Commission in Enugu, before sending them up to the head of the West African department for transmission to the deputy under-secretary. Throughout the morning, he suffered from wind, but it had not affected the purity of his beautiful, italic script (he always used blue-green ink) as he wrote in the margin a few carefully chosen words.

'The events of July 1966 were highly regrettable, but, of course, they had been coming a long time, and nobody can say that the Ibos did not ask for everything they got,' he said to Oliver Twickerley. 'In any case, these so-called massacres have been much exaggerated.'

'But how can they be sure they won't happen again.'

'Of course, nobody can be sure. Quite frankly, that will be their own look-out. Most of the Ibos have gone back to live in the Eastern region again, and that is probably the best idea for all concerned. They were always a disruptive element in the rest of Nigeria. One can feel sorry for them, but they ought to have thought of it before. We never asked them to upset the applecart in the first place. It's quite another thing to say they must be allowed to break up the Federation after what has happened. If Nigeria breaks up, the whole of Africa will break down on tribal lines. It will be the end of everything we have ever worked for.'

'But surely' said Oliver, 'there is no danger of that now?' The Nigerian regional leaders had all met in Ghana, and reached agreement on a solution which was acceptable to all of them. Oliver found himself disliking Burns-Oates.

'Don't you believe it,' said the counsellor. 'Between ourselves, the Aburi agreement is no good at all. We look at it as a formula for disintegration.'

'But there's nothing we can do about it, if that is what the Africans want,' said Oliver.

'Don't you believe it. We both know perfectly well it's no good leaving things to these Nigerian johnnies. Of course their new man is absolutely first class. Do you know Jack Gowon? First class man, with immense charm, of course. We've had to tell him that this Aburi thing won't do at all. I think he sees our point of view. We assured him, you know, that we'd support him up to the hilt with any measures which might be necessary to keep his country together. That was all he really wanted to know.' Burns-Oates spoke in a bluff, man-to-man sort of way. 'Now he's getting his civil service boys to draw up a new map of Nigeria, dividing it into twelve states. The Eastern region will become three states, and the Ibos will be shut into one of them, without access to the oil, or to the sea, or to any foreign frontier. We think it is probably the best way to deal with the Ibos – clobber them good and hard, before it is too late and they take over the whole country. This way, they're isolated inside their homeland, without a friend anywhere else. I haven't told you any of this, of course, because it is all secret. I don't even think the Secretary of State knows quite what is going on. So far as the House of Commons is concerned, we are not interfering in any way with the internal affairs of a sovereign, independent country, but we earnestly hope the unity of the country will be maintained and to this end we have promised any assistance requested by the recognised government.'

It was seldom Mr Burns-Oates was called upon to make such a long speech. He hoped that the parliamentary under-secretary was impressed. Within the Commonwealth Office, such things were communicated by the twitch of an eyebrow, the hint of a smile, a careful pause in speech – or even by a wildly indiscreet exclamation mark at the end of a neutrally worded memorandum. Mr Burns-Oates felt somehow debased by having to reveal all these subtleties of meaning in plain speech. Nevertheless, it was most important that the House of Commons should be kept out of it. No end of harm could be done by debating another country's internal affairs. He thanked his lucky stars yet again that the Socialists were in power, bound to support the decision he had made about six months earlier, after luncheon one day all alone in the canteen, and suffering from wind.

Oliver Twickerley looked at the Order Paper again: Mr Stan Kark, Labour Member for Neasden South, to ask the Secretary of State for Commonwealth Affairs what steps have been taken to implement the Aburi agreement be-tween the regional military governors of Nigeria; what compensation has so far been paid in connection with the massacres of June, September and October of last year; and whether Her Majesty's Government will be prepared to reconsider their recognition of the present regime in Lagos, if the Aburi agreement is discarded, in light of the fact that the regime has never been recognised by all the constituent regions of Nigeria.

'This Stan Kark is, I understand, what is generally described as a left-winger,' said Mr Titus Burns-Oates with the tiniest lift to his left eyebrow. This would have spoken worlds to the Head of the West African Department, an insignificant fellow with bad breath; the deputy under-secretary would have evaluated it accurately enough; journalists in the diplomatic, Commonwealth and political lobbies would have nodded to themselves and chuckled, delighted at their own cleverness, and the way they were entrusted with such sensitive information – never to be printed, of course – that would be an unthinkable breach of trust – for background information. And the joy of the situation was that if anything ever went wrong, if a journalist betrayed his trust, or if it was unmistakably proved that the information given by that lifting eyebrow was false, *Mr Burns-Oates had never actually said it.* He had never said that Mr Stan Kark, Labour M.P. for Neasden South, was a fellow traveller, or a Russian agent in the pay of the K.G.B., or a Trotskyite. He merely lifted an eyebrow and let others draw their own conclusions. To do them justice, some of the press people were quite quick at the uptake: Daniel Chamberlain, Aubrey La Touche, Bernadette Zunz. You never had any trouble with Bernadette Zunz.

Oliver, however, who used to be described as a left-winger himself before accepting a job in the government, gritted his teeth and scowled. Mr Burns-Oates's impertinence was the only reason that he continued asking questions.

'But will there be a civil war when your friend General Gowon repudiates the agreement?'

Mr Titus Burns Oates put on his man-of-the-world face. 'I doubt it very much. The Ibos can see they're absolutely isolated. We've told our man in Enugu to make it plain they won't get any help from us. If they try to play silly-buggers, Jack Gowon will go through them like a dose of salts. It would be all over in about a week, and they would be even worse off than when they started. They're not fools, the Ibos – nor is their leader, this man Ojukwu.

We've told him we won't stand for any secessionist movements in West Africa; the Americans have told him that. He knows he wouldn't stand a chance.'

'You sound very confident. But perhaps the Ibos really are concerned with their security, after being massacred all over the Federation.'

Mr Burns-Oates looked thoughtful. 'Of course they might try to make trouble. We've got to take the possibility into account. If they do, then Jack Gowon will just have to put it down. Do you know Jack Gowon? Absolutely first-class man, you know, with great charm. Some of his boys are rarin' to go and have another crack at the Ibos in their home base. One doesn't like to think what they'd do when they got there. It would be mincemeat. Quite honestly, one hopes the Ibos will come to their senses before it happens. They've been asking for this for a long time. Talk to any Nigerian you know.'

Oliver felt lonely and sad. 'Why must we be involved?' he asked. 'What has it got to do with us whether the Nigerians stay together or not?'

Mr Burns-Oates realised that he had been on the wrong tack. He put his papers together and looked sincere, mature, compassionate. What he was going to say now was something he really did feel most strongly. Or so he imagined.

'Now, Mr Twickerley, I won't try to impress you with a list of British investments in Nigeria.' A bright, wet sparkle of mucous appeared on the end of his nose and began forming itself into a drop. Oliver watched, fascinated. 'I know that there are more important things in life than that, although an investment of £2,000 million is not to be sneezed at nowadays, of course. I wouldn't even ask you to consider the 12,000 British subjects living and working in Nigeria.' The drop grew and sparkled in the now, clear sky which appeared through his window. 'Their lives, of course, would count for nothing if we

168

turned our backs on the Lagos government as soon as things got difficult. I wouldn't even expect you to ask yourself what right the Ibos have to wreck the entire Federation, although if you had watched them over the past eight years as I have, throwing their weight around and treating everyone else as their social and intellectual inferiors, you might reasonably ask yourself that question. But I would like to put one proposition to you: that Nigeria is the only hope left in Africa.' The drop must surely fall soon, unregarded, to land on the large blotter.

'We saw what happened in the Congo, in Ghana, in Rwanda. Nigeria has got the people and the resources to show that there is hope in the world for the independent state run by Africans for Africans; that African society need not always break down under the pressure of tribalism. If we are prepared to stand aside and let Nigeria disintegrate, we had no business to be there in the first place.' For all his British phlegm, Mr Titus Burns-Oates was visibly moved by his own eloquence. He took out an evil black pipe and began sucking at it cruelly. 'That is all. I am sorry if I have bored you, or been over-emphatic. There are some matters one just happens to care about more than others.' He wiped his nose brusquely with his wrist. Perhaps it had all been a trick, to hold Oliver's attention.

Oliver Twickerley was surprised to find that he, too, was moved by what had been said. 'Thank you very much, Sir,' he said. Something in the Counsellor's manner encouraged one to call him 'Sir', although one was a Parliamentary under-secretary and he a mere counsellor. 'I am very glad I had a talk with you. I think you can trust me not to let you down, if they ask any awkward supplementary questions. Of course, I shall follow what happens in Nigeria with much greater interest than before. Thank you so much.'

'It is a pleasure,' said Mr Titus Burns-Oates, handsomely.

Important businessmen never lobby ministers in a delegation. For this reason, Oliver was surprised to recognise among the dim, avaricious faces of the Nigerian lobby no less a person than Mr Frederick Robinson, managing director and acting chairman of Robinson Investments. He had brought with him a lieutenant, Mr Truefitt, and a stenographer, whom he introduced rather coyly as Miss Stella Intersan. Frederick Robinson had only to pick up a telephone at any hour of the day or night and he could come round and see the Secretary of State – even the Prime Minister – for as long as he liked. But he would not be able to bring a stenographer with him. It was most unusual to have any record of these conversations. Oliver would have to watch his tongue very carefully.

'Good afternoon, gentlemen,' he said. 'No doubt you have all seen my statement in the House this afternoon.' He recognised two M.P.s who had been asking supplementary questions on the floor of the House. Mr Runnyman and Mr Crozier were no longer the representatives of the people, they were simple, honest business men with an interest to safeguard.

'Obviously I can't add anything to what I said then, but if you have any special anxieties, or some point which you consider needs clearing up, I shall be delighted to do so on an informal basis. Needless to say, nothing said here can be regarded as official or binding.'

'Why not?' said Mr Robinson.

'Because it is only said for general guidance,' said Oliver.

'General guidance,' said Mr Robinson to his stenographer.

'I have a point which needs clearing up,' said Mr

Crozier heavily. 'How on earth are we supposed to export and do trade with a country if one half of it doesn't recognise the authority of the government? My work is absolutely vital.' Mr Crozier had somehow acquired the Nigerian monopoly in surgical goods, including condoms. 'Everybody agrees they've got to have birth control. It is humanitarian work which should have first priority. Are you prepared to bring pressure to bear on the government of the Eastern region to accept my goods at Port Harcourt?'

'Our man in Enugu is doing everything in his power to persuade the Ibos to face reality,' said Oliver.

'Of course,' said Mr Burns-Oates, 'you might also say that most of the Ibos are Roman Catholic; so long as the Ibos have control of the whole Eastern region, you have very little chance of getting anything very humanitarian through Port Harcourt. *We* favour a twelve state division which would keep the Ibos in a corner around Enugu, turn them out of Port Harcourt and Calabar, and give the minorities a chance to run their own affairs in the other two states.'

'We consider it absolutely vital that the rights of minorities should be protected,' said Mr Crozier.

'And the integrity of Nigeria be maintained,' said Mr Runnyman.

Other voices chimed in. 'Essential British interests.'

'Friendly Commonwealth country.'

'Traditional trading partner.'

'Russian infiltration.'

'At last they've got a really first class man.'

'Do you know Jack Gowon?'

'First class . . . got enormous charm . . . went to Sandhurst . . . really straight fellow.'

Frederick Robinson's voice broke over the babble, and everybody kept quiet in deference to his enormously greater wealth. 'So you can give us an assurance, er,

Twickerley, that these very dangerous proposals contained in the Aburi agreement will never go through, and that the British government will support Gowon in any measures necessary to preserve the unity of the country.'

'So far as the first part is concerned,' said Oliver, 'Everything depends on the Nigerians themselves, but I can tell you in confidence that we are urging Gowon very strongly indeed to press ahead with his original twelve-state plan and to forget about this Aburi nonsense. So long as he feels we're a hundred per cent behind him, I think he'll go ahead.'

'Even if it means civil war?'

'Of course, we all hope it won't mean that,' said Oliver hastily. 'We hope the Ibos will come to their senses and behave more sensibly in future, so there won't be any need for these massacres. Our man in Enugu does say that emotions are running very high there.'

'I think we can disregard him,' said Mr Burns-Oates. 'The Ibos will come to their senses when they see how the cards are stacked.'

'In any case, they couldn't resist the whole Nigerian army for more than a matter of days,' said Oliver. 'They haven't the arms or the trained soldiers. By nature, the Ibos are shopkeepers, civil servants, money lenders – that sort of thing. As soon as they feel the pinch, they will pack it in. And as soon as they try to secede from the Federation, all the minority tribes in the South and South East will be up in rebellion. The Ibos will be flattened, and by then, of course, they will have forfeited any claim to anything. We can get them out of Port Harcourt, away from the sea altogether, and the oil, shut them up between Enugu and Aba, then they won't be able to make any more trouble at all. They won't even have a foreign border to escape over – theirs will be the only state without access either to the sea or to a foreign border. I think we can trust Jack Gowon to look after any little local difficulties which might be presented by the Ibos.'

Oliver was mildly appalled by the ease with which he adopted Mr Burns-Oates's manner of speaking. He had never met Jack Gowon of course; a few weeks ago, he had nothing against the Ibos whatever, whoever they were. His feelings towards Nigerians had been one of general, undiscriminating benevolence.

'But has General Gowon the government's assurance that we will support him in any civil war?' asked Frederick. 'How can we be sure that some left-winger like this Mr Kark will not carry the day?'

Everybody smiled at this. 'I don't think we have much to fear from Mr Kark,' said Oliver. 'I am a left-winger myself, as you very well know. Not many left-wingers are going to help a great African country like Nigeria to fall to pieces.'

'What did he say at the press conference?' Frederick Robinson sat in his brother's desk at Robsec House, feeling like a king.

'As I've explained, it wasn't a press conference. It was a background briefing only for trusted journalists in the political, commonwealth, diplomatic and city branches,' said Daniel Chamberlain. He was looking very nice and above the board this morning. 'Few bothered to turn up. There was me, Aubrey La Touche from ITN, Bernadette Zunz from the *Business Telegraph*, Jeff Squiffy from the *Mail* and a couple of hacks from the parliamentary lobby.'

'Was *The Times* man there?'

'Yes, he was there. And the BBC man. They all took it pretty well straight. I don't think there'll be any difficulty with the press. Very few people are interested in Africa, and most of those are on our side, for one reason or another. The public is bored with being told we mustn't sell arms to anybody, and the left don't like the thought that we'll sell arms to whites but not blacks. Twickerley seems solid. By the time anyone else takes an interest, the matter will have gone too far and they'll have to defend everything they've done to date.'

'Burns-Oates told me Twickerley was solid. Funny the way we two have to arrange to keep Nigeria together. Never been there myself, and never want to go. If we left it to the nig-nogs they would let it fall apart, and where would seventeen million pounds of Robsec's hard-earned money be then, Danny?'

Daniel Chamberlain swelled with pride. 'If we left these things to the British government of either party, there wouldn't be any money for the nig-nogs to throw away,' he said.

'I want you to keep an eye on the Nigerian affair for me,' said Frederick. 'Especially watch the other journalists. If any of them start getting too interested, tip me the wink and we'll see if we can get them transferred to other fields. Alternatively we'll tell Burns-Oates to let it be known on the grapevine that they're unreliable. Meanwhile, I have another little favour to ask you.'

Daniel Chamberlain sat forward with such a frank, intelligent, humorous, approving look on his handsome face that Miss Intersan would gladly have taken him to her bed that night and damned the consequences.

T. BURNS-OATES C.M.G. WEST AFRICA.

The light burned in Titus's room at three o'clock in the morning. Editing, commenting and re-writing reports which came in from Lagos, Enugu, Benin and from the foreign service in the 'Q' bag. Titus sat in his shirt sleeves, perspiring slightly. The military governor of the Eastern region was buying arms and equipping an army, was he?

Titus Burns-Oates would soon put a stop to that. He drew his elegant fountain pen straight through the report from Her Majesty's deputy High Commission in Enugu. The governor of the Eastern region was no longer buying arms or equipping an army. Gowon had been trying to get in touch with Ojukwu again, using the communications facilities at the High Commission. Burns-Oates deleted that from the report which would go to the Secretary of State. Things had gone too far for a peaceful solution. The Ibos would twist Nigeria round their little fingers again. There had been demonstrations at Enugu and Nsukka, calling upon the government of the Eastern region to declare secession immediately, in reprisal against the Federal stoppage of all payments to the east. How did that fit into the scheme of things? On the one hand, it might give an undesirable picture of the East's determination to resist; on the other it might show that Federal sanctions were beginning to bite. Titus decided to let it remain, where it rather worried Oliver next morning. Titus sighed. It was a terrible business, being the only person who really knew what was happening.

CHAPTER EIGHT

There were few visitors at Williams Farm in April, 1967. Occasionally Charlie Winter, from Hatch Bottom, would drive in his tractor to deliver some livestock or a barrel of cider, or merely to pass the time of day with Wee Willie Williams, who had become much more bland of late and greeted his old friend almost hospitably. Charlie couldn't make head or tail of Walt Izzard, though; nor could anyone else these days. Walt constantly made incomprehensible remarks in the sort of voice which suggested he was saying something clever, always with an odd, crooked smile on his thin, furtive little face. Constantly he stared at Rosalind and winked at Orlando in a suggestive sort of way, but nobody paid any attention to him. People supposed he had his uses.

Once, the policeman called from Combe Mendip, pushing his bicycle over two miles of cart-track, trousers neatly tucked into his socks. He had heard a rumour – from Mrs Winchcombe, at the Post Office – that there were foreigners at Williams Farm, and came to assure himself that they had work permits, residence permits and all the other paraphernalia of bureaucratic civilisation. On being assured that there were no foreigners, he stayed long enough to have a cup of tea. The occasion at least provided an opportunity for Jaques to give them a little talk on the nature of existence:

'What *he* means by existence,' said Jaques, pointing at P.C. Weevil, who was almost certainly innocent of the charge: 'is to be contained in a coded reference number on

176

a microfilm stored at Doncaster for an electronic computer belonging to the Ministry of Pensions and National Insurance. Just as medieval theologians used to suppose that our existence owed itself to the continuing exercise of divine will – that we were a figment, if you like, of God's imagination – so nowadays we exist only in the mind of a computer or, to be more accurate, in its information storage facilities.'

'Amen,' said Walt Izzard. He stared at Rosalind who blushed. 'How do computers have babies, then? Do you have male computers and female computers screwing each other?'

'Babies just drop into the national "In" tray, I suppose,' said the Duke.

'Oddly enough, I've never fucked with a computer,' said Beauty thoughtfully. 'There were really horrible things, though, called vibrators, which some girls used to have in the like apartment I shared with them before I mean you know Black Stone here came and turned me on properly. I never knew they could give you babies, though.'

'They can't,' said Dumpling. 'Jaques has got it wrong.'

Macbeth said: 'I don't think Jaques really knows what he's talking about. Not when he talks about fucking, I mean. He's quite good on God, I expect, and all that sort of thing, having been like a priest, and I expect he was quite a good one too, and I must say he knows quite a lot about Africa and like all those you know Nigerian babies, but when it comes to fucking I don't think he knows anything.'

Silence greeted this. It was very seldom that anyone made such a long speech, except Jaques, the Duke, or occasionally Beauty. Plainly Macbeth felt very strongly on the subject. Some of them even racked their brains to remember what this was. Jaques nodded his head many times, and large salt tears ran a watercourse down his face.

'I expect you are right,' he said. 'I don't know anything about that sort of thing. I wasn't really talking about that.'

'Of course you weren't,' said Beauty, moved by pity. 'I've never liked computers any way. They always seem sort of polluted.'

'I mean fucking,' said Macbeth, obstinately unpleasant.

'If Jaques wants to know anything about that, he has only to come to me,' said Beauty, the earth mother. 'There's no mystery about it, honestly, Jaques, and there's nothing difficult, either. You must just trust me to look after you. It doesn't matter if we don't get anywhere the first few times. The great thing is not to worry. Come along with me whenever you feel like it. That's what I'm here for.'

Jaques continued weeping, his ugly, absurd face puckered in misery, and he shook his head wretchedly, completely closed in on himself.

'Don't take it to heart,' said Macbeth. 'I only meant there was no need to lecture us about it.'

P.C. Weevil said: 'Well, if there aren't any people from overseas at the farm, I don't really know what I'm doing here. Thanks for the cup of tea, I'm sure. You seem quite a happy community, for the most part. None of my business to disturb you. 'Bye, 'bye and God bless.'

'God bless you, P.C. Weevil,' they all cried.

This visit had a strangely disturbing effect on Touchstone, however. Perhaps it was the sight of a policeman's uniform which revived memories, perhaps it was his naturally suspicious mind, but when Daniel Chamberlain arrived one day at Williams Farm, in a gleaming new Land Rover, Touchstone did not join in the general excitement.

The rest of the family grouped itself around the jeep chattering as excitedly as if they had been primitive head-hunting villagers in Borneo. They fingered the bonnet and somebody – nobody ever discovered who – stole a badge of the Royal Automobile Club.

'Who are you?' said Beauty, greatly daring.

Danny looked distracted, cleared his throat, and said modestly: 'As a matter of fact, I'm called Daniel Chamberlain.'

In London, this announcement invariably caused a quick thrill of excitement, carefully hidden. The name Chamberlain was exciting enough, but many people on meeting the dashing young journalist of that name experienced something approaching a religious ecstasy.

At Williams Farm, the name caused a similar sensation, but it was much less muted:

'He can't be serious . . .'

'He must be absolutely out of his fucking mind . . .'

'What an absolutely I mean *amazing* name. What can he mean, this guy, coming here and saying these strange things like these absolutely *incredible statements*.'

'Oh my God, did you *hear* what he said? Do you think we ought to get Jaques to come and take a look at him. I mean, do you think that he's *safe*?'

'He's very small,' said Beauty. It was true. What with one thing and another, Danny had never grown much above five feet. But he made up for it by flicking his hair back from his eyes in a most engaging way. 'I think he's quite handsome in a way. I mean like it's unusual to be quite so small nowadays, from that point of view, if you see what I mean, and he might be sort of hungry, which accounts for some of these *strange utterances* like, "Ahum, ahum, es a metter of fact Oh'm called Dennielle Chambermaid".'

'I wondered,' said Danny patiently, 'if I could see the owner of this establishment.'

The family considered this for a while.

'He wants to see Willie Williams. He must be a friend

179

of Willie Williams. Tell Willie to come and talk to this perfectly amazing friend of his.'

'Ung, Oi've never seen on un. Him'll have to go away ung, us'll put some paraffin on 'ee. Mr Chambermaid, Mr Chamberpot, ung, us'll have all the pisspots us wants already, thank 'ee, un, us'll have piss in un, tew, har, har, har.'

'Good old Willie,' cried Beauty. 'Isn't he the most incredible I mean individual? Isn't he I mean quite incredible?'

'As a matter of fact,' said Danny – patient, modest, diffident Danny; there was scarcely a woman or a man in Fleet Street who would not happily die for him when he looked like that – so patient, so modest, so charming. 'I was rather hoping to meet Mr Robinson.'

'Mr who?'

'Here we go again. What *is* this man saying?'

'Es a matter of fact, Oh'm looking for Mistah Robinson. Eh'm *rather* hoping to see this quite completely unbeliev-able cat called Mistah Robinson.'

'Mr John Robinson,' said Danny – patient, modest, thoroughly likeable.

'No, baby, you've come to the wrong patch for this man called John Robinson.' It was Rock who spoke, in his Wild West manner. Soon, he relapsed into Slough psychedelic, with curious undertones of the Brains Trust pundit. 'Wrong patch of ground, wrong century. There was a farmer called Stone Killer Robinson lived at Avebury in Wiltshire, middle of the eighteenth century.'

'It was the violent things he did,' explained Beauty. 'He had this really evil kind of hang-up, you know, against stones. Well, naturally, living at Avebury, he had some of the *biggest* and really most significant stones in the entire world right there on his doorstep. So first he lit a kind of fire out of wood, you know, underneath them, and then when they were red hot, he poured a great jug of cold water over them, so that they split.'

Noises of wonder and disbelief were heard all around the family circle. 'Oh my God, what did he want to do a thing like that for? He must have been out of his mind, I mean really far gone.'

'Fancy wanting to spend your time like breaking up these magnificent old stones. I mean, could they feel it? Did they know what was happening to them even?'

'There is a picture of it in Dr Stukeley's book,' said Black Stone. 'I could tell you how to get to Avebury now, if you've got a compass, but of course you almost certainly won't find this guy Robinson there. I mean, if you did, he would be so old you couldn't make out a word he was saying. His teeth would have fallen out years ago, you know, and his hair etcetera.'

'I wanted to meet Mr John Robinson, the chairman of Robinson Securities,' said Danny. 'I happen to know that he is here. In fact, he invited me down to join him at a tea-party he gave in Robsec House about a year ago. Could you please tell him that it really is most urgent I should see him as soon as possible.'

This announcement caused dismay and pity in about equal proportions:

'Poor man. He's come a long way. He keeps having delusions about this guy Robinson. Poor man.'

'We all have funny ideas sometimes. This fellow really has got a big thing on about someone – or some *thing* – he once thought of called Robinson.'

'Perhaps if he stayed here a few days and got all that pollution and shit out of his system. I mean, fancy demanding to meet someone who's probably been dead like *three thousand years*.'

Eventually a thin, small voice spoke up, sounding mysteriously like the Queen of England: 'I think he wants to see my father.'

It was Rosalind. In her seventh month of pregnancy, she

looked lovelier than ever, and somehow more significant. Only Orlando had noticed she was pregnant – unless Walt Izzard is counted as a human being – although her beautiful, round tummy now jutted like a puffball in front of her. The others may have sensed it, but they said nothing, only treating her with a greater respect than usual.

'He wants to see her *father*. Pisspot wants to see *the Duke*.'

'What a *strange* way for anyone to set about seeing the Duke, shouting his head off about how they broke stones a million years ago.'

Once again, Beauty took pity on him. Rosalind had recognised Danny as soon as he appeared. A sudden, quick contraction in her belly – it might almost have been a labour pain – warned her that Danny's intentions were malignant. She felt weak and slightly sick.

Danny treated her to that quick, handsome grin which everyone in London liked so much. Although his height brought him only to her chin, an awareness of his own charm and masculinity seemed to add inches to his stature. 'I wondered when you were going to recognise me, Rosie,' he said. Cocky and self-assured as ever, the ghost of Sir Henry Campbell-Bannerman, or some such fool, smirking over his shoulder.

'You must come this way, Mr Pisspot, if you want to see the Duke,' said Beauty. She led the way into the kitchen, followed by the nice-looking Daniel Chamberlain who was now limping so heavily that he needed to put a hand on Beauty's shoulder. After them came the whole family, except Rosalind, who stayed behind with Orlando.

'He's kicking around like a shark out of water,' she said.

Orlando put his hand on her proud, stretched belly. 'I think we'll call him Lunchtime Vinegar,' he said, giving her a kiss on her soft, sweet-smelling neck.

'Or Grimalkin,' said Rosalind. 'I always rather like Grimalkin, as a name, for a boy.'

Plainly, they were not going to agree about the matter, so they went for a slow and stately walk in the field, murmuring to each other about animals and woolly things, in the way that lovers do.

'This is Mr Pisspot,' announced Beauty importantly.

'Hullo, Danny,' said the Duke. 'Have you decided to come and join us?'

'Not exactly,' said Danny. 'I wondered if I might have a word with you.'

'Of course.'

'Alone.'

'That would be quite impossible, I'm afraid. We live here as a family. I couldn't persuade them to leave the room if they didn't want to. They would think I had gone mad.'

'Es a matter of fact,' said Beauty, in her best satirical voice, '*Ai* would rather laike to be left alone with Mistah Pisspot for a few moments.'

Everybody groaned. 'Beauty's such a bore. She only thinks about fucking.'

'Shut up, Beauty. Can't you see Pisspot's got something serious to say?'

Only Dumpling was prepared to come to Beauty's rescue on this occasion. 'Not at all,' she announced. 'I think he is a very nice-looking young man.'

This announcement caused a major sensation. '*Dump-ling*,' they screamed. 'What on earth has got into you? Have you lost your mind I mean to this *amazing* stranger?'

'Dumpling's fallen in love with this guy Pisspot. Isn't it like unbelievable? I mean he'd be like a fly settling on top of an elephant.'

'Mind you,' said Rock, 'it would be a very beautiful and you know meaningful sight, a fly trying to make love to an elephant.'

'You mean every time like the fly started getting really excited the elephant would just move its tail a little, or blow out of its snout or something and the fly would fall off and have to start again,' said Beauty. 'Poor Pisspot has let himself in for rather an exhausting evening.'

'Dumpling hasn't got a tail,' somebody pointed out, 'or a trunk.'

'Every fly,' said Strong Arm, more solemnly than the occasion really warranted, 'should *aspire* to fuck an elephant.'

'You are wrong,' said Jaques mournfully. 'Most profoundly and utterly wrong. That is the formula by which wars, revolutions and tyrannies are born. Oh Pisspot, Pisspot, I charge thee. Fling away ambition. By that sin fell the angels.'

'Jaques fancies Dumpling himself,' said Touchstone. 'I've noticed that's always the way with religious gentlemen.'

Jaques treated him to a pitying smile.

'What did you want to see me about, Danny?'

'Perhaps it might be easier if we could discuss things in a little more privacy,' said Danny. 'At least without Mr Jaques here.'

'Jaques has many interesting opinions,' said the Duke. 'In any case, he may want to stay.'

'I shall leave,' said Jaques. 'I shall go and talk to Orlando and Rosalind in the field. It seems to me that the time has come when those two should think of getting married.' He turned to Danny, and stared at him balefully. 'My poor, polluted little cripple,' he said, 'I should pray for you if I thought it would do you the slightest bit of good.' Before he left the room, he turned, pointed his finger at Danny and shouted: 'Where is your wife, Pisspot?'

'You see,' said Danny. 'He doesn't like me.'

'I mean, where *is* Mrs Pisspot?' asked Beauty, all polite and interested. Danny resisted the temptation to say that had he been called Pisspot, which he wasn't, his wife's correct style of address would have been Lady Deidre Pisspot, not Mrs Pisspot, since she was the daughter of a marquis, no less, and it was customary for daughters of the higher nobility to retain a courtesy title even after their marriage to commoners such as himself. But he judged the moment inopportune. In London, everybody already *knew* these things, just as they knew who Danny was, and thought him charming, brilliant, important. One never had to waste time in London pointing these things out. He decided to ignore Beauty.

'What I really wanted to see you about, Mr Robinson, was to enquire whether you had any particular plans for directing the investment policy of Robinson Securities, either in the short term or the long term, especially in the present conditions of uncertainty about sterling and the extreme uncertainty of conditions in Nigeria which must affect pretty well all your West African subsidiaries and, of course, also, the uncertainty which is being expressed in certain quarters concerning the . . . ah . . . government's competence to handle the next exchange crisis when it comes and also of course the somewhat disappointing performance of your Tube Group in Doncaster . . .'

Danny's voice trailed off. 'No,' said the Duke, 'I have no plans about any of that.'

'Do you think,' said Danny, keeping his voice judicially neutral, 'there might be a case for your making way, in that case, for some other person who might be prepared to make decisions and run the company in the light of the present . . . er . . . situation?'

'You mean my brother Frederick,' said the Duke. 'No, I don't think he has quite the breadth of outlook required for a job like that. You know how it is, I am not sure that he is quite completely the right person . . .'

'What is wrong with him?' asked Danny breathlessly.

'We just feel down here,' – the Duke's wave embraced Dumpling, Audrey, Willie Williams, Ruby Wednesday, Walt Izzard, Touchstone, Beauty, the old fool Adam who had fallen asleep, Macbeth, Strong Arm, Rock or Black Stone, Celia, Snowman, Buttercup and anyone else who happened to agree – 'we just feel that Frederick is not perhaps entirely gathered together, if you know what I mean.'

Celia looked hurt. She was more beautiful than ever, after twelve months of fresh air and organic food. Somehow, nobody ever took much of an interest in her. Perhaps she, too, was not quite gathered together.

'It is not that I have anything against my brother, personally,' said the Duke, hastily. 'In many ways I think he is quite . . . good-looking, you know, and careful. But sometimes we wonder down here whether he is quite sufficiently collected, as it were, you know, together . . . *integral* . . . rounded . . . what is the word? *Complete* if you like.'

'Total,' said Strong Arm.

'Developed,' said Macbeth.

'Like a gentleman, you know,' said Audrey.

'Gentle,' said Rock.

'Like, kind of nice,' said Beauty.

'No,' said Ruby Wednesday. 'The Duke's brother doesn't sound at all the sort of man who should be running things.'

Danny wondered if he dared take out his notebook and pencil. He was terrified in case he forgot any of this. As soon as he wrote this story up, John Robinson would have to resign from the chairmanship whether he liked it or not – even if it required an Act of Parliament. The government could scarcely sit still and watch a madman control the destinies of some eighteen thousand working families in Britain alone.

'So your plan, Mr Robinson, is to stay down here and do nothing, while preventing your brother from moving in and taking any necessary decisions as chairman?'

'Ah, yes. As I mentioned to you, Frederick has never impressed me as possessing the necessary qualities, and I have no doubt you will agree that what the world needs now is a general rest from people making decisions. With modern technology, the choices before us are quite terrifying. All our energies should be spent preserving what we have, and far the best way to do that is by doing nothing and changing nothing.'

'What are your plans down here, then, Mr Robinson?'

He should not have asked that question. The Duke was soon well away on his standard speech about founding a community to create its own life-style away from the mental and chemical pollution of the technological society.

'But why?' Danny was disturbed, even through his cockiness.

'Because everybody has become so hopelessly, so incompetently materialistic. At one end of the scale, the working class has been encouraged to indulge every brutish instinct as if it was the expression of its freedom and its dignity that it should do so; the result is that it has lost any idea of enjoyment. At the other end of the scale, among the educated, refined people of superior intelligence, there is belief that all goodness, all morality consists in helping the workers to indulge their brutal appetites even more fully, encouraging those who lag behind and even pushing the stragglers forward, with cries of pity and of pain that they have not yet been corrupted as fully as they might have been.'

'I see,' said Danny.

'I see, too,' said Touchstone. 'Although I don't know that the Duke need be worried. That's what the police are here for, to make sure the lower orders don't get too materialistic and start taking what doesn't belong to them.

187

That would never do, would it, Duke? We wouldn't like them to get too materialistic for their own happiness.'

'It is not their happiness which concerns me so much as their sense of their own dignity. It is that which society is destroying.'

'Now let me see,' said Danny. 'What would you say in particular has this corrupting influence? Would it be better schools, better hospitals, better housing, better food? Or would it be just having more money in their pockets, more leisure, more security than ever before?'

'No doubt all those things have contributed,' said the Duke, somewhat subdued. 'What worries me is the state of mind they have produced. There is the smell of murder about England nowadays. As soon as people begin to feel these things threatened, they will see naked murder committed rather than lose any of their comforts. They will encourage tyranny and massacre, rather than lose an ounce of butter from their regular grocery order.'

'So we should all go back to the slums of Victorian England, or perhaps to some pre-industrial society where we lived the simple life on the land?' Danny spoke bitterly, just as every one did in London when they spoke about the slums of Victorian England. For some reason, it was the smart thing to mind terribly about them.

'In this six-roomed house there live eighteen adult people,' said the Duke. 'We have no central heating, no hot water, and only one lavatory.'

'It's really disgusting,' said Beauty. 'Have you seen it? I mean, would you like me to show it to you? It really is disgusting.'

'Perhaps in a minute when I have finished,' said Danny.

'Two of the bedrooms have leaky roofs, and at least one has a broken window. Although we have television here now, we have no other comfort. All I am trying to say is that people should stop worrying about these things, see how unimportant they are, and learn that there are other things which are much more fascinating in the world than unnecessary bodily comforts.'

'Yes, but you have all the money you want. You have no need to worry,' said Danny.

'Nearly everybody in England has far more money than he needs. It is just that we are trained to want more and more. I would like all my workers to come to me and ask for half of the wages in exchange for half the work. Then they would realise how they had been wasting their lives at work all this time.'

This was too good to miss. Danny wrote it down in longhand, pressing firmly on his pencil.

'I used to have to write things down, once,' said Touchstone. 'Then I asked myself, what's the point? You can live here without writing down a word, all week. The food's not so good, I grant you, and the life isn't so satisfying perhaps as it was to be Sergeant of the Metropolitan Police, but then I ask myself, what the hell? The trees are quite nice at this time of year.'

'. . . in exchange for half the wages,' murmured Danny to himself, his tongue sticking out of the side of his mouth in concentration. 'Now, perhaps, I will avail myself of your kind offer, and see if the lavatory is as bad as you describe.'

'It really stinks, I warn you,' said Beauty, as he limped out after her.

Snowman had caught nearly thirty young rooks from the two rookeries over the hill. Nobody asked how he did it, but people assumed that magic was somehow involved, or at any rate mesmerism. Black Stone also discovered that he had magical powers. They found an old bicycle wheel and knocked the spokes out. Black Stone charged it with magical properties and it was an undeniable, inexplicable fact that anyone who put his hand through it thereafter felt a cold chill. Walt Izzard described it as weird and laughed a lot; but even the Duke confirmed the phenomenon. Another property which attached itself to this wheel was that whenever it was suspended by a string from a beam, it ended up in the same alignment, which Macbeth identified as being the Dragon Ley. Macbeth interpreted these phenomena as meaning that they were extremely close to the hiding place of the Holy Grail. They were never able satisfactorily to test other properties which Black Stone claimed for his wheel – power to cure demonic possession and even to control certain minor devils, power to divine gold and counter the evil influences of electric current. But every time Orlando, in secret, asked the wheel to indicate the sex of Rosalind's unborn baby in the following weeks, it answered that Rosalind was carrying a boy, and they awaited the boy's birth with the quiet confidence of a conjurer who knows that the rabbit is already concealed in the lining of his hat.

Knowledge of these magical powers residing in the community had fortified many of them, especially the younger ones, throughout the rigours of winter. Even the Duke thought of the magic with pleasure whenever his confidence in the greater dignity and self-respect of the new life-style was threatened by a particularly childish squabble between the elect. But when they asked Danny to stay to dinner, and later to stay the night, it was not to show him the magic of the wheel; it was simply the kindly, hospitable gesture of people who were proud of their rook pie, prepared by Audrey and Dumpling with endless debate throughout the afternoon.

So Danny stayed. His story did not have to be in his newspaper office until Friday, and one never knew what the evening would bring in the way of lurid disclosures about the present circumstances of Robsec's chairman, perhaps the most powerful single man in the private sector of British industry. As he ate his way through various pieces of young rook, listening to the wild prattle of Mr Robinson's family, he could scarcely believe his luck in finding such a story for his newspaper. It was Frederick Robinson who had given him the idea – a man who helped Danny in many ways, not the least being a quarterly payment of five hundred pounds into his bank account. But Danny did not doubt that it was his own personal combination of qualities which brought him there; and he was going to use them ruthlessly – yes, quite ruthlessly – to show the world that he was the cleverest midget in London.

'I was speaking to you,' shouted Beauty.

'I am so sorry. My thoughts must have wandered.'

'I said I hope you like your rook pie. Dumpling cooked it specially for you.'

Danny glanced at Dumpling, who looked down at her plate and blushed. Danny thought it funny that anybody quite so unattractive should fancy him, and laughed condescendingly. 'I think it is very nice,' he said.

'You never told us what happened to Mrs Pisspot,' shouted Beauty, who had decided that he was deaf. Everybody was listening, now. Danny cleared his throat.

'We don't like to talk about that,' he said.

'Why not?'

Danny felt himself cornered. It was something nobody ever asked him in London. But then in London, of course, everybody already knew. 'She ran away with a Swede,' he said quietly.

In London, everybody would have looked at their plates in embarrassment, mumbling: 'I'm sorry,' or something like that. Not so in Williams Farm.

'Har, har, har,' chortled Wee Willie Williams, who had suddenly joined the discussion. 'Oi aren't half wonder. Ung, hers called Mistress Buttercup, hims called Master Turnip-top. Oi wouldn't trust my wife with 'alf a potato these days, let alone a Swede, hur, hur, garp.' These are rough phonetic approximations to the rich variety of noises which came from Willie's throat and from other parts of his body. Quite plainly he was most amused by the fact that Danny's wife had run away with a Swede.

'I knew a Swede once,' said Beauty dreamily. 'He had long, golden hair and very thin you know trousers. Unfortunately, he had to go to Africa and build houses there. I'd have run away with him very happily, only he said that white women were a disaster in Africa, and in any case he couldn't afford the fare. If Mrs Pisspot ever bumps into a really beautiful Swede – I think he was called Carl Thorensen or something like that – with this unbelievable golden hair, huge colpons you know like tumbling over his shoulders, she might give him my love.'

The way Beauty mentioned her love was so gentle, so humble, so utterly sweet that everybody paused for a moment to think about it. Then Dumpling said: 'The only thing to do with swedes really is to mash them. I usually put a clove or two in as well, but even then there are lots of people who refuse to eat them.'

'This wasn't a vegetable,' explained Strong Arm gently. It was seldom that Dumpling contributed to debate. 'It was the real thing, you know, which comes from Sweden.'

'Yes, but why did she *run* with him,' said Dumpling obstinately.

'I suppose she wanted to get away from Pisspot here,' said Beauty, with more candour than charity. 'Or perhaps he was just the most incredible kind of Swede who'd never learned to walk.'

'I expect she found Pisspot too small for her,' said Macbeth.

'Maybe she didn't like the way he sticks his tongue out whenever he's writing.'

192

'No, I expect the Swede was just much better,' said Beauty.

'I expect so,' said Danny quietly. What a shame there was no sane person present who could recognise the fantastic dignity, restraint and maturity with which he was comporting himself.

'Did you have any children?' asked Rosalind, sitting in regal dignity at the opposite end of the table to her father.

'No,' said Danny, staring at her stomach.

When dinner was cleared away, the Duke deemed that in honour of their guest, they should have four joints circulating at the same time. This had been tried before, but without much success, because they all had a way of ending up with Macbeth, who liked to reflect a little between pulls, as he put it. But Snowman was put to work again, rolling the cigarettes.

Nobody who watched Snowman at this task could doubt that there was magic in his fingers. With a packet of cigarette papers, a tin of tobacco, a cake of hashish, and a candle, Snowman produced his works of art – as fat and as compact as cigarettes from Messrs Sullivans and Powell, more intoxicating than the finest brandy.

'Tell me . . . ah . . . Duke,' said Danny, descending to the vernacular, 'Do you often smoke marijuana here? Don't you have trouble with the police? How do you reconcile this with all the . . . ah . . . high ideals which you set out in founding the community.'

'I often think about that,' said the Duke. 'Jaques, of course, never touches it, and I hoped that others of us, in time, would find it possible to focus our minds on what I like to call the alternative awareness, if you know what I mean, my dear . . . er . . . Pisspot, an awareness which is entirely coloured by charity, by a sense of the most extraordinary well-being and benevolence, you know, to your fellow creatures. But we found in one way and another it was more agreeable to go on taking the hash, you know, while supplies last.'

'When my wife ran away, it was quite honestly as if the bottom had fallen out of my world,' said Danny unexpectedly.

'Of course,' said Jaques. 'Poor wretch. Do you know what happened to her?'

'They say she was killed in a car accident. I don't know. It was no concern of mine.'

'Was it not?' said Jaques. 'I prefer to think that all sorrows are our concern, and all moments of happiness. Poor woman.' Great tears began to form in his eyes, as they did so often.

'The other thing I wanted to talk to you about . . . ah . . . Duke, was this Nigerian business. No doubt it has escaped your attention entirely.'

Very much to Danny's surprise, the Duke was extremely well-informed on all the latest developments in the Nigerian crisis. On March 31st, the government of the Eastern region had put in its claim for money owed by the Federal government in compensation for the massacres. On April 4th the Federal government had stopped all payments of salaries to people living in the Eastern region, had seized all property outside the Eastern region which belonged to its government; ordered Nigeria Airways to stop flights to Eastern Nigeria, and withdrawn import licenses in the region threatening to blockade Port Harcourt. 'All because the military regime in Lagos refuses to implement the Aburi agreement,' said the Duke. 'I wonder who put them up to it. If we aren't careful, there'll be one of the nastiest civil wars of all time.'

'Naturally, Her Majesty's Government are most anxious that Nigeria should not be allowed to disintegrate,' said Danny smugly. He had just come from talking to a Minister on the subject – two days ago, but it seemed an age. Did nobody realise how important he was, down at Williams Farm? 'I should have thought you would feel the same way.'

'Why?' asked the Duke. 'The Ibos have been appallingly treated. I would gladly give my fortune to helping them, if I thought it could be of any assistance. There are worse things in life than disintegration. Society can only go so far. We must now have a breaking down, a gentle drifting apart. Those at the centre always want to keep control, and they manage to convince the rest of us that they are necessary. The Africans should be left alone for a while now. We have pushed them around too much.' His speech was beginning to be slurred and hesitant. Others felt that he needed help:

'Like disintegration doesn't mean anything nasty,' explained Beauty. 'It is a slow kind of dreamy thing, like people who just drift away from each other and think about it. That was what everyone was kind of trying to say like at Aburi, I think.'

'And what do you know of the Aburi agreement?' Danny nearly added 'my little woman'. The smoke from Snowman's masterpieces – he had been holding a cigarette now for fully five minutes, inhaling it deeply and greedily – made him strangely truculent.

'My own opinion is that the really like *key* passage in the Aburi agreement is to be found in the passage devoted to the reorganisation of the army,' said Beauty, with her lovely, childish eyes fixed on Danny's face. 'Without that, none of the you know military governor's like rights of veto inside the Supreme Military Council can mean anything. The governors *must* be responsible for internal security within their own region.'

Noises of assent were heard around the room. 'It's as fundamental and as inalienable as that,' said Strong Arm.

'We can't just sit here but, I mean, what *can* we do? Buttercup is knitting mittens and things for the Ibo refugees, but I can't even knit,' wailed Ruby Wednesday. 'Do you think we should write to this man Gowon?'

'Or we could write to our own Prime Minister – Wilson or whatever he's called,' said Black Stone, but his voice was sad. 'I'm sure he could do something to make the Nigerians see sense.'

Danny's frustrated self-importance suddenly burst out. 'You are all talking absolute rubbish,' he said, laughing helplessly. He realised it was only the effect of the marijuana which caused him to laugh, but this realisation made it even funnier somehow. 'You are all so fantastically silly. You none of you know what you are talking about at all.' Laughter was making the tears run down his cheeks now, and he began to feel an ache behind his eyes. 'Harold Wilson doesn't *want* Nigeria to break apart. It's the British government which is preventing those bloody Ibos from setting up their own nation – nobody else could give a damn. The Ibos simply haven't got a bloody chance; they're outnumbered nearly four to one by the rest of Nigeria, and we're going to keep the Nigerian army supplied with arms. I've just been told so. Oh my God, you're all so bloody ignorant. You don't know a single bloody thing. I was talking to a cabinet minister about it only yesterday.' This was not completely true. Danny had been talking to a minister below cabinet rank two days before. But it created a stir among those assembled.

'What did he say?'

'Will it be all right?'

'I can't waste my time talking about it to you. You've got it all wrong,' said Danny. 'You don't know a single bloody thing. Can't you see that I'm different to you lot? Can't you see how . . . important I am?'

There was a pause. 'Pisspot is stoned out of his tiny mind,' said Beauty. 'I think we should take him to bed.'

'Poor man,' said Jaques. 'Of course I realise how important he is. He is immortal, indestructible, the highest

196

point of creation, the purpose and end-product of all that has gone before, the shaper of everything that is to come. He is like every one of us, we are all God's children, the proudest and most wonderful boast in the world. Yes, even the poor, polluted cripple we call Pisspot.'

'Where should he sleep?' asked Dumpling.

'I'll sleep with you, gorgeous,' said Danny.

'You'll have to share with someone,' said Dumpling. 'There isn't room otherwise.'

'All right, I've said, I'll share with you,' said Pisspot. Through the haze of intoxication, Dumpling appeared a homely, comfortable sort of body to have for the night.

'I think I'll come in with the two of you,' said Beauty thoughtfully. 'It should be quite interesting.'

So the three of them shared a bed. Nobody enquired what happened between them, or if anything did. It did not seem to concern anybody but them. Dumpling, however, looked even more serene than usual for the next few days, and she became more friendly with Beauty than ever before.

Pisspot left next morning before anybody else was up. When the Duke read what he had written in the Sunday newspapers, he remarked that they should hide their remaining supplies of hashish down the well. Nobody else referred to his betrayal in any way, and the name of Pisspot was never mentioned again at Williams Farm.

197

CHAPTER NINE

Nothing very memorable happened in England throughout the months of April and May, 1967, but in West Africa they are still remembered with a certain amount of interest. On April 13, angry East Nigerians hijacked a Nigerian Airways aeroplane in the Midwest. Throughout this time, the government of the Eastern region, led by the Ibo Colonel, Chukwuemeka Odumegwu Ojukwu, continued building an army, purchasing arms from abroad, and preparing all measures necessary for secession. On April 24, the Supreme Military Council of Nigeria ratified the British High Commission's political and administrative programme of action for preserving the Federation of Nigeria. A total blockade was imposed on Eastern Nigeria after April 25th, and the High Commission in Lagos ordered the evacuation of British citizens from the region. Still, however, the Africans held back. Demonstrations in Enugu, the capital of the Eastern region, demanded secession; Gowon, the military commander in Lagos, announced various punitive measures against the East which had still failed to recognise his authority after the coup which brought him to power nearly a year earlier. The stage was being set for the last and greatest crime of Britain's colonial record.

Events there were watched with a certain amount of anxiety in Robsec House. Frederick Robinson had reason to be grateful that a Labour government was not going to let the Federation disintegrate. The Secretary of State for

Commonwealth Affairs seemed an eminently sensible little man, called Thomson, who was at least prepared to take advice from people who were well informed. He had an agreeable twinkle in his eye, which reassured Frederick that there would be no left-wing nonsense while he was in control. British interests came first, and no interest could be more British than those of Robinson Securities. Even better, the little fellow really felt that we had a moral obligation to help the country stay together. That was even more important.

Frederick was always interested in the moral side. He took Communion on Easter Sunday in the Church of St Michael, Chester Square, reckoning that God would forgive him his joyless, ritual couplings with Miss Stella Intersan, the efficient stenographer. He felt that these were undertaken for the benefit of the export drive, as much as they were for anything else, and God surely approved of the export drive. No, Frederick thought there was much to be said for good, old-fashioned morality. There was far too much materialism nowadays, until the moment had been reached when it began to threaten the economic health of the nation. Personally, he deplored the nation's choice of a Labour government, but he could quite understand the need for something with more moral backbone. Again, he wholeheartedly supported the Labour government in its attempts to impose a wages freeze. He was nothing if not a balanced, mature sort of person. What would the government think if his brother John had been an active chairman of Robsec throughout these difficult times?

'I ask myself, Twickerley, what sort of life is that child going to have. Your brother Orlando has no job, no money of his own as far as I can make out. They have not even married, and probably don't intend to. You may not believe it, but I look upon Rosalind almost as my own daughter. She is going through a very difficult phase at the moment – most girls go through it, in one way and another, some more violently than others – and I think it would be *criminal* if we allowed her to ruin her entire life in this way, not to mention bringing an unwanted baby into the world . . .'

Frederick's voice trailed off. They had discussed the Nigerian situation, and run out of conversation on the matter finding themselves completely in agreement. Oliver, Frederick detected, was very nearly an enthusiast, like the intelligent Mr Burns-Oates. He felt it would be the greatest tragedy if countries like Nigeria were ever to break down through the internal pressures of tribalism. So did they all. It was so nice to be on the right side. Nearly everybody who knew anything about the matter agreed with them, and so did many people who knew very little, judging the matter quite correctly as another manifestation of the perpetual struggle between government on the one side and the forces of anarchy on the other.

Titus, of course, had his own, peculiar reasons for supporting the right side. Sometimes Frederick suspected that these derived from a general hatred of the black races, although Titus was always most particular to emphasise that Ibos were the problem – ambitious upstarts, arrogant, clannish, avaricious, dishonest . . . In any case, and whatever the reason, Titus Burns-Oates had arrived at the right conclusion, as had Mr Daniel Chamberlain, the distinguished City journalist, Mr Aubrey La Touche, the scarcely less distinguished television Africa expert, Miss Bernadette Zunz – highly intelligent – Jeff Squiffy of the *Mail* and Mr Oinpin M.P., the stalwart trade unionist of left-wing sympathies. If they all disliked Africans, then Frederick could only conclude that they were all probably quite right to do so.

'There are two loop-holes in the law at present,' said Oliver. He was glad to be away from the subject of Nigeria. He had made up his mind on that subject; further discussion could only be boring. 'In the first place, we are still not allowed to terminate pregnancies without the consent of the mother. You may think of this as a tiresome formality, but it is one which has done a lot of damage, holding everything up and producing untold suffering in the world from babies being born who could otherwise have been prevented. In the second place, if Chamberlain's article is correct, your niece must be well past the statutory three-month period after which doctors are still most reluctant to . . . ahm . . . effect the necessary termination. They do make exceptions, of course, in extremely urgent cases, and there is a particularly good man, Dr Trelawney, of Devonshire Place, who specialises in these late terminations. But we must somehow obtain Rosalind's consent.'

'It is absurd to suppose that girls like that know their own mind. Half the time they're blotted with drugs – I read somewhere drug addicts almost invariably produce children who are either physically or mentally deformed. There she will be, stuck with a deformed child for the rest of her life, a husband who cannot support her, living in some sort of gypsy encampment in Somerset. What can we do?'

Oliver did not point out that Rosalind had enough money of her own to keep about a hundred Orlandos in the greatest comfort. He remembered Orlando's irresponsible attitude to national insurance contributions, and decided that, once, again, he was on Frederick Robinson's side.

'I think we should both write to our brothers.'

'John is most unlikely to listen to me,' said Frederick. 'Goodness knows why he wants to remain as chairman of Robsec. He has never taken the slightest interest in our investment policies; he only occasionally sends these lunatic directives to executives on the board. Look at this scrawl which reached Mr Truefitt, our chief executive investment analyst in the oil and metallurgical fields.'

Alas, Frederick had not exaggerated in describing the letter as a scrawl. The document had been drawn up, after endless debate, on the kitchen table at Williams Farm one evening. It did not look quite such a fine, imperious thing when produced in the chairman's office of Robsec House, in the Haymarket:

3rd April 1967.   The Williams Community, Williams Farm,
Combe Mendip, Nr. Glastonbury,
Somerset.

My dear Truefitt,
  Kindly inform Gowon that we shall withdraw all investment from Nigeria unless he can find a peaceful solution to the present crisis.
                    Yours ever,
                    J. Robinson. Chairman.

Oliver missed the point of the letter at first. 'But he can't do that. It would tie Gowon's hands. The Ibos would get away with all their plans, if this became known.'

Frederick was laughing, rather unpleasantly. 'Of course, we have not the slightest intention of doing anything about it,' he said. 'Even if we wanted to, no African government would let anybody withdraw about sixteen million pounds from its currency reserves. Foreign companies can only threaten to stop further investment. But this gives you some idea of my brother's state of mind. If it were not for two aunts, whose representatives on the board are still appointed by my brother, I should have him removed. You would have thought there would be no difficulty in having him certified insane, if only half what Chamberlain said in his newspaper story is true.'

'I am sure it is all true,' said Oliver; but Frederick looked less sure.

'In any case,' he said, 'I will write to my brother, and I

shall also take steps to bring my own daughter back to London. Clearly, she is in moral danger down there. Celia may be able to bring Rosalind to her senses, but if she can't, then there is only one person who can – your brother Orlando.'

'I am afraid that he is very irresponsible,' said Oliver.

'Never mind. We must simply persuade Orlando to do the decent thing by my niece and let her have a quiet abortion. Otherwise I might even have to take action on these directives which constantly rain down upon us from my brother. You would not like it very much if I started making approaches to the Nigerian government, and told them to stop all this nonsense about splitting the country into twelve new states. What would you think of that?'

'The government would take a very dim view of any private concern interfering in the affairs . . .' Oliver had only begun his speech when he was struck by the full enormity of what Frederick had said. 'You can't be serious,' he finished. 'Nobody could be so wicked.'

'Perhaps not. But I think you should go down to Somerset and have a word with your brother. I would also like to hear an unbiased account of what is going on down there. Now that I am acting chairman of the company, you might suppose my interest is purely academic. But John can vote me off the board any time he chooses to call an extraordinary meeting and actually attend it. I would like to know if he really is certifiable. We have been working quite well together over the Nigerian business; now we must try to work together over this family matter.'

Miss Intersan brought them some tea. She walked with a curious, hobbled motion. By the way she handed Oliver his cup, you would have thought she did not like him; but if Oliver had been her employer, she would have expected to sleep with him. She was the perfect secretary. Frederick, who paid her £2,500 a year, thought he was extremely lucky to have found her. She was so clean, so competent, so straight forward. She had no life outside the office, although at Christmas she went to stay with her mother in Devon. She had a flat in Kensington and a few friends. She was what had happened to the human race.

'You are absolutely certain, of course, that we are doing the right thing,' said Frederick, suddenly anxious. He liked to have moral scruples from time to time. Only the rich could afford to be human, nowadays, and Frederick was not ashamed to let it be known that he was very rich indeed.

'About Rosalind?'

'No not her. We need have no worries about that. She has made her bed, and we must try to save her from the consequences. I meant Nigeria.'

'Do we really want the whole of Africa to disintegrate on tribal lines? Haven't we a duty to help them?'

'Exactly. I mean, there won't be a bloody and atrocious civil war, will there, just because we have refused to let the Nigerians settle matters their own way?'

'If I seriously thought there would be, I would back out of the whole business,' said Oliver. 'But of course the Ibos will knuckle under as soon as they see they're on their own. Ojukwu isn't an idiot. If it comes to conflict, the Nigerian Army will be through them like a dose of salts. Ask Titus Burns-Oates. He's got all the facts and figures.'

'I thought so,' said Frederick. 'I just wouldn't like to be responsible for about half a million deaths, you know.' Frederick had always suspected that inside the horrible businessman known to the world as Frederick Robinson there was a good man struggling to be recognised. Perhaps the good Frederick would appear sooner than anyone expected. 'Stella, did Mr Twickerley bring a coat?'

Titus Burns-Oates's window looked out on the back of a huge stone statue, representing Time, or Industry, or Fruitfulness. He liked having an office you entered through

Downing Street, but he liked much more the way this statue enclosed him like an earth mother.

Perhaps his favourite occupation was editing and annotating the various messages which came in from the High Commissions throughout West Africa, bringing his own unique experience of the area to amplify, modify and sometimes even in the most unobtrusive way to reverse the judgments of the men on the spot.

The High Commission in Lagos reported that the deputy High Commission in Enugu expressed the gravest misgivings about the assessment in Lagos and London of the Eastern region's determination to secede in the event of General Gowon's refusal to implement the Aburi agreement. What children they all are, thought Mr Burns-Oates. We know perfectly well that the Eastern region will attempt to secede. We also know perfectly well that the attempt will be unsuccessful. It was essential in the scheme of things that there should be a military defeat or he would never put the Ibos out of Port Harcourt. He read on. Lagos described almost hysterical reports coming in from Enugu of the determination to fight; of huge arms purchases; of the recruitment of mercenaries and the enlistment of a huge army. Mr Burns-Oates shrugged his shoulders. If they really intended to found a new republic called Biafra and if they had enough arms to defend it, they would plainly have to be starved out, which would be extremely easy, although harder for them. It was no business of his if they chose the hard way. But there could be no useful purpose in passing on these biased messages from Enugu. Lagos did not give much credit to them. Nor did Titus Burns-Oates C.M.G., possibly the greatest living expert on the subject. His final *résumé* which went to be filed in the permanent under-secretary's department made no mention of arms, or of mercenaries, or of an army. Mr Burns-Oates slept happily that night, secure in the knowledge of a job well done.

CHAPTER TEN

Letters were left in a wooden box on the road about two miles from Williams Farm. They arrived so seldom that the box was inspected very rarely, but they caused great excitement when they came. Once, there was an incomprehensible circular for Willie Williams, describing the advantages of some new brand of chicken pellets which, inserted in a cockerel's neck, caused it to lose all sexual desire and become enormously fat. This intelligence was debated at considerable length from every possible angle: the sensations of the cockerel, while undergoing this treatment; the aesthetic question of whether cockerels looked more handsome when slim and agile or plump and glossy; the morality of inserting pellets into the neck of another creature and, coupled with this, the whole tortured question of contraception, its morality and desirability, coupled once more with the world population explosion.

To Macbeth, for instance, it seemed that these pellets offered the complete solution to the problems of the third world. The family had already decided, long ago, that it disapproved of bribing Indian peasants with wireless sets if they would agree to be sterilised. This was plainly immoral. There was nothing to be gained by encouraging innocent, doe-eyed Indian peasants to listen to all the poisonous, corrupting rubbish which came out of the wireless every day. Only that morning the family had been listening to a discussion programme on the wireless, in the course of which an extraordinary woman had suggested that if a dog made a mess in its owner's house, this was invariably the owner's fault. The typical Indian peasant could not begin to cope with that sort of thing. As often as not, he lacked the sophistication to distinguish what was true and wise from what was false or meretricious. There could be no justification for distributing wireless sets among them at this stage.

But Macbeth argued that if a small number of Indian peasants would agree to accept one of these pellets in the neck, this would not only help the birth rate but would also encourage other peasants to ask for the same treatment when they saw how recipients became enormously fat. The entire picture of the sub-continent would thus be changed. Instead of seeing peasants who were little better than walking skeletons, with enormous families of beautiful but under-nourished children, we would have the spectacle of great fat capons, epicene and childless, waddling over the land. Aesthetically, this might not be so appealing as the present arrangement, but Macbeth argued that other criteria should prevail, and that by the stern balance of suffering and happiness his own system must be preferred. If it proved necessary to bribe the first peasants to get the process off to a good start, Macbeth suggested that they should be given musical instruments of a pleasant but inexpensive sort: recorders, whistles and mouth organs — rather than wireless sets. This would provide a harmonious background of noise and be an adequate substitute for the noise which children make.

The Duke was by natural inclination opposed to any remedy for any problem, pointing out that remedies almost invariably created further problems, often worse than those they sought to cure; that the desire to remedy problems was of itself evidence of some social or emotional maladjustment, producing the desire to dominate, govern, influence events; that it was this attitude of mind which had led to every recorded case of brutality and repression in history. One's charitable obligations were to humanity in particular, rather than humanity generally, he said. Better communications may have increased the sphere of our awareness but they had not increased the area of our personal involvement. Moreover, he was most especially opposed to any remedies which involved whole-sale medication of those who were not sick. When Strong Arm (supported in this by Buttercup, Beauty, Walt Izzard, Audrey and Wee Willie Williams) argued that there was no need to make Indian peasants both fat and sterile, since either would do the trick equally well, the family decided not to accept the generous offer of these pellets at a reduced price, and the twenty or so chickens which pecked their way around the farm by day were left unmolested. Only Touchstone argued that since the purpose of making Indian peasants sterile was to enable them to become fat, the two phenomena were largely inseparable. He was over-ruled. Nobody ever took his contributions very seriously.

London forwarded no letters to the Duke, although once, mysteriously, a company report slipped through the net and reached Williams Farm, where it caused much puzzle-ment. It also announced a share issue which required to be signed and returned to the company, but none of them understood that. Eventually, Ruby Wednesday decided that the list of figures must have some cabbalistic signi-ficance, and took it away to unravel in the privacy of her bedroom, where she forgot about it.

So when Snowman returned one day about two weeks after the visit of Daniel Pisspot and announced dramatically that he had found two letters in the box, he caused a major sensation. One, for Jaques, appeared to have travelled all over the world before reaching Somerset. It had been posted in Nigeria four weeks ago, travelled to the headquarters of the Holy Ghost Fathers in Dublin, where 'The Rev.' was deleted in favour of a somewhat ostentatious 'Mister', and then from address to address in London. When opened, however, it was seen to contain about ten pages of very thin paper, written close, so attention immediately focused on the other letter, which was for the Duke.

'It is from my brother, Frederick,' he said.

'Frederick!' they all exclaimed, startled. What sort of person could possibly go round being called by such a really evil, wrong-sounding sort of name as Frederick?

'As a matter of fact, he's my father,' said Celia. This, again, caused a stir. They listened to an endless story from Beauty about various fathers she had known, while the Duke read his letter with a puzzled frown.

'What does it say?' they asked.

The Duke, his face a picture, started to read: 'My dear John.'

'*What*?' screamed Beauty.

'He always calls me John,' explained the Duke.

'What an amazing name to call your own brother. I mean don't you think that's absolutely fantastic? Of all the things in the world, I mean what does he *mean*?'

'It's like just a name,' said Rosalind. 'Lots of people out there have it.' Her gesture indicated the entire world outside Williams Farm, a most dangerous and wrong-headed place, but one requiring tolerance and under-standing.

'Yes, I know, but I mean what do people *do* all day with a name like that?'

'Oh well, some of them go to their offices, you know, and like write letters to each other, all starting in that sort of groove, like very cool: "My dear John, you know, then zonk, bang, here it comes, pursuant to yours of fourteenth inst. I have pleasure in enclosing the requested estimate, yours truly, old man, like, love from all of us here," you know, then your name.'

'Do you mean to say that's what he's written?' Beauty

could scarcely contain her excitement. 'What an absolutely beautiful sort of letter suddenly to receive.'

'If you'll let me read it to you, I will tell you what.it says,' said the Duke. Everybody kept quiet after that.

'My dear John,
I was very much concerned to learn from a friend who has just visited you in your Somerset retreat that Rosalind is expecting a child . . .'

This was too much for the company. Half found the idea uncontrollably funny, the other half asked if it was true. Buttercup said, 'You mean you're going to have a baby, Rosalind? How beautiful.' Orlando and Rosalind looked modest and demure. Eventually, it became clear to everybody that this was indeed the case.

'But why didn't you tell any of us? I mean, what are you going to call it?'

'It's a boy,' said Rosalind. 'I thought you could probably all see.' She indicated her stomach which now, in the eighth month of pregnancy, swelled in front of her like a proud standard before some victorious, crusading army.

'It does look rather big, now you mention it,' said Beauty. 'I suppose it just grew like that so gradually that nobody noticed it.'

The Duke looked positively feeble in his happiness. 'Such wonderful news, Rosalind. What a glorious thing to learn quite suddenly. When is he expected?'

'On about May 30th, we think,' said Orlando.

'May 30th 1967 will go down as one of the watersheds of history,' said Black Stone. 'The spring point is now entering Aquarius. Events are moving towards the pattern foreshadowed by centuries of prophecy and portents. Bit by bit, we are beginning to discern the impermanent nature of the structure evolved in the past two thousand years, the age of Pisces. Old secrets rise to the surface and dissolve into the consciousness of the human race to fertilise the seed of evolutionary growth.'

'Yes, yes, but what are we going to call him?'

'That is just the trouble,' said Rosalind ruefully. 'We can't agree. I have always liked Grimalkin, for a boy, but Orlando thinks that something like Lunchtime Vinegar would be more, you know, dignified and important.'

'Grimalkin is quite nice, or Belisarius,' said Strong Arm.

'What about Wonder Boy,' said Buttercup.

'For unto us a child is born, unto us a son is given,' said Strong Arm, reciting from memory, 'and the government shall be upon his shoulder: and his name shall be called Wonderful, Counsellor, The mighty God . . . Isaiah IX 6, I think.'

'Actually, I was thinking of Wonder Loaf,' said Buttercup. 'You know, the bread.'

'It certainly does put some zip into you,' said Walt Izzard. 'I don't know what it's got in it, but it certainly does do that.'

'I don't like Counsellor as a name for a boy. It sounds too much like Councillor and Mrs Blackbottom, the Mayor and Mayoress.'

'No, Counsellor's no sort of name to give a boy these days.'

'Who suggested we should call him Almighty God, anyway,' said Beauty. 'I think that would be most unfair. He might grow up into you know like a six-stone weakling, then everybody would laugh at him.'

'I would still love him,' said Rosalind.

'That's not the point,' said Beauty. 'The point is why do you have to go and call him a really stupid old-fashioned name like that and invite people to laugh at him.'

'The point is that we can't agree on a name,' said Rosalind. 'I think we may have to call him nothing.'

'What, nothing at all?' Beauty was intrigued. 'Or do you mean that you'd just call him, you know, "Hi, you over there", or "thingummebob" or something like that?'

'We don't really know,' said Rosalind sadly. In her world, this inability to agree on a name was the thing which worried her most.

'The letter goes on, if you'd like me to finish it,' said the Duke. 'I'm afraid the second half is less pleasant.' He read it in full:

'My dear John,

I was very much concerned to learn from a friend who has just visited you in your Somerset retreat that Rosalind is expecting a child. Since nobody has informed me of any marriage, (as her guardian and trustee, I think it reasonable to suppose that I would have been informed) I can only suppose that she is still unmarried, and that the father is one or other of the male inhabitants of your hostel, or whatever you call it.

I do not intend to comment at this stage on the attitude you show to your own responsibilities as a father. Suffice to say on this occasion that my own attitude is entirely different. I must therefore require you to send Celia back to London within the week, unless you wish me to institute court proceedings.

The case of Rosalind is clearly more urgent. I do not know exactly how long she has been pregnant, but my informant suggested that immediate action is required. If you allow her to bear this child – by goodness knows what sort of father, and conceived under the influence of goodness knows what drugs – you will not merely be showing your own extra-ordinary irresponsibility, you will also be ruining a young girl's life, and bringing an unwanted child into the world to face heaven only knows what sort of existence. One must also, just occasionally, dear brother, try to think of other people. This island is over-crowded enough already, and housing in short enough supply, especially for the weak and infirm, without your making your own contribution to everyone's misery.

I am sensible that Rosalind's pregnancy is long past the stage at which it is normally considered desirable to effect a termination. However, there is a Dr Trelawney, in Devonshire Place, who specialises in these late terminations, and who has agreed to accept Rosalind in the light of her extreme need. Accordingly, I have made an appointment for Rosalind to see him at 11.0 o'clock on Monday, May 10th, for a routine check-up before she goes into his nursing home. We have agreed that it would be better for her to stay overnight so that she can be kept under observation, in the light of the lateness of her operation. For this reason she will need to take her night things, toothbrush etc. with her.

I am afraid that I must also ask you to signify your agreement with this arrangement by telegram. In the event of your deciding not to co-operate, I have seen to it that two other doctors will be making arrangements to have you taken into care; this saves the embarrassment of a police prosecution, but will unfortunately necessitate having you certified as insane. This is something which you will realise I am most reluctant to do.

Your affec. brother
Frederick.'

There was a shocked silence when the Duke had finished reading, then loud cries of sorrow and dismay.

'Aren't we going to be allowed to have the baby then?'
'What does he mean?'
'Poor man, he *must* be hung up over something.'
After endless debate, while Rosalind wept silently in a

corner, comforted by Orlando and Celia with small nibbles of chocolate fudge which Audrey kept in a biscuit tin, the following reply was drafted and sent by runner (Snowman) to the post office in Combe Mendip.

DEAR BROTHER FREDERICK WE HAVE READ YOUR LETTER OF SECOND INST. WITH SOME ATTENTION AND ANXIETY COMMA SINCE IT SEEMS BASED ON UNSOUND MORAL UNDER-STANDING OF THE WORLD AS IT ACTUALLY IS AND ERRONEOUS REASONING STOP JAQUES HAS MADE APPOINTMENT FOR YOU TO SEE FATHER RASPUTIAN AT JESUIT HEADQUARTERS FARM STREET MAYFAIR W.1. 11 A.M. MONDAY MAY 10th STOP MUST REQUEST YOU ATTEND UR-GENTEST YOUR LETTER DOES LITTLE TO REASSURE US YOUR SUITABILITY AS POSSIBLE FUTURE CHAIRMAN ROBINSON SECURITIES GROUP LOVE FROM BROTHER JOHN ROSALIND GRIMALKIN STROKE LUNCHTIME VINEGAR CELIA MELANCHOLY JAQUES AUDREY WIL-LIAM WILLIAMS ALBERT TOUCHSTONE COMMA PHILOSOPHER COMMA ORLANDO TWICKERLEY WALT IZZARD BUTTERCUP AND STRONG ARM RUBY WEDNESDAY ROCK OR BLACK STONE MACBETH DUMPLING BEAUTY AND SNOWMAN THE HUNTER AND ADAM THE GENTLEMAN'S GENTLEMAN.

'We are the good people,' said Beauty, reading the list appreciatively. 'Do you think I should be called Beauty the Good? I am sure I have become a good person since talking with the Duke and Jaques and everybody else like that.'

'We can call you that, if you like,' said Touchstone. 'We can call ourselves anything. If you call me beautiful

214

I'll call you good. That is what society is all about. We're no better than anyone else, really. We're just a collection of drop-outs who happen to have fallen on our feet with the old Duke here to pay for us. Others aren't quite so lucky.'

'It is one of the glories of bourgeois society that it can afford to maintain any number of parasites on the body economic.' The Duke spoke flatly.

'I am a fugitive from justice, that is why I am here.' Touchstone completely ignored the Duke's interruption. 'When I was at home I was in a better place. But travellers must be content.'

'We are all fugitives from justice,' said the Duke. 'Justice is the most inhuman and repulsive concept, designed to harness men's avarice into whatever repressive social system the leaders and political people impose.'

'You don't do too badly from it, though,' said Touchstone. 'Without the law courts and the police force behind them, the workers would grab all your fortune in a second.'

'It wouldn't make them any happier.'

'How do you know it wouldn't? Anyway, perhaps they don't want to be any happier in your sense of the word. A taste of your money will be quite good enough for them.'

'The tragedy of it is that you're probably right,' said the Duke.

'Yes, that's the real tragedy,' said Snowman, looking very thoughtful and sad. He was just about to leave with the telegram for Mrs Winchcombe at the Post Office, but had to wait for Jaques to write to Father Rasputian.

'It's too terrible, really. I can't begin to think about it,' said Dumpling, who cleared away the breakfast plates.

'So sad, so sad,' muttered Ruby Wednesday, indescribably tragic.

'They have been duped into thinking that money is the only thing that matters. So they go on, making each other richer and richer all the time, with no joy in it and no end in sight.' This was the Duke, of course.

'Funnily enough,' said Touchstone, 'this does not accord with my own observation. There always has to be an end in sight. It's only when someone has reached the end, and is as rich as the Duke here, that he starts complaining.'

'I know I am right when I say that nearly everybody in England has more money than he really needs,' said the Duke. 'If everybody worked half as much for half the amount of money, they would be happier and better off. But the system won't allow it, because the system demands that rich people should always try to get richer. It is only because so very few people yet share our perception that we must retire from the world. It is a waste of time trying to persuade people. In any case, persuasion never solved anything. What we want is a process of gentle disintegration. That, thank heaven, is what we are getting in England. But while this is happening, and while public awareness is so abysmal, we must all agree that it is better to drop out of the system than it is to stay inside it and try to make it work.'

'Hear, hear,' said Strong Arm. The others were a trifle taken aback. Touchstone said: 'Says you,' regretting that he had ever started the conversation. Adam, breaking one of his interminable, disapproving silences, said: 'That's the trouble nowadays. Everybody is always trying to make himself better than he really is. You need to be born to the gracious life, like our friend the Duke, here. Some of these people asking for more money have no idea what to do with it. Gentle disintegration is the word for them, I'd say. Apart from anything else, they've got no respect. I started work as a boy of ten. We were proud to be in service, in those days.'

Nobody ever paid any attention to old Adam. The modern age had long ago buried the old Adam in its children. The system of thought in which he believed was no longer even of antique interest. But the Duke had made one of his major pronouncements, and the family supposed that this should be discussed.

'What does Jaques think?' asked Ruby.

Jaques had been sitting in a corner, reading his interminable letter. Ruby's mention of his name reminded everybody of the second letter; they all crowded round him to learn what on earth could have happened in the world that anyone should think it worthwhile to write a letter on the subject.

Jaques was distraught. 'There are things going on in London at this moment which are wickeder than anything this country has known before,' he said.

'Wow!' said Beauty.

'Shut up, Beauty. Can't you see he's serious?'

'Are they cutting all the balls off, now, to stop people expanding. Is that what is happening?'

'Nearly,' said Jaques. Then in rather unfavourable circumstances, with a bored and distracted audience, he started telling them the story of his letter:

'It comes from Father O'Flannelly, an old friend of mine, back in Nnewi village, some sixty or eighty miles from Enugu. He tells me how they've more refugees from all the other parts of Nigeria than they can possibly feed. Do you remember I told you about what was happening in Nigeria?'

'Yes,' said Beauty. 'It all depends on whether General Gowon agrees to implement the Aburi agreement.'

'It now appears that the British government won't let him,' said Jaques. 'The people are terrified and don't know what is going to happen next. There is talk of breaking away and announcing the new republic of Biafra.'

'Biafra,' said Rosalind. 'That is a beautiful name.'

'It could scarcely last very long if it has Nigeria and Britain and America against it.'

'And Russia,' said Jaques. 'The Russians have promised to help Nigeria in any war to prevent secession.'

'Wow,' said Beauty. 'Poor old Biafra. Everybody seems

to have it in for her. Why has everybody got such a hang up on Biafra?'

'Biafra does not yet exist. All the governments of the world have a hang-up against secession,' said the Duke. 'Because they are composed of mean, small-minded people who cannot bear to see power slipping from their grasp.'

'Biafra won't stand a chance. Perhaps they would be better not even to try.'

'No, we must hope they try, whatever happens afterwards,' said Jaques. 'It is better to exist and die when a day old than never to have existed. But there seems to be a false moral perception in England nowadays. Everything is judged by whether it makes people richer or not. What in God's name has happened to the English? I shall mention it in my letter to Father Rasputian.'

'Yes, but what can we do?' wailed Beauty.

'We can think about it, and suffer with them,' said the Duke. 'That is by far the best thing to do.'

'I was knitting a little woollen jumper for my son,' said Rosalind. 'I could send it to your friend at Nnewi instead.'

'I'm sure that Father O'Flannelly would be most grateful,' said Jaques. 'Often we used to need clothes for the babies out there, when the mothers did not have any.'

'I can knit, too,' said Buttercup.

'I can only do French knitting,' said Beauty. 'You know, with a cotton reel and pins. It comes out in a long worm which you can curl into a table mat or even a tea cosy, if you do enough.'

'That would be better than nothing,' said Jaques. 'There won't be any abundance of table mats and tea cosies for a very long time.'

'I can make them some marmalade and potted ham,' said Dumpling.

'I can give them the pressed flowers I collected in the summer,' said Ruby Wednesday.

'I will give them my wheel,' said Macbeth. 'It might not

be so powerful when it is taken away from Glastonbury, but it should be charged enough with all the currents it has absorbed to last twelve months. Then they can send it back again for further charging.'

Everybody agreed that this was extremely generous of Macbeth. They would make a parcel of all these things and send them to the Holy Ghost Fathers in Dublin, since all ports were now cut off between Eastern Nigeria and the rest of the world. Then everybody looked at the Duke, wondering what contribution he was going to make.

'I suppose I can send some money,' he said, tentatively.

'Are you sure that is what they need? You know what a corrupting effect money can have. Perhaps they wouldn't even know what to do with it.' The debate went on for a long time. In the end, it was decided that since money was trying to destroy the family's adopted children in Eastern Nigeria, money should be sent to combat it. Not just a bit of money, but an enormous amount.

Two days after the excitement of the telegrams and the letters, a car drove up in front of the farm. It was a taxi, which had come all the way from Bath station. Out of it, on a beautiful, bright spring morning in May, 1967, stepped Mr Oliver Twickerley, Under-Secretary of State at the Commonwealth Office. The pious might also suppose that his guardian angel stepped out of the taxi at the same moment. His taxi driver, however, stayed inside and sat there for a full hour until Oliver came out, paid him his money (demanding a receipt) and sent him away. A group gathered at the farmhouse door to watch him drive along the pitted cart-track, out of sight over the brow of the hill.

CHAPTER ELEVEN

Lunch consisted of black pudding for all of them, pigs'
trotters for some. Rosalind was given the kidneys, because
of her condition. Oliver and the Duke were given first pick
at the liver, which was delicious, while tripes, lights and
other parts of offal were shared by anyone who liked the
look of them. Snowman and Macbeth had killed a pig the
day before. He was called Percy, and had been a great
pet with the girls. Nobody asked how he had died, although terrible squeals were heard coming from a deserted
stable at the back of the farm where the deed was done.
Wee Willie Williams showed great cowardice, as he
always did where pigs were concerned, but both he and
Walt Izzard watched the event from over the stable door,
returning to the farm in a state of high excitement.

They would be eating various pig dishes for a week.
Even as they all sat, a cauldron bubbled away on the fire,
containing the two parts of Percy's head, split down the
middle by Walt Izzard with a saw so that Dumpling could
make some brawn. Audrey, Buttercup and Strong Arm had
all declared themselves vegetarians after the family's
first attempt to kill a pig, nearly six months ago. But they
ate rabbits, pigeons, rooks, trout, grayling, sticklebacks,
perch, chickens, moorhens, coots, and almost anything else
they were given. As Audrey said, they had to keep body
and soul together. But not by eating pigs; still less by
eating Percy. You might as well ask them to eat one of
their own children (they said).

Oliver sympathised with this point of view as, indeed,

he sympathised with almost any point of view he ever heard. That was what being a constituency member of Parliament was all about. He felt, indeed, almost as if he were among a gathering of his own constituents at the moment – particularly half-witted ones, of course, poor dears, but we can none of us have all the advantages. If voters were brighter than M.P.s, then M.P.s would have to become voters and let the brighter people become M.P.s. That was what it was all about, was it not? As things stood, being rather brighter than the others, Oliver was in the position of organising and arranging everything to ensure that the right things were done, the wrong things were left undone. He felt rather like a king, in any case, being waited upon by Beauty. There was another girl, sitting at the far end of the table, a blonde – he did not know her name – who kept catching his eye in the most disturbing way. She was extraordinarily beautiful, too, with such a generous, loving expression on her face, amused but curious, shy but greatly daring, willing him to do something, willing, willing, willing. Oliver found himself confused and blushing. He must stick to his brief.

'It was very rash of me to send the taxi away. I really don't know what time I shall get back to London now,' he said.

'What makes you suppose you will ever wish to return to London,' said the Duke.

' 'Fraid I must. There's a Division tonight at 10.30.'

Jaques looked very disturbed about this. 'There are enough divisions in the world already, without it being necessary for you to create some more artificially. Nothing whatever divides the benches in the House of Commons, and it is absurd to pretend otherwise. You both believe the ultimate good on earth is that Englishmen should get richer, you both believe in the same methods of government, you both believe that you are the best people in the country to do it. These divisions of yours are only ritual,

but they are an unhealthy ritual, symbolising quite un-
necessarily the much grosser divisions which exist in the
world and which lead to oppression and killing.'

'I suppose that is a point of view,' said Oliver, in a
clever sort of voice. Personally, he preferred to think that
the Labour government was achieving a lot of good in very
unfavourable circumstances – helping the pensioners, the
less-well-off, the not-so-competitive. He had no time for
the cheap cynicism which was so fashionable nowadays
especially among young people about Parliament and the
parliamentary institutions. If only they knew what the
alternatives were, what men like him (only a little older)
had fought the war to protect us from, what a beautifully
intricate system it was which had produced Oliver
Twickerley as Under-Secretary of State for Commonwealth Affairs – something which no foreign system could
probably ever do . . .

'What?' he said.

'I said why did you come here? Was it just to see your
brother?'

There was definitely something unfriendly in the Duke's
manner. Perhaps he did not like being addressed as 'Mr
Robinson' in his own lunatic asylum, as it were. As a
general rule, Oliver preferred the term 'mental hospital',
or even just 'hospital', but an asylum was quite plainly
what Williams Farm had become. Perhaps it fulfilled the
function of Glastonbury Abbey before the Dissolution of
the Monasteries in providing sanctuary for fugitives from
justice. Now he came to think about it, this was a most
improper thing to do, and he was surprised that the
medieval church was allowed to get away with it. How did
those ecclesiastics justify the deliberate frustration of
justice? It was a most flagrant abuse of privilege, and
must have made government very difficult. Oliver thought
of all the criminals who really made him angry – drunken
drivers, dishonest manufacturers of candyfloss who in-

creased their prices without good reason, racialists – and tried to imagine these people escaping from justice every time by simply applying to a monastery for asylum. He decided that the dissolution of the monasteries had been a very good idea.

'I said why did you come here?' There could be no mistaking the Duke's hostility now. Oliver felt inexplicably reluctant to mention the two purposes of his visit – to persuade Orlando to prevail upon Rosalind to have an abortion, and to dissuade Robinson from sending vast sums of money to aid a rebellion in Nigeria. The second purpose really was most terribly urgent, he told himself. It would be the height of irresponsibility to give the slightest encouragement to the rebels; this course of action could only lead to more bloodshed, greater insecurity in Africa and less prosperity for all concerned. Rebellion was the vilest of crimes, threatening everything which generations of social progress had worked to create. But he could scarcely be expected to go into all that now.

'Well, Duke, I thought I'd come along and see how you were all getting along if you see what I mean,' he said lamely. The Duke immediately became more friendly.

'You weren't sent by my brother Frederick?'

Up to a point, Oliver supposed he had been sent by Frederick, but it all seemed such a long time ago. Mr Burns-Oates had also been most insistent that he should come. There was great over-excitement in the Commonwealth Office when an intelligence report came in that Mr John Robinson's bankers had approached the rebel agents. He could see the beautiful blonde girl staring at him in a worried fashion, waiting for him to say something. But he could scarcely plunge into such complicated matters without warning.

'Well, there are a few things I would like to discuss with Orlando and also, as it happens, with you. But I don't really know where to begin.'

'Poor man,' said Jaques. 'His mind is all tied up in knots. I know exactly what he needs.' Nobody spoke for a moment while this remark was being considered. Dumpling cleared away the plates, Snowman took out some needles and started knitting; so did Buttercup, Rosalind and the Duke, while Beauty fumbled disconsolately with her cotton reel and some pins. Suddenly, she brightened. 'A smoke,' she said.

The cry was taken up by all of them. 'A smoke, a smoke.'

'Would you like to smoke?' asked the Duke.

'Thank you very much, but I gave it up some time ago,' said Oliver.

'You *need* a smoke,' said the Duke. 'Snowman, go and see if you can fish some shit out of the well.'

Snowman put down his knitting, tied a rope round his chest, removed the heavy iron cover and made to climb down the slimy, vertical sides of the well.

'Why is everyone knitting so much?' asked Oliver, at a loss for anything to say. Perhaps it was some sort of therapy. Then it occurred to him that it was probably for Rosalind's baby, and he wished he had never spoken.

'For Biafra,' explained Celia. She spoke to him for the first time, although their eyes had scarcely been away from each other since his first appearance.

'Biafra?' Oliver was overcome by confusion under those limpid blue eyes.

'Of course you would know nothing about it. The country does not exist yet, but we think it is about to be born. For the first time in African history the people are going to create a country for themselves. Of course, everybody is trying to stop them, and they'll have a terrible struggle. That is why we are knitting for them.'

'Oh,' said Oliver, feeling slightly sick. 'You mean Eastern Nigeria?'

'That's what it's called now,' said Celia. Oliver had no

doubt that she had sought him out. Perhaps she was interested in politics, and wanted to meet a genuine under-secretary of state. Oliver could scarcely believe that she fancied him. 'I am so sorry, we haven't been introduced,' she said, with such a sweet smile as would melt any politician's heart. 'I'm Celia.'

'Celia Robinson?'

'Well, here I'm sometimes called like the Moon, or Celia Moonface,' she glanced around conspiratorially. 'You are quite right, though. My real name is Celia Robinson.'

'Very pleased to meet you,' said Oliver, inadequate as always. 'I know your father.'

'How is he?'

'Very well. He wishes you would join him in London.'

'I wish he would join us down here. It's much purer, you know, cleaner down here.'

'I'm sure it is.' Oliver spoke with feeling. Anywhere which contained Celia Robinson was by definition purer and cleaner than anywhere else.

Their conversation was interrupted when Snowman returned with a package wrapped in polythene. 'We have to keep it like this, against the hash hounds,' he explained. 'There is an extraordinary junk heap at the bottom of the well. I think I am going down again.'

Snowman was the one who usually prepared the cigarettes. As Macbeth was holding the rope at the top of the well, Celia was left with the cake of hashish, a candle, some paper and a tin of tobacco to get on as best she could.

'I don't know whether I should really have anything to do with this,' said Oliver heavily.

Celia replied impatiently: 'It's all for your benefit. Will you hold these two skins while I lick this one?'

It is an extraordinary fact, of which feminists should take note, that the woman has not yet been born who can get out a decent joint. Perhaps it is something to do with their biological function. In any case, Oliver needed to help Celia a lot, while she fumbled around in the sweet incompetence of her fingers, licking bits of paper, the tobacco, Oliver's hand – before Strong Arm took the equipment away, and rolled six beautiful cigarettes in almost as many minutes. One was sent to Macbeth to smoke on his own. Experience suggested that this was the best way.

The Duke's hash was not just any old stuff. Perhaps it came from Afghanistan, smuggled by donkeys over little known passes through the mountains. Perhaps it came from Acapulco, flown in the athletic support of an airline steward from Mexico City. Whatever it was, it burned with a deep ochre light, pure and fragrant, an invitation to love your neighbour, to be consumed by simple, wholesome goodness and relaxed enjoyment.

'One of the reasons I came was to try and persuade Orlando to do the right thing by Rosalind?' said Oliver, eventually.

'You mean they've got to get *married*?' asked Beauty. 'Luckily, we've got a priest on the premises, before it is too late.'

Oliver took another long draw on the cigarette before passing it to Buttercup, his eyes melting into Celia's face, and decided that marriage was exactly what he had meant.

'We must arrange a great wedding feast,' said the Duke. 'Snowman must kill another pig and at least four chickens. We might even have to take little Adolphus.' Adolphus was a heifer calf of about three months, so named by Beauty before Snowman pronounced on the animal's sex. They had bought her from Charlie Winter, at Hatch Bottom, after the mother had died.

'I hope you will stay for the wedding,' said Celia.

'Of course I will,' said Oliver. Divisions were forgotten, so was Britain's struggle for economic survival – even the urgent requirements of social justice – as he lived in her mild and magnificent eye. They were holding hands, touching each other's faces, grinning fatuously to each other when there was a shout from Snowman in the deserted laundry from which the well was sunk, some eighty feet down into the Mendip lime.

They found Snowman white and shaking over the prostrate body of Macbeth. Macbeth was not dead, but heavily concussed, with both eyes open. The small room was full of extraordinary pieces of metal, wood and even a decayed leather collar or yoke of a carthorse. The room had a strong watery, metallic sort of smell.

Snowman stood in his bare, wet feet and started to tell them what had happened. He had been standing at the bottom of the well, tying things to the end of the rope for Macbeth to pull up. He had not found anything very interesting, although one rusted, cruciform piece of iron might once have been a sword, he supposed, but Macbeth was getting more and more excited, telling him to search harder, to dig in the bottom of the well, to feel around the sides in case there was an alcove there.

'He seemed to have got a scent for something,' said Snowman. Normally, he spoke very little, and seemed to find the telling difficult.

'Then what happened?'

'I got bored of standing up to my waist in this freezing water, so I collected together a few more bits of junk from the bottom – that old bucket without a handle and a few others – and told him I was coming up.'

When Snowman had reached the top, Macbeth asked him what he was carrying. And then all that Snowman could say was that Macbeth had attacked him.

'Why?'

'I don't know.'

'Didn't he say anything?'

Macbeth had said plenty of things, but none of them made any sense. He had had an extraordinary, wild look in his eye, half blissful, half what could only be described as mad. He had been shouting about his eyes, in some strange way, then things about Glastonbury and St Joseph of Arimathea.'

'He's often like that,' said Ruby. 'It's one of his things. But why did he attack you, Snowman?'

Snowman could not be absolutely certain whether Macbeth wished to attack him, or hug him, or what he had wanted to do. He had rushed at him all of a sudden. Then he caught his foot on the iron well-cover which lay on the floor, and fell sprawling. For a nasty moment, Snowman thought he was going to fall down the well, but he merely hit his head a heavy blow against the floor. That was all Snowman could say because it was all he knew. He hoped Macbeth would be all right.'

'You must get out of those ghastly wet trousers,' said Beauty, helping him to pull them off. Snowman looked strangely appropriate in a short shirt with no trousers – there was something almost classical and semi-divine about his lower nakedness, as Beauty dried him with a towel.

'Can anybody explain what has happened?' said Jaques. He had picked up a flat dish-shaped object of indeterminate age which might have been made of pewter, or lead, or almost any other base metal.

'That was the thing which seemed to excite him most,' said the Snowman. 'He kept shouting to ask if there were bloodmarks on it, then he said that his whole life was fulfilled, that he felt like some guy or other in history who kept saying like Lord, now lettest thy servant depart in peace.'

'Screwy,' said Beauty.

'The Nunc Dimittis,' said Jaques. 'The song of Simeon.'

'Simeon who?'

'Oddly enough, there are marks on it which look strangely like bloodstains,' said Jaques. 'Of course, they could scarcely be that, after such a long time.'

'Ugh, how unhygienic,' said Beauty.

'I could clean it up for you, if you wanted, sir,' said Adam. 'It is amazing how well things will sometimes polish up, even after the worst treatment. Of course, this object doesn't really look as if it was anything much in the first place.'

'No,' said Jaques. 'I don't suppose it was ever much to look at, even in the first place.' Tears were streaming down his face, but nobody paid much attention, as this was a frequent occurrence. 'To think that Macbeth should sing the Nunc Dimittis. Lord, now lettest thou thy servant depart in peace, according to thy word: For mine eyes have seen thy salvation, which thou has prepared before the face of all people; A light to lighten the Gentiles, and the glory of thy people Israel.'

'Amen,' they all sang, with varying degrees of solemnity. Macbeth slept on, his eyes open and unseeing. After a time, he began to move.

'One thing Macbeth *did* tell me,' said Ruby Wednesday. 'Only it was sort of secret to me, you know, not for general publication.'

'If it has any bearing upon this accident, it is your duty to tell us,' said the Duke, in a terrible voice.

'Macbeth told me that some time ago he had this really bad acid, you know, really evil substance like with which he wanted to get rid of for, so he told me he emptied it down the well.'

'But he wasn't drinking, was he?' said the Duke.

'I don't know,' said Snowman. Beauty had brought him some rather fetching light blue jeans. 'I was down the bottom. He could have been drinking out of this dish-thing, or the bucket, or anything, but the acid would scarcely have hit him so quickly.'

'It was very quick acid,' said Ruby. 'Filthy, filthy, filthy stuff. Macbeth thinks it had been siphoned into the underground from the C.I.A., you know, in order to discourage the people from taking acid. Of course, acid and pot are what is going to bring the capitalist system down. Naturally, the C.I.A. are interested.'

'Naturally,' said the Duke. 'Although personally, I find the capitalist system, for all its faults, preferable to anything which is likely to replace it.'

'I think there is some writing around the rim of that dish you are holding.'

'I know,' said Jaques. He seemed reluctant to let anyone take it from him.

'What does it say?'

'I don't know. I can't read Hebrew.'

'Who?' said Beauty. 'It looks like Turkish to me.'

'Or Persian,' said Buttercup.

'I think it's Pakistani. They used to have their own newspapers, you know, in Birmingham. Dreadful really, because nobody could understand a word of it. They might have been saying, you know, like let's go and cut their throats for all anybody knew.'

'It might be quite valuable,' said Walt Izzard knowingly. 'If it's old.'

Suddenly, Jaques made up his mind.

'If the well is polluted, I think we ought to seal it up,' he said. 'And I think we should put all this . . . junk' – he seemed to choke over the word – 'back inside first. It has no place, no possible usefulness in the modern world. We now know that it is there, which we did not know before, but the world has changed since the olden days . . . and we would not necessarily wish . . . to add to the . . .' Jaques, in the grip of some violent emotion, seemed to run out of words.

'Garbage,' said Ruby Wednesday.

'Pollution of the environment?' said Celia.

'Loss of amenity,' said Oliver, who was holding her round the waist from behind, fondling her breasts in an embarrassing proprietorial way.

'... the vulgarity,' said Jaques, 'and the tastelessness, the lack of reverence, the cheapness, the greed, the *thoughtlessness*, that is it, that is why God has withdrawn from the world, nobody has time to think, or wishes to think.'

'They are afraid,' said the Duke, who was always ready for this sort of conversation. 'Afraid of discovering their own nakedness. Anybody who steps outside the consensus will always seem to threaten the system. That is why people are frightened to think, for fear their thinking takes them outside the consensus and into the cold.'

'Still, I definitely feel we shouldn't throw anything away until we've discovered whether it's valuable or not,' said Walt Izzard. 'Even scrap metal has its value, nowadays.'

While this conversation droned on, Jaques dropped the metal object down the well shaft. It took nearly two seconds to fall, once striking the wall, once some other object, probably an iron beam put across the bottom of the well to keep its sides apart. With each noise, Jaques flinched. Afterwards, he stood over the well and seemed lost in prayer. For an ugly moment, Oliver thought he was going to jump after it, but nobody else noticed at all, being absorbed in questions of social theology:

'Would it not be possible to imagine a state, a society, where everybody in it had every material possession his heart desired,' said Strong Arm. 'Fire, refrigeration, hot swimming baths, an air-conditioned garden outside, seven colour television sets, washing machines, a lavatory which played the Eroica Symphony when you sat down on it? Could not then the hearts and minds of God's children on earth return to thinking about God?'

'No,' said the Duke.

'People feel God's a bit old fashioned, if you see what I mean,' said Beauty.

'Now, we must fill in this well,' said Jaques.

'Fill it in?'

'Yes. The water has been polluted and the modern

231

world has no further use for anything else it may contain. We must fill it with stones and earth, cement, clay and anything else which will prevent people from knowing that there ever was a well on this spot.'

Snowman and Black Stone set to work, happy to be engaged in a task which seemed somehow significant and historic. They were destroying a monument – what other ways are there for modern people to leave their mark on the world?

The womenfolk helped Macbeth to walk, still dazed and uncomprehending, to his bed, where he immediately fell into a deep sleep. They undressed him and bathed the slight wound on his head, then Ruby Wednesday took up her vigil by his bedside.

Oliver said yes, he thought he would quite like to try another joint, if everybody else was going to, and if nobody minded. Celia said oh dear, would Oliver ever forgive her for her incompetence in trying to make a joint hold together, she was just so funky like she couldn't get anything together in her life. This really cracked Oliver up, who said he thought Celia was one of the most together chicks he had ever met, you know, really sweet and deeply committed into giving off these nice vibrations. Then they started fondling each other again, which was all very well, but somehow out of tune with everybody else's mood, which was more businesslike at this particular moment.

Snowman pushed a wheelbarrow of old stones through the kitchen, saying that he and Rock were demolishing the kiln which had stood crumbling and disused in the orchard for as long as anyone could remember, using the stones to fill the bottom of the well, where the water was. A few members of the family crowded through to watch. First they threw in the bucket without a handle, the carthorse yoke and various other bits of junk which Snowman had brought to the surface, then they emptied the wheelbarrow of stones. On the second barrow load, all the struts and beams which kept the soft clay sides of the well apart, at its bottom, collapsed. Subsequent barrow loads made no splash, until soon the well was half full.

'That is enough work for today,' said the Duke. 'We must now discuss arrangements for the wedding, since Rosalind's baby is due any day now, and children require a settled family background for their satisfactory development. Jaques, will you marry them tomorrow afternoon?'

'We want to be married, too,' said Celia. She and Oliver had emerged from one of their huddles, both as stoned as the proverbial crows, eyes bright, cheeks pink, ready to die for each other, to love and to hold, in sickness and in health, until death did them part.

'Oddly enough,' said Touchstone, breaking in with his ugly, persistent voice, 'me and Audrey here were thinking of getting hitched also. She's not much to look at, I grant you, but she cooks quite nicely, she doesn't smell, and she's got all it takes to satisfy my simple and what might be called diminishing requirements in the sexual field.' Audrey gave a squawk of pleasure. 'If Mr Jaques would consider marrying all three couples, it would save on the expenses,' said Touchstone.

'No,' said Jaques. 'Not that. I can't go through all that tomfoolery with altars and vestments any more. Of course true marriages are made in heaven, of course they are for ever, not dissoluble at will – that is not a marriage at all, it is nothing. Of course God's church will survive, but it can only survive in the hearts and minds of those who seek it. Altars and vestments and assemblies are only for people who wish to suppress and pervert the promptings of goodness.'

'So you won't marry us, then?' said Touchstone.

'You marry each other in God's sight,' said Jaques. 'I can't marry you.'

'It will be more convenient from the tax point of view, if we remain unmarried,' said Oliver.

'And from the point of view of our pensions,' said Touchstone. 'It seems odd that anyone gets married nowadays, if what the reverend gentleman says is true.'

Audrey still looked sad. 'I always dreamed of a white wedding,' she said. 'I have been what might be called saving myself for the moment.'

'Very nice, too,' said Touchstone, loyally.

Jaques took pity on them all. 'If you really wish to indulge in all that flummery, I know a friend in London who will do it for you, a venerable and holy man called Father Rasputian. He will give you lights and smells and sweet fluting noises, so that you can believe the moment has some greater solemnity than the promises you make in your heart.'

'You mean to say,' said Oliver, 'you have no objection if Celia and I go to bed with each other tonight, even though we are not married?'

'It has nothing to do with me. In any case, I am not God. It is totally unimportant.'

'Good,' said Oliver, and left the room with Celia.

Touchstone and Audrey eyed each other speculatively. 'Time for supper, Audrey,' said Touchstone.

She trounced out of the room.

'Comport yourself more seemly, Audrey,' shouted Touchstone. Clearly, he, too, was asserting his marital rights in advance.

'Snowman, will you kill the calf, and a pig, and at least five of our chickens? Don't worry about doing it. Animals scarcely notice whether they are alive or dead. We have to believe in an after-life, whether it is true or not, because our intelligence abhors the idea of its own death. We have to believe in the idea of nobility and purpose as well, but the only purpose in a pig's life is to make a pleasant smell when it is cooking, a pleasant taste in our mouths and a pleasant feel in our bellies.' The Duke never seemed to take animals very seriously.

'After that, they end up in the toilet,' said Beauty. 'How sad.'

'Perhaps our own lives are just as useless,' said Jaques. 'Perhaps the child which Rosalind will soon bring into the world is just another meaningless object on the conveyor belt. But at least we are granted the imagination to think otherwise, and anyone who does not take advantage of that gift is a fool.'

'I wonder what I should wear for the wedding,' said Beauty.

CHAPTER TWELVE

The last screams of a slaughtered pig had scarcely died away when Frederick Robinson drove up to Williams Farm in a large car, with a large, sleek, and well-fed man in clerical costume beside him. Snowman received them with mild hostility at the door. More guests would mean more meat and more meat would mean more slaughtering. Snowman was always worried by the atmosphere in Williams Farm when a slaughtering was due to take place, like the atmosphere in a prison before someone was hanged.

He wiped his bloody hands on the apron he always wore for slaughtering. 'Nearly everyone's out,' he said. 'They're picking flowers for the ceremony tomorrow. Are you the doctor, come to see Macbeth?'

'No,' said Frederick. 'I wanted to see my daughter, Celia.'

'Perhaps you had better see Macbeth,' said Snowman. Just as he, by studying the spoors of wild animals in the wood, had somehow divined how to thatch a roof, slaughter a pig and collect the blood to make a black pudding, how to thresh corn and mill the grain – so he assumed that men who so obviously came from the town would know all about modern technology and medicine. 'Perhaps the reverend had better come along too,' said Snowman. Macbeth's problem seemed as much religious as medical.

Frederick was a little put out to find himself immediately cast in the role of a physician, but he felt a new man since his conversation with Father Rasputian. On the journey, he once found himself weeping on Father Rasputian's shoulder, while the Jesuit smoothed his hair and murmured words of comfort, persuading him to make a complete confession of all his sins. Rasputian was quite easily the most successful fisher of souls in London at this time.

Macbeth lay propped up in bed, a strange and unnatural light glowing from his eyes. Ruby Wednesday slept on the floor like a dog, her mouth open. Strong Arm was making a bag out of string with a crochet hook at the end of Macbeth's bed. The sight of Father Rasputian set Macbeth gabbling again. His eyes had seen the glory of the coming of the Lord. His hands had touched the Holy Grail. Now he was at peace, God's servant, treading the paths of righteousness, singing God's praises, there was no need to eat any more, the Lord had fed him on the honey from heaven. Father Rasputian felt distinctly flattered.

'Oh good,' he said. 'I expect we'll get you out of bed in no time. How are you feeling today? Mouth a bit heavy, nose a bit gummed up? There's a lot of it around, at present. The only thing is to take it easy for a few days.'

'Father, Father, why hast thou forsaken me,' shouted Macbeth.

'No, no, I'm still here,' said Father Rasputian smugly.

'My fingers have touched the Holy Grail itself, my eyes have seen the stains which were left by the Most Precious Blood.'

'I know it's absolutely mouldy having to stay in bed,' said Father Rasputian. 'You should always reflect on how much worse off other people are. Think how mouldy you would feel if you were in an iron lung with your mega-colon cut away and all your dinner dribbling out between your legs, that's what I always say. There's nothing makes one feel better than reflecting on the misfortunes of others.'

'Father, Father,' whined Macbeth.

'Oh very well,' said Father Rasputian. 'If you like, you

can say two Hail Marys after every meal. I would not say more than that.' It might be dangerous to exceed the stated dose, his tone suggested, although he knew perfectly well that this was not the case, that he was dispensing no more than a placebo. 'Now I must leave you to get better by yourself. Try not to make too much of a nuisance of yourself to other people. Always think of other people. In the name of the Father and of the Son and of the Holy Ghost.'

'Amen,' said Macbeth intensely.

Father Rasputian left the room importantly, followed by Frederick and Strong Arm. 'What on earth has got into him?' he asked vulgarly, as soon as they were outside.

'He became very excited when they found the Holy Grail. You see, he has spent the last ten years looking for it.'

'The Holy Grail?' Father Rasputian suspected that it was some sort of annual conference for young people, organised to encourage religious vocations. The young man had not looked very promising material to him, but the priesthood was desperately short of recruits, and this was no time to be choosey. Perhaps he should have shown more interest. What a coup it would be if he could return to Farm Street from his expedition into the country with a captive oblate.

'The Holy Grail is the name given to the dish or shallow bowl from which Christ is said to have eaten the paschal lamb on the evening of the Last Supper with his disciples,' said Strong Arm.

'Oh really?' said Father Rasputian. 'And have they found it? That should be jolly interesting.'

'I think we probably did find it,' said Strong Arm. 'But of course, as Jaques pointed out to us, it is of no use to the world now. The stories of the Arthurian legend are merely fantastic and extravagant if one understands the quest for the Grail to be the search for an interesting historical relic

– even one with sacred connotations. The essence of the legend is that long before Joseph of Arimathea brought the Grail to Glastonbury, he received into the vessel many drops of Christ's blood which issued from the still open wounds on Christ's feet, hand and side when he took Christ down from the Cross. This matter, which Tennyson and many modern writers overlooked, is plainly essential to an understanding of the whole conception.'

'No doubt,' said Father Rasputian. 'Where is this vessel now? I am no expert, but some of my colleagues in Farm Street have an almost morbid interest in old relics of this sort. I'm sure that they would be prepared to look after it, if you really have no further use for it, as you say.' Father Rasputian was careful to sound slightly bored. He did not approve of this sort of thing at all, but something told him that if he returned to Farm Street with the Holy Grail, it would be judged even more of a coup than to return with a half-witted, God-touched oblate, useful as the latter would be for cleaning shoes and other necessary chores about a religious house.

'We decided that the Holy Grail could have no relevance in the modern world,' explained Strong Arm. 'You see, nobody can ever understand why it should have been so important to find the Holy Grail who does not accept the old Catholic doctrine of the hypostatic union – that where the body or the blood of Christ is, there, by virtue of the hypostatic union, are His soul and His divinity.'

'Even His dead body and His dead blood?' asked Father Rasputian shrewdly. 'Quite honestly, I think you are stretching the whole concept of hypostatis in your efforts to over-sell your merchandise. No, I would be quite prepared to pay as much as forty pounds, in cash, for anything which was unmistakably the authentic Grail, but for something less certain I could not possibly pay more than twenty pounds.'

'Are we to suppose that the hypostatic union ended at

the moment of Christ's death on the Cross and resumed at the moment of His Resurrection?' Jaques had joined the company, wearing a daisy chain, as it happened.

'Very well then, twenty-five pounds,' said Father Rasputian.

'Twenty-five pounds seems remarkably cheap for a piece of God's own divinity,' said Jaques.

Father Rasputian had not reckoned on having to barter with another Catholic priest, even if a spoiled one. If nobody else had been present, they would certainly have reached some agreement between them. Rasputian decided to appeal to Jaques's better nature.

These are hard times for the Church, you know, Jaques. 'Things have got worse since you left us. Time was, we would have paid the earth for this sort of relic. Nowadays, there simply isn't the money, even if there was the general interest in this sort of thing. I'd be in serious trouble if I gave you more than forty pounds. As it is, I'm doing you a favour.'

'Alas,' said Jaques. 'Strong Arm was quite right, I would not like to rob you. The modern world has no use for what we found, which is nothing more than a lump of old tin, completely valueless, a bit of old junk lying with several other bits of junk. Now it has been thrown away.'

'I knew there would be nothing in it, anyway,' said Father Rasputian. 'But when you see the old pieces of rag and bone which simple people are still prepared to reverence, I thought I ought to look into the matter. This young man you call Macbeth plainly needs looking after. I wonder if he would like to come and live at Farm Street? No doubt we could find something useful for him to do.'

'Ruby would expect to go with him,' said Strong Arm.

'I expect it will come to that,' said Father Rasputian. 'We shall have to enrol her in the choir as an honorary castrato. There is a desperate need in religious life nowadays for holy, enthusiastic people prepared to clean the shoes. Well, well, we can discuss all that later. Now we must turn to happier things, must we not, and discuss the weddings. Do the . . . ah . . . participants want the service in Latin, or according to the Anglican rite, or something unpretentious, without too much religion in it, or is it to be a "pop" wedding, with electric guitars and what people sometimes call *all that jazz*?'

Rasputian spoke without distaste. Plainly he was ready for anything.

'I think the best place for a wedding round here would be on the site of the old ruined chapel of St Michael, on Glastonbury Tor,' said Jaques.

'Where Abbot Whyting was hanged for refusing to accept the English king as head of the Church,' said Strong Arm.

'Exactly,' said Jaques. 'And Rasputian can deliver whatever sermon he thinks appropriate to the occasion and the place.'

'Quite right,' said Rasputian. 'We should never let ourselves forget the past in our enthusiasm for the present, should we?'

'Quite right,' said Frederick. 'Nowadays people think only of the present.'

Celia who had ox-eye daisies behind her ears, pale white forget-me-nots from the meadow plaited into her hair and darker blue forget-me-nots from the garden in a necklace, bounded up to her father and threw her arms round his neck.

'Daddy, how lovely of you to come down for the wedding.'

'To tell you the truth,' said Frederick, quite overcome, 'my original idea was to put a stop to it.'

'Man, what a crazy, screwed-up, sick old notion,' said Oliver, clicking his fingers rather inexpertly.

'Hello . . . ah . . . Oliver,' said Frederick. 'I sent you down here to stop my brother giving vast sums of money to some absurd African rebellion and to persuade Orlando to talk my niece into an abortion, and now I find that you are going to marry my daughter.'

'You'll love him, Daddy, when you get to know him,' said Celia.

'I already know him perfectly well,' said Frederick. 'I suppose there could be worse sons-in-law than an under-secretary in the Commonwealth Office, even if it is in a Labour government. Anyway, since talking things over with Father Rasputian, I have decided to retire from business and devote my energies to SHELTER.'

'SHELTER!'

'A charity to provide homes for the homeless,' said Frederick. 'I would like to appoint Oliver to my place on the board of Robsec, except that his conduct of certain African transactions makes me wonder whether he has sufficient moral stamina.'

'Oliver's quite changed about all that now,' said Celia. 'He's on our side. He's even starting to learn crochet-work so that he can make string bags for the Biafrans.'

'The Biafrans?'

'It's what the Eastern Nigerians are going to call themselves when they declare independence. I hope they do, don't you, Daddy? They are the ones we have got to think about.'

'I think I almost agree with you,,' said Frederick. 'Father Rasputian feels I might like to become something called a worker priest. You wear ordinary clothes, just like everyone else, but work in a factory or something like that, and all the time, secretly, you're a priest.'

'How fantastic!' said Celia, clearly puzzled.

'It is fantastic,' said the Duke who, with about eight of

his followers, had joined them. 'I feel we are all beginning to lose our grip on reality. But fantasy is surely the refuge of a troubled mind. Your church, Rasputian, has grown fat through the ages by sustaining the fantasy life of its members. We must all believe in an after-life, whether there is one or not, or we shall be destroyed by the squalor and pointlessness of our existence on this earth. Those who plainly cannot reconcile themselves to the possibility of an after-life, like you, Rasputian, must escape from an awareness of their own futility in other ways. Audrey has prepared some fudge for us, as a treat, before the excitements of tomorrow.'

'Hash fudge,' everybody cried. 'Christmas is here again.'

'I do assure you,' said Rasputian, 'I do not consider my own existence futile.' He delicately helped himself to a large slice of fudge. 'Today I have persuaded your brother to abandon his harmful struggle to get richer, making everybody else richer around him and causing untold desolation at home and abroad. Tomorrow I marry your daughter, your niece and your housekeeper to the men of their choice. How can you say that my existence is futile. What does anybody else do which is more worthwhile?'

'You miss the point,' said Jaques, wringing his hands. 'The Duke was saying that without an after-life, *everybody's* existence is futile. What is the point of making other people happy – like a writer, making them laugh, or like a politician, removing their physical discomforts – if it all ends with death?'

'What is the point in not doing these useful and kindly things,' said Rasputian blandly. As the miraculous hash fudge began to take effect, he spoke more slowly, spacing his words with the greatest care. 'To tell you the truth, I was confronted by exactly that problem when teaching dogmatic theology at Heythrop. It suddenly occurred to me, a few years after my ordination, that I no longer believed in the existence of any supernatural being, let alone an after-life, or anything like that. What should I do? Leave the priesthood, like Jaques, and live the life of a tramp, or a schoolteacher, or worse? Why? If I was right, what possible harm could there be in not going on as before?'

'Villain,' breathed Jaques, who had taken no fudge, 'I always knew you for a villain.'

'Now you have heard my position, would you like to conduct the wedding service tomorrow, Jaques? You, at least, still believe in the existence of God, even though you have given up the priesthood. I can immediately recognise other priests who, like me, no longer believe in the central proposition, that there is a God. No doubt they recognise me, too, but we never communicate our recognition. We merely recognise it in each other, and are happy to keep silent, performing our slightly absurd function. Would you like to conduct the service tomorrow, Jaques?'

'No,' said Jaques. 'I may sometimes dare to speculate on the nature of God, but organised religion has become a mockery. When they announced that the Mass was no longer a sacrifice, it had become a meal, I realised that the institutional form of the Church had become no more than an empty shell; if the Church survives, it survives in the individual consciousness only – rather like the awareness you recognise among priests who have lost their faith. I will never go through the mockery of a church service again.'

'And yet,' said Father Rasputian, 'if you share my perception, that there is not and never has been a God in the sense of some super-natural, all-loving, all-powerful Being, then it scarcely seems to matter. You can call it a Mass, a sacrifice, a meal, or you can simply call it macaroni. You are doing something slightly ridiculous to make people happy – no more ridiculous than helping to build a hydro-electric dam, or anything else. If we feel the need of a serious purpose, we explain that since God is Love, and Love, God, the only thing that religion has ever meant is to love your neighbours, be nicer, kinder, more considerate to everyone you meet and then, if you are lucky, they will be nicer, kinder, more considerate to you. What is the harm in that?'

Frederick's only contribution to the expense of the wedding was to hire a char-a-banc which took the family from Williams Farm to the bottom of Glastonbury Tor, and brought them back again afterwards. The chairman of Oliver's constituency Fabian Society came, representing himself and his wife, but the Commonwealth Office sent nobody, since the marriage was not going to be solemnised according to the rites of the State. The Prime Minister, very broad-mindedly, sent a personal telegram of congratulations to Oliver. This was read out by Father Rasputian in the course of his sermon, while the congregation sat around on the grass at his feet and the wind played with his cassock so that Beauty, squinting up from below, had a tantalising glimpse of thick elastic sock suspenders on hairless, white legs. Miss Stella Intersan, the hygienic and sensible secretary, came and took everything down in shorthand. Mr Partridge, the local agent, and Mr Charles Winter, the farmer, came as friends of the family. A brother of Touchstone's, called Alfie Touchstone, came down from Leytonstone, where he trained greyhounds.

Rosalind had the greatest difficulty climbing the steep, grass hill to the top of Glastonbury Tor where the tower of St Michael still stands above the Somerset countryside as it stood in the year of our Lord 1539, when Robert Whyting, sixtieth and last Abbot of Glastonbury, was hanged on a gibbet before being taken down, his body quartered and his head stuck on the portals of the ancient abbey. Orlando feared that her labour might start at any moment. Eventually she was carried to her wedding by her father and her bridegroom, in a fireman's lift, with her belly sticking out in front of her like the round prow of a merchant ship.

'We are gathered together in God's sight . . .' said Father Rasputian, the lying, hypocritical villain. But it was almost impossible to believe that God did not have his eye on Glastonbury Tor throughout the afternoon of Tuesday, 30th May 1967, being celebrated as the Commemoration of St Felix I, Pope and Martyr, in the diocese of Clifton. A few sheep joined the congregation and listened as attentively as anyone else, occasionally bleating in a self-satisfied way. Father Rasputian took their attendance as a compliment, judging his own role to be something between that of St Francis of Assisi, preaching to the animals, and Jesus, delivering His well-known Sermon on the Mount.

He started off by observing that none of the partners intended going through a legal form of marriage, either for tax reasons, or because the old age pension was greater for two single persons than it was for a married couple. This was most irregular, but the great lesson of religion at the present time was that we must all be adaptable. There followed a reading of Mr Harold Wilson's telegram to Oliver and his bride:

' "Kind regards from us both on the occasion of your marriage and best wishes for a long and prosperous life together. Harold and Mary Wilson handed in at Downing Street Special Post Office eleven thirty a m thirtieth of May 1967" Amen. It's very suitable that I should be reading this telegram here on the spot which has witnessed, in its time, such violent confrontations between Church and State; it should fill our hearts with thankfulness and optimism to reflect how much things have improved since then.

'There are those, of course, who maintain that the only thing which has really happened is that the State has won the argument; the Church as an institution now disintegrates before our eyes, while the State goes from strength to strength. Do not be deceived by appearances, my brothers and sisters. All that has happened is that the Church, with greater wisdom than our political masters can show, has decided to go underground. There are those who complain about the new order of services. The Mass, or what passes for the Mass, is now meaningless, ugly and an affront to religious sensibility. Nobody has yet understood that this may, through the ancient wisdom of the Church, be intentional, its purpose to discourage people from the empty gesture of church attendance, to drive them back on their inward spirituality, where all hope for the Church's survival must reside. This is an age of formal disintegration, which the Church realises and the State does not. The State cannot realise it, since the State has no existence outside its form, unless you adduce the self-important and obsequious longings of a few individuals as evidence of a soul. The Church is now engaged in a process of voluntary, formal disintegration, while the State is fighting the irresistible forces of disintegration with more and more hyperbolical measures, unfounded in human aspirations or convenience, towards greater cohesion. Nobody can know what violence and what suffering will attend the State's final disintegration, or for how long the wretched people who exercise their authority and feed their self-importance through the machinery of the State will manage to delay the moment, but of one thing we can be sure: when the moment of disintegration comes, the Church will re-emerge, through the will of the people and in response to their needs.'

The sheep set up a great bleat at this point, and a few of the congregation, lying sprawled in the sweet-smelling spring grass, moved their positions and wondered when the service would be over. Rosalind felt an unfamiliar tightening in her stomach, and wondered if her labour was about to start. Beauty felt an entirely familiar warmth between her legs, and put her hand there, wondering if she would ever get married and, if so, why.

'That's why I am standing here in a field, preaching to the grass, some sheep, and a motley collection of drug addicts, deranged or eccentric, according to taste. You could scarcely hear me even if you wanted to listen, but that is not the purpose of this gathering. The purpose is to mark the moment in time at which these six people decided to share their lives. I am sure we all wish them the best of luck, and I hereby pronounce them man and wife – Albert and Audrey, Oliver and Celia, Orlando and Rosalind, till death do them part. *In nomine Patris et Filii et Spiritus Sancti* Amen, you may kiss each other at this point, if you wish, and now we'll all join together in singing *Faith Of Our Fathers* as we wend our way down the hill and back to the char-a-banc.'

The singing was frankly weak, although nearly everybody joined in as best they could. An Anglican clergyman from some neighbouring parish, dropping in out of curiosity – ignominious heir to an ignominious inheritance – led the singing in a fine baritone. He was called Mr Jones, like so many Anglican clergymen:

> 'Faith of our fathers, living still
> In spite of dungeon, fire and sword . . .'

Rosalind, walking alone with Orlando, felt a sudden lurch in her stomach. She was sure that her baby was going to be born any minute. But Orlando sang away lustily, his voice lost on the sweet, open air:

> 'Our fathers chained in prisons dark,
> Were still in heart and conscience free.
> How sweet would be their children's fate,
> If they, like them, could die for thee.'

Perhaps there were more pleasant places on earth than Glastonbury Tor, in Somerset, England, on that afternoon of May 30th 1967, with the sun shining down on the warm, fragrant grass and a happy carefree collection of people who knew nothing at all about what was going on and cared even less. Perhaps it was pleasanter in the Bahamas, or in Florida; even on the Cote D'Azur. At least nobody present was worried by the fear that this might be so:

> 'Faith of our fathers, Mary's prayers
> Shall win our country back to thee:
> And through the truth that comes from God
> England shall then indeed be free.
> Faith of our Fathers! Holy Faith!
> We will be true to thee till death.'

The Reverend Mr Jones, of Combe Polden, sang as if his heart would break, proud consummation of the oecumenical movement, but he was not asked back to the marriage feast at Williams Farm, so he returned to his ugly modern rectory, his ugly, modern wife and his interminable worries about money.

The party at Williams Farm was everything that such a party should be. Oliver and Celia retired early to bed, where, no doubt they made love – tenderly, passionately, silently, noisily, or however they best felt inclined; nobody knows exactly how they did it, because nobody ever asked. Touchstone and Audrey joined with Jaques, Snowman and others in a sort of country dance until a cry from the old dairy told them that Rosalind's baby was on the way. Snowman hurried through to assist at the delivery.

Macbeth wandered through the company, a seraphic smile on his face, blessing everyone and distributing fudge doctored with hashish, which Audrey had made as a treat that morning. It was as if the sun shone from his face. Wherever he went, he was followed by Ruby Wednesday, swamping him in great waves of tenderness and love. Alfie Touchstone, the brother of Audrey's husband, tricked Frederick out of four pounds with a card game, called *Spot The Lady*. Then he taught the trick to Walt Izzard. Buttercup and Strong Arm sat watching television, holding hands. Wee Willie Williams smoked himself into a stupor and lay, with a foolish grin on his face, babbling about cider, a dog called Titch and a horse called Kirstie. Beauty had a brief but exhilarating moment of passion with the chairman of the Fabian Society in a cupboard under the stairs. Dumpling was kissed by Sergeant Touchstone's brother – old enough to be her father, but still distinctly a compliment. Everybody was happy.

Rosalind's baby was born with so little fuss that one could have been at the party and never noticed, except that everybody started dancing and kissing each other. It was the perfect end to a wedding day. He was born at eleven o'clock, during the news on Independent Television. Strong Arm and Buttercup, watching the news, were able to announce that the military governor of the Eastern region of Nigeria, acting on a mandate from the Consultative Assembly of the region had declared the independent Republic of Biafra, the first Republic to be set up in the history of Africa by the Africans in response to the needs of the African inhabitants. This set off a new round of rejoicing, and the baby boy was christened on the spot by Father Rasputian: Biafra Sunshine Ojukwu.

So the infant Biafra was toasted in cider, and it began to look as if there would be no end to the evening. Eventually Frederick departed in his car with Jaques, who had decided to leave the Duke and attach himself to Frederick. Miss Intersan stayed at Williams Farm, having decided to try the alternative way of life and see if she found it agreeable. Poor woman, she had tasted hell in London. Rasputian travelled back to Farm Street with Macbeth and Ruby Wednesday. Macbeth started a new life next day cleaning the shoes of the Fathers and praying fervently in the church during any respite which the Fathers allowed. Ruby Wednesday stayed around at Farm Street for a short while, than ran away with a young Dominican priest who renounced his priesthood and wrote rather unpleasant book reviews in the secular press.

Orlando and Rosalind bought a house near Glastonbury, where Celia and Oliver visit them from time to time. The Duke stayed on at Williams Farm with a shifting population of guests. Of the original company, Buttercup and Strong Arm disappeared one day, on a walk, without warning; Willie Williams, Audrey, Touchstone, Dumpling, Rock and Beauty stayed on, so did Miss Intersan, who turned out to be a treasure. She was never expected to take down another word of shorthand, or sleep with another man, and she was unbelievably happy. Walt Izzard became bored and went away, returning when he felt like it. Old Adam eventually died, and was buried by Snowman, without the assistance of Father Rasputian, beside a path which led down from the valley into the marsh. Snowman grew into something like a son to the Duke, and neither left Williams Farm at all, except to make one-day excursions to Glastonbury, or Bath or to the house of Rosalind and Orlando.

The child Biafra grew up beautiful, intelligent, and thoroughly pleasant. In his own person he combined everything necessary to the happy ending of a love story. If nobody lived completely happily ever after, that was scarcely to be expected. But at least they all tried.

EPILOGUE

Sophie Nizam's party on election night – June 18th 1970 – was not nearly so well attended as it had been four years earlier. Among the many dim newcomers was an assistant under-secretary at the Foreign and Commonwealth Office called Sir Titus Burns-Oates, who became drunk and truculent as the evening wore on – he was the only person in the room who would admit to having voted Conservative – and made a violent pass at his hostess in the kitchen, as she spread biscuits with a paste made from cheese, vegetable oil and caraway seeds. Fortunately, only the plate was broken.

But in the four years since Mrs Nizam had last given a party, Burns-Oates had broken more than that. The Republic of Biafra was dead, at a cost of about two million lives, mostly children, starved to death in a war which dragged on for two and a half years. The defeat of Biafra vindicated British policy which was to support the Federal government with arms, money and diplomatic encouragement. It also vindicated the then Mr Burns-Oates, although there had been some awkward moments. He it was who saw that Britain never wavered, sending consignment after consignment of arms in the teeth of what is laughingly called world opinion.

Conversation ebbed and flowed around the room. After the first numbing realisation that the Conservatives had won, traditional English obsequiousness began to reassert itself.

'One thing I will say for this man Heath, he has got

integrity, not like Wilson. He says a thing and he means it. And he does believe in putting Britain's interests first,' said Daniel Chamberlain, the distinguished journalist, rumoured to be junior assistant editor designate of *The Economist.*

'One almost sometimes thinks,' said Bill Nizam, who had just joined the party. He was clearly going to say something incredibly clever and paradoxical. 'I mean one does sometimes *almost* think that we might be better off with the Conservatives, at any rate for a short while. I mean Wilson made such a mess of things. Look at Vietnam, look at Biafra . . .'

But this time Bill Nizam had gone too far. A pale young woman with bad sexual vibrations nearly struck him. She looked as if she was going to spit in his face. Angry murmurs were heard from every side.

'And forget about the pensioners, I suppose.'

'Bring back the cat. Flog the queers. Golden hand-outs for the bosses. It's good to know which side Bill is on.'

'I wondered who would be the first . . .'

'Come on, Nicholas. There's no need to stay here and be lectured to by a fascist.'

'Now look, folks. I voted Labour,' shouted Bill Nizam, but it was too late. Everybody wanted to leave. Nicholas patted him on the shoulder sympathetically.

'Don't worry, old man. It's nothing personal, but it's been rather a shock for Claire, and she probably doesn't feel she can take any of your jokes tonight. She likes them normally of course.'

Sir Titus sat alone in the corner with thoughts of his own. He loved London, he loved the English way of life. Her sights and sounds, dreams happy as her day; and laughter learned of friends. It had not all been easy, of course. There had been that awkward moment when a young under-secretary – Atcherly? Twitcherley? Twicker-ley, that was it – had threatened to resign, and the Prime

Minister himself had to plead with him to keep his conscience for another day. Then there was the 'genocide' scare, put around by mischievous elements. Of course, it had never been his intention to exterminate the entire Ibo race. Even now the accusation made him angry. The idea had been merely to teach them the sort of lesson they would never forget, and to clip their wings enough to put a stop to any question of their threatening to take over the Federation in the foreseeable future. This was the purpose, and this had been achieved.

Sir Titus Burns-Oates had been vindicated. He took his hat, his umbrella and his overcoat. He kissed Sophie Nizam warmly on the cheek. She would not betray him. Women never did. He might return one evening, when her husband was at work, if he could be bothered. How he loved England, her gentleness in hearts at peace, under an English heaven. Pausing in the doorway, he filled his lungs happily with the pure, sweet air of freedom.

THE END

15.11.1970 – 26.10.1971   Chilton Foliat
                                           Wiltshire